DONATED IN MEMORY OF

ANADEAN FELTY FLANNERY

BY

RONALD & HELEN FLANNERY HEMELGARN
RHONDA HEMELGARN
JAMES CECIL & DONNA FLANNERY
DAVE & MARCIA FLANNERY
AND
THE JESSE STUART FOUNDATION

Goodbye Kate

Goodbye Kate

BILLY C. CLARK

Edited and with an
Introduction by
Jerry A. Herndon

Illustrated by
Harold Eldridge

The Jesse Stuart Foundation
Ashland, Kentucky

1994

Goodbye Kate

Library of Congress Cataloging-in-Publication Data

Clark, Billy C. (Billy Curtis)
  Goodbye Kate / by Billy C. Clark ;   illustrated by Harold Eldridge
; edited by Jerry A. Herndon.
    p.   cm.
  Summary: Follows the misadventures of a country boy from Kentucky
and his mischievous mule.
  ISBN 0-945084-41-2
  [1. Mules—Fiction.   2. Kentucky—Fiction.]   I. Herndon, Jerry A.
II. Eldridge, Harold, ill.   III. Title.
PZ7. C535Go   1993
[Fic]—dc20   94-2193
                                                                  CIP
                                                                   AC

Published by:
The Jesse Stuart Foundation
P.O. Box 391
Ashland, KY 41114
1994

*To my wife Ruth, my son Billy,
my daughter Melissa, and
my three grandchildren Benjamin,
Timothy, and Jodie Elisabeth.*

CONTENTS

INTRODUCTION

Goodbye Kate, Billy C. Clark's sixth novel, is based in part on a mule he once owned. He got Kate free of charge by agreeing to pay her owner $1.50 for her bridle. He wasn't long in finding out why her owner was willing to let her go so cheaply. "She gave me a lot of trouble with my neighbors," he recalls, because this friendly, docile little mule had an ornery streak in her. She gave her new owner no trouble by day, but she spent her nights wandering about the neighborhood raiding corn patches and gardens and stomping through flower beds. Putting her behind a six-rail fence didn't stop her wandering ways. When the notion struck her, she easily jumped the fence and went about her mischievous business.

But Billy loved the little mule. When she died, he didn't just drag her carcass off for the varmints and buzzards to clean up. He dug a grave for her on a hill near the Big Sandy River. The spot overlooks the point where the Big Sandy empties into the great Ohio River; from the hill, one can see the borders of Kentucky, West Virginia, and, across the great river, Ohio. Billy covered Kate's grave with flat sandstone rocks to protect her remains from marauding varmints and dogs.

In the novel, Kate is found far back in the hills by a lonely country boy named Isaac Warfield. He lives close enough to Tatesburg, the nearest town, to walk to school there, but it's a small town, and his home is isolated. Isaac has graduated from the little country school he has attended and the other members of his class will be moving on to another school, or to no school at all. He won't have much contact with his friends anymore, and the nearest neighbor, a money-hungry man named Simm Johns, has no children and is "mean as a striped snake." Isaac finds Kate when he goes back into the hills to pick some blackberries for his mother. The little mule is apparently as lonely as Isaac is, and she adopts him and follows him home—as far as the pine grove above the house, that is.

Kate had been left in the remote hills of Simm Johns's farm by a man who had once worked for Johns as a farm laborer. Johns believes in progress and has no use at all for a mule. He is a "tractor man" and proud of it. When he finds out that Kate has been stealing his corn and that Isaac has been seen riding her up and down Bear Creek, he goes to the Warfield place and confronts Isaac. Isaac's father pays for the corn and Isaac has to work out the debt. Kate gets Isaac into more trouble by following him to school and disrupting the teacher's history lessons. But he finds a new friend, Elwood Sperry, and they devise a scheme to make some money by renting out Kate for rides during the lunch hour. They expect her to stay hidden in a grove of woods near the schoolhouse. Elwood is a puny kid, but his mind is sharp as a razor, and he is the brains of the operation. Unfortunately, their plans are exposed when Kate follows Isaac into the school building, and the principal marches the boys into his office and makes them tell him all about their little business enterprise. The boys have to give up their dream of easy money, but Kate really gets Isaac into trouble with the town (and his mother) when she follows his new route to school directly through town and starts trampling flower beds and getting into gardens. But the big trouble comes when Kate gets caught eating feed at John Naper's feed store. Naper is Tatesburg's biggest merchant and Simm Johns is his prime supplier. Naper has Kate arrested, and the two-man police force puts her in jail.

What happens next is sheer comedy, but with a very serious side to it. If no one stands up for Kate, the little mule will have to go to the tannery, where she will be killed for her hide. Isaac and Elwood hatch up a scheme to free Kate, but they have to use both the legal system and public opinion to do it. The comedy is provided by the bumbling attempts of the town policemen to cope with Kate, and the wild tales Elwood gets his classmates to circulate to stir up public sympathy for her.

It takes some doing to remind people well into the gasoline age of how much they and other country people like them owe to the labors of mules like Kate, but the boys get it done with the help of their classmates and the ladies of the town. Even Isaac's mother, who is embarrassed by his getting mixed up with the mule, is won over, and Isaac's parents do their part to get Kate released.

Kate does her part in providing the tale's comedy, for she is capable of her own little jokes. She even makes faces at people, and everyone in town comes to know her loud bray. The story is an endearing one, and anyone who has ever loved an animal, whether a dog, a cat, a horse, or a mule, will be able to identify with Isaac's affection for Kate. It helps in appreciating the story to remember that Billy Clark grew up, as Isaac does, as a poor man's son. One senses the sincerity of his picture of how hard it is to live this way, and one can easily see how important an animal's companionship can be for someone who has to create his own pleasures and pastimes.

You will enjoy reading about how Elwood and Isaac awaken the town's conscience and create sympathy for the broken-down little mule, and you will be interested in how Kate finally proves herself to everyone, including the skinflint Simm Johns. If you have ever thought the world sometimes moves a little too fast, and if you like to read about slower-paced, simpler times, you will like Kate's story.

If you want to know more about Billy Clark, you should read his autobiography, *A Long Row to Hoe*, which vividly portrays the life of a poor boy growing up in an Ohio River town, Catlettsburg, earlier in this century. Its vivid detail and realism puts it in a class with Mark Twain's *Life on the Mississippi* and *Huckleberry Finn*. In writing it, Clark has done for Catlettsburg, Kentucky, what Twain did for Hannibal, Missouri.

Dr. Jerry A. Herndon
Murray State University
July 30, 1993

Goodbye Kate

CHAPTER 1

Finding a Mule Is Just Ordinary

It was pure and simple the way me and the little mule met. It was on the Fourth of July, Independence Day, and the beginning of wild blackberry season here in the Kentucky hill country. The sun had peeped over the top of the ridges early, hot and red. I was standing along the fence line above the house looking over all that country that belonged to one man—Simm Johns. Me having about as much use for Simm Johns as I had for the heat of the sun.

And just as I was thinking that I sure didn't want no truck with either, ma hollered out at me. She met me in the yard, handed me a bucket, and said: "Isaac, why don't you go into the hills and fetch this bucket full of wild blackberries and I'll make you one of them good blackberry cobblers you like so well and been doing a heap of talking about."

That's just the way ma was. I mean when she wanted something she always asked for it in a way that made it sound like you were craving it for yourself.

Now the point is, I didn't have no taste for wild blackberry cobbler on this day. I had my mind set to cross the ridge and scoot over to Bear Creek and be thumbing my nose at the sun from about the center of that creek come noon.

But I knew not to argue with ma whenever she had her mind set. I also knew that I had been looking for an excuse to cross the ridge. And gathering blackberries was a reasonable one sure enough. Ma saw the look in my eyes. She said:

"And I mean blackberry picking and not a trip to the creek. There's deep holes in that stream and snakes too."

Ma was forever stretching that creek out of size. Flat on your back you could touch one bank with your fingers and scratch your initials on the other bank with your toes. And snakes wouldn't be in the water today; they'd be out sunning on the roots of trees. But it wasn't a woman's way to know much about creeks that were made for boys. Or about mountains, either, big mountains that women couldn't see through. Made that way so a boy could scoot down the other side and be lost in a world of his own. That it was so saved me many a whipping. Look out crawdads, I'm coming, I thought. I'll fill that berry bucket fast as a cricket's wink and spend the day in the creek. Later I'll tell ma that berries were surely scarce.

"Why you ought to have this little bucket filled in no time," ma said. "There were no May storms to worry the berry blossoms. They ought to be hanging blue and juicy. I wouldn't be surprised if you ain't home by noon."

Ma might not have been able to see through a mountain but she had made up for it by being able to see through my head and then some. About the only thing she missed seeing was all the loneliness that was there, specially now that school was out and me with no one to loaf with. Simm Johns was the closest neighbor, mean as a striped snake, and no family to boot. Pa said that he was too stingy to raise children and ma said pa had no right to judge a man.

Figuring that I was going to have to scoot to even have time to stick my toe in Bear Creek water I hurried to the house to get dressed for berry picking. I searched out the worst clothes I had which wasn't hard, since they were all about the same.

I made my way toward the ridge, the grass still holding enough morning dew to wet my clothes. I turned toward the roughest land, land that would be too rough for Simm Johns to pasture cattle.

On top of the ridge I stopped to catch my breath. I could see the lowlands below. I could see my home, looking no bigger than a walnut. I tried to judge the distance—wondering if ma could see this far. I caught a scent of wild rose, turned to watch the bees swarm over the blooms, and saw a hummingbird hung in the sky above them. Close by a green snake worked his way up a thorny bush to wait lifeless for bugs. I looked at the bucket, empty and as deep as a well.

If I was to have time to get to Bear Creek the bucket would have to be filled fast. So I decided I would stand a better chance if I went deeper into the hills to search them out. For the deeper I went the less chance there was of another berry picker being ahead of me. I turned down the side of the mountain.

There were stompings of berry pickers on the second ridge so I went on to the third. I stopped only long enough to catch my breath on the fourth and buried my head against the side of a white oak on the fifth, winded and almost too tired to move. I looked down the long slope, rubbing my eyes to free them of wind-tears so I could see. It was then that the old shack came into focus. Either a squatter's shack or a shelter for winter hay. I couldn't tell at this distance. It could be either, for the land this far still belonged to Simm Johns and he had both. Whichever it was it was old, sitting under the shadows of the hill, quiet as a mountain rock clinging to the red earth.

Never mind, I thought. There is no better place to find berries than around deserted shacks. For the land about is moist and rich, and once deserted, berry vines claim it like ghosts and grow so tall they bend like the back of an old man. And the berries grow lonely, cool, big, and juicy.

Maybe here would be my bucket of berries. I wiped my eyes again and looked down the slope.

That's when I first saw her. No more than a brown speck at first, but growing in size with each step I took, bowing more in the back and looking worse. And then we were face to face.

"I'll be dogged," I said. "It's a mule!"

She looked up at me as if I were a sorry sight. She didn't even pay me a second look. Just went back to trying to pull up a pod of crabgrass that looked as old and tough as her. And I sorta grinned and said:

"If you aim to get that grass, little mule, you better have some teeth in the back you ain't showing. Them ones up front ain't as long as sheep grass."

She sized me up once more, looked like she was saying something like "just watch and see," and so I decided to sit for a spell and end up with a laugh. I got comfortable enough. There was a big split oak a few feet away and so I stretched out in the forks knowing full well that little mule was in for a licking.

And while she worked around the grass making no headway I got to thinking about where she had come from and who she belonged to. She didn't belong to Simm Johns. That was for sure. He wouldn't let a mule on his land. I had heard him say so.

"They ain't no laying off a piece of land to corn and fodder a tractor during the winter," he had said. "You can just sell that strip of corn and feed the fodder to cattle, and put the tractor in the shed snug as a bear. A little gasoline in the spring and she's out of hibernation."

And that was that.

"Poor little thing," I said, still watching her tug at the grass. Then I glanced at the shack. I looked over the old railing fence around it; old, hand-hewed and laced together like shoestrings until it stood nearly six feet tall.

What caught my eyes the most were the berry vines that matted and held it together. Shadeberries hung from them like clusters of grapes. I followed them with my eyes to the big post that held a half-rotted gate.

Inside the yard the grass was tall; so tall that it bowed over, laced itself in knots and peeped skyward again. I closed my eyes, saw the berries, Bear Creek and the mule. I say to myself to go down there, open that gate so as to be able to pick from both sides of the fence and get my bucket heaping. Each berry is a step toward Bear Creek.

5

I walked toward the gate. I heard a shuffle in the grass behind me. I turned and there she was, following like she belonged to me. Just looking at me like she was saying something like "well, go on and open the gate and let's be at it."

I touched the gate and it fell and I looked at her and walked in. I set my bucket down under a big bush and started picking those berries like milking a cow. And they echoed up from the bottom: clink, clink, clink. Like drops of rain. And then something nudged my shoulder. I turned and there was that mule, ready to nudge me again. But now that she had my attention she wallowed a clump of grass with her tongue and made pretense to pull it loose. She couldn't do it. She just didn't have the teeth up front—or back either. Then for ever so spare a moment I glanced at the sun, knowing my time was short. I closed my eyes, expecting to draw up a picture of Bear Creek and pay no attention to anything—like a mule—that could keep me away from the cool water. But to save me it wasn't there. The creek, that is. First time it had failed. Instead, I just saw scrawny mule with teeth too short to pull grass.

I jerked up a handful, tossed it to her and turned to pay her no more attention. Believe me if you want or not, but she let out a bray that nearly pulled me out of my shoes. I never heard anything like it. I figure you might get close if you could pull a saw of lightning over a log of thunder:

"*He-haw-e-e-e-e-e-e-e-e-e!*"

How could such a noise come from a thing so little? I fairly expected the berries to come falling from the

6

bushes. I figured too that after a blast like that there couldn't be anything left to that mule but a pouch of old hide. But I was wrong. She just stood there, her front legs crossed just like you wouldn't expect a mule to be standing. And she nibbled at the grass.

It didn't take me long to know I was picking more grass than I was berries. And I finally figured it was time for me to put that mule in her place. I looked at her just like ma looked at me whenever I was pestering, her hands on her hip, her mouth puckered and a look in her eyes that said I was plainly in for it. And for a moment it felt real good being on ma's side of the fence.

But the good feeling lasted only until I looked into the eyes of that ornery mule.

I couldn't see the little mule the way I wanted to see her: trifling-like. All I could see was her old shaggy coat of hair matted with cockleburs so long with her that they had rubbed sores on her hide. And there was a grayness to the hair that marked her next to as old as the mountains themselves. I saw her eyes, brown as a butternut and hollow as the loneliness of a summer day.

I saw myself in the tiny pupils of her eyes, a speck as black as a crow, and so small to the world about that a single wink would rub me out. I was alone to wander the hills and the creek for the summer, but was soon to face a new world I saw as less important. For I wouldn't be going back to Bear Creek school this year. Bear Creek had taken me as far as the ninth grade and then shoved me out to scratch for myself, away from my friends. No more riding the county school bus, putting lizards, frogs, bugs and things on the girls to make them miserable and jump. I would miss that. And the other things, too: the big oak where I ate lunch each day, and hunting snakes in the hills about. The rest of my class would go to another school. Some to no school at all.

I had plumb educated myself into the city school at Tatesburg where pa operated his shoe cobbler's shop. Pa would even have to pay tuition for me to go there since we lived outside the city limits. All that trouble to get me educated so I wouldn't end up a simple shoe cobbler like him, hands rough as leather and curved by time and a shoe hammer—which was the way I wanted to end up. Me wanting no truck with that city school and ma saying she wouldn't have me grow up like a woods rabbit.

"You'll meet new friends there, Isaac, and get yourself a heap of learning besides," ma said. "You'll learn there's more to this world than just hills and creeks."

But I named the time to come "Doom's Day" and didn't look forward to much afterwards.

I might have thought more but the little mule blinked her eyes and rubbed me out. I looked now at the sky. The sun was overhead. And it would race me over the ridges toward home, trying its best to end up in the lowlands before me.

And then I said it. I don't know why. It just came as natural as breathing.

"Come on, little mule, let's go home." Can you imagine? Me with no home for her to go to, no pasture, no nothing but a ma who would skin me alive for carrying in as little a thing as a green snake.

And she turned with her head down and followed.

It just seemed so natural for her to follow that I didn't

8

lose my breath until we were looking over the ridge and seeing home. I turned then to look at that brown heap of trouble. I just couldn't go down that slope, my chest out like a mountain and an old mule behind me. I looked into her eyes, and saw moisture there. And something more that said she knew what must come now. She looked as old and gray as a moss-covered rock.

Then I looked at the pine grove above the house. Got to figuring just how dark it looked inside it from the yard. A dark green shadow even on the brightest day. I said to the mule:

"You're a sorry looking sight. Just sorry enough to get me in a heap of trouble. But it's mighty lonely around here just now and I can't be too particular. You'll spend the night in that pine grove down there. And I'll study about where we go from there."

Ma watched me cross the fence, then gauged the sun and the look of her eyes told me I was long in the hills.

"Berries scarce?" she asked, taking the bucket.

"No'm," I said.

"You've been long in the hills," she said.

Sometimes, you probably know, answers come at a time you need them most. Just fall out of nothing to pull you from the jaws of a licking. Where they come from, I don't know. But I'm grateful.

"I didn't want to pick you a bucket of little sunberries, ma," I said. "I knew you always liked them big, juicy shadeberries, that make the best cobblers."

Ma gave me a look that said she was having some doubts about the truth of my answer but was giving me credit for it being a good one. She turned to the house.

9

I didn't say much that night to pa. We usually sat around and talked a little. But I needed time to think. I did say to him:

"Pa, you think mules will ever come back to the mountains?"

"What's that?" he said, squinting at me.

There came another one of those answers.

"I was just remembering the time last summer Simm Johns saying that mules were gone forever. Being of no use anymore."

Pa grinned and rubbed his chin. "Mules. I'm afraid he's right." The grin was gone now. "Can't say I'm glad, either. There was a warmness to them little critters. They came in here, and did enough work to give man time to come up with a machine to kick them out."

"That's progress," ma said, looking up from a sewing hoop.

"Maybe so," pa said. "But me, I'd heap rather push up to the warmness of a mule than a cold piece of machinery."

"Machinery don't stink," ma said. "Mules do. That's the way I remember them."

"You just never got real close to one," pa said, grinning.

"Don't ever intend to, either," ma said. "I'm as close now as I ever want to be."

Pa yawned. "I don't 'spect you'll have to worry none about it. Not as long as Simm Johns owns the whole county. Worst mule hater I ever saw. Never had a mule that would work for'im. Never knew how to treat one, that's the reason. They knew he didn't like'em. They

10

wouldn't work. Stubborn little critters."

Ma looked at me now and grinned. "I don't know about mules," she said. "But that Isaac is a fine berry picker. Going again early in the morning, he says. If the urge stays with him to gather enough I'll do some canning."

I yawned, too, and went to my room knowing that I had me a way to get back in the hills when daylight came; a way to go to the pine grove without a sight of suspicion.

Funny thing: As I lay thinking that night the fartherest thing from my mind was the fear that the little mule would leave during the night. She seemed to belong there. Close to me. Real close. What to do next was something else.

CHAPTER 2

A Mule Ain't Hard to Teach

Morning broke with unbearable joy. I was up and on my way to the berry fields by way of the pine grove before you could say jackrabbit. And the mule was there waiting. We sneaked to the top of the ridge, hurrying to step over the rim and into the blackness of the hills on the other side. And for ever so spare a moment I stopped to think how strange the world around me was; so big and yet able to change in the blink of an eye. Just yesterday I had come up the same path. I had heard the lonesome caw-caw of a crow; saw the slowness of a terrapin spending a lifetime trying to reach the top of the mountains where he would find less than he had below; and stood to watch the sun glinting from a silver path a snail had traced over a gray sandrock old and wrinkled from time, wind and snow.

Today I saw none of these things. The sky was all blued out like a robin's egg. There was magic in the wind and coolness in the shadows.

The mule had changed it all. She made me feel purposeful and important. I felt like bragging that mule against something—something like a tractor. It wouldn't be a fair brag; a tractor was a dead thing, mute as a handful of old clay. It took a key instead of a heart to make it move. You couldn't make it happy or you couldn't make it sad.

I stood under the trees on the other side of the ridge and patted the old mule across the nose, knowing that neither of us was big enough to make one particle of difference to the world ahead. But she nudged her nose into my hands and I knew then that none of it mattered. All that mattered was that we belonged together. It seemed natural. And yet at the snap of a twig we jerked our heads back toward the way we had come, knowing that we were going to have to do a lot of fooling to stay that way. For we knew that we were in a heap of trouble if we were caught and not knowing why except that we were a boy and a mule.

We moseyed along, me stopping here and there to pick a handful of berries for the bucket and her taking advantage of tender grass that showed itself whenever I lifted a berry bush. And now and then she reached out and plucked a juicy shadeberry from a bush. Well, I thought, I sure never heard of a mule eating blackberries. Then I got to thinking that never before had I had reason to know whether they did or not and decided I'd find a way to question pa about it later on without giving out that there was a mule about.

For the present I just looked at her tongue all blued out from berry juice and I got to laughing and telling her what ma would say if she should just go to the house and stick that big, blue tongue out.

"She'd take a board to you," I said. "She says that eating berries in the field before your bucket is full is dead wrong. One berry leads to another and before long you get too fat and lazy to pick them anymore and so you start eating from the bucket. Then you go home with an empty bucket and a stomachache and there's dead sure to be something else hurting before ma gets through with you."

She watched me as carefully as a sentry crow. Maybe knowing that somewhere along the line I was going to have to stick out my own tongue for all the world to see. I did when I laughed. She took a look then, saw my tongue was almost as blue as hers and then she flopped to the earth and rolled over and over in the brush, making a whinnying noise that sounded enough like a laugh to me to be one. I looked down at her and said:

"You want to roll there all day like a dead leaf in a low wind, or are you aiming to scoot over to Bear Creek with me?"

She jumped to her feet, brayed to high heaven, and stood swishing her tail. Her mouth puckered in the silliest grin you ever saw. And judging the sun filtering through the tops of the trees as well as the distance from here to the creek, I decided then and there that a mule was made to ride. So I hopped on her back. She looked back with that silly grin, and set her eyes on the berry bucket as much as to say that I was finally catching on to the likes of a mule, but if I rode I paid. I picked a big juicy berry out of the bucket and watched her woller it with her tongue. She dropped her head low to the earth and walked off like she had been cheated out of her hide.

We turned now toward the lowlands—to where the creek trailed. And . . . where Simm Johns' long bottoms of corn stood shoulder high. It was tall enough to tassel out good and proper, with the corn setting on the stalks, yellow kernels under the green shucks with a brown mustache on the end. If you peeled the shuck back, and stuck your fingernail into the kernel, the sweet juice would jump out and pop you in the eye. It had me; I had been to the patch three days ago.

But today I had no intentions of spending time staring at corn. I stripped off my clothes down to my birthday bathing suit, stuck a toe in the water and thought about how lucky that mule was, able to go in the water as is and trust the sun to take care of her on coming out. Each piece of my clothing had to be hung over the low limbs of the willows and I had to be careful not to get my hair wet. Ma knew the black loam mud that belonged only to the creek and she knew that wet hair dried by the sun was bushier than a crow's nest.

I waded into the creek and turned to coax the little mule to follow, bringing her into the stream where it lay shallow and caught the rays of the sun. For I had a streak of meanness in me now and here where the water was thin and warmed by the sun the big crawdads gathered, clung lifeless to the bottom with only their big pinchers bobbing the surface like small splints of driftwood, ready to latch onto anything that was close. She walked half-heartedly, her eyes still on the corn. She lifted each hoof, paying no attention to the crawdads that slid from them like boys from a slicky slide. If she knew that some had made it far enough up the slick hoofs to latch their pinchers into the hair of her leg she paid no mind. She just looked at me like I was plumb crazy for trading a field of corn for a little water over my back and she turned and walked into the field dragging crawdads with her. And they scooted from her like fleas when she reached the bank, dropping to the sand and backing toward the water for all that was in them. That mule was going into the cornfield with pure intentions of doing a little thinning.

I splashed from the creek, grabbed my britches, and felt the water soak through them as I pulled them on. I tore after that mule as fast as I could run. Not that I was so pure in heart that I thought it wrong to steal a little corn for eating. But there was more to stealing corn than just going in the patch and pulling it where you pleased; that is, if you wanted more than one mess, which I did. The mule was just a few steps from ruining it all for both of us. And then I'd have to be content to eat my corn from ma's table which wasn't any way to eat corn. Ma saying: "Eat your corn, Isaac, without slurping." And that was it. From that time on I would sit there listening for the noise of my eating and not a sound anywhere to help me steal a bite. Each kernel popped inside my mouth like a firecracker and I never had no way of knowing how much of the noise was staying inside and how much was sneaking out.

It was different at the creek. That's where I learned to eat corn and like it. Built me a little fire and covered those ears of corn with mud and stuck them under the hot ashes and cooked'em in their own juice. And there was the flavor of knowing you just might get seen and have to dive through the bushes. Then just sit back under the shade of a willow with the coolness of the creek coming up at you and the birds furnishing music in payment for

17

the cob and you just slurp with all the noise of eating you like and you got corn the way it was made for a boy to eat.

The thing is, you just couldn't go pulling those ears of corn off the way that mule was intending to do, leaving your tracks there in the soft earth for everyone to see. You had to know the trick, a whopper of a trick that I had learned last summer.

For several evenings I had been watching the muskrat come up from the creek, slip up the cornstalks for an ear, and drop back to earth dragging the corn back to the water where he could outswim a hant if he got caught while eating. I set my eyes on those little tracks he left in the earth. So I sat myself down and went about becoming a painter with only one picture in the world to paint: the tracks of a muskrat. I went into the cornfield with a willow sprout in each hand—one bushy with leaves to brush out my tracks and one cut to a point to scratch out the prints of a muskrat's paw, with me backing to the creek like a crawdad. I got so good that I couldn't tell to save me which were the doings of muskrats and which were my doings. I got so good in fact, that I heard Simm Johns say to pa one day:

"The varmints are cleaning me out."

It was a good trick, all right. Now, here was that ornery mule a few feet away from ruining it. For if she reached the corn both me and the muskrats were in for it good and proper-like. For Simm Johns could easily enough reason out a mule's tracks. He'd come looking. He'd find that mule and trace her to me since we had no intentions of being separated. He'd bird-dog that field from this day forward until a rabbit couldn't pass through it without being spotted.

She had pawed up the earth leaving tracks that a ground mole could follow. I ran and caught up just as she was about to slip her first ear from the stalk. She pulled at the stalk purely intending to uproot it and forever sign away me and the muskrats' rights to the creek. I grabbed her around the neck and made no progress. So I dived and caught the stalk at ground level, slipping my fingers through the tiny rain roots for a hold. She fairly set her hoofs into the dirt with intentions of pulling the earth from under me. We yo-yoed back and forth for the better part of five minutes, the only thing saving me being those short teeth of hers. They just kept sliding up the top until her head popped off the top of the corn. And I took the chance to grab her around the neck and yell:

"That ain't no way to do it! That ain't no way to do it!"

She kicked and stomped to break free. The corn blades touched my naked hide and left red welts that itched worse than nettles. They cut my forehead and sweat moved in to burn like fire. I was plumb disgusted. I turned her loose and stepped back.

"Go on!" I said. "Go on, you old fool. You're too big for me to stop. Just go on and me and you ain't ever going to be together again. Maybe that's the way you want it."

She reached again for the corn, got inches away and then twisted her silly head and popped her eyes up at me. And as old and bowed as she was I could see mountains of power in her muscles that she hadn't bothered to use on me at all. She closed her mouth, turned to stare at the corn and then just walked over and shoved her nose against my chest. The wind came up from the creek and the blue jay screamed from the willows and the warm smell of the little mule was everywhere about me. I could feel her heart beating soft and fast right through her nose, up and down like the bobbing of a sandpiper's tail. And for ever so spare of a moment I wished she could look different so I could say something mean to her for what she had been about to do and how close she had come. Instead, she just stood there the only way she had to; so old that some of her hair had fallen out leaving bare patches of rough hide to spot her like the bark of a sycamore tree. Most of her hair had been claimed by cockleburs, matted and twisted. And her hoofs were broken by a lifetime of walking rocks, found mostly along the steep ridges, I thought, which was the best place for something to hide that had reason to. She was, at this moment, the ugliest and pitifulest creature I had ever seen. Lonesome enough to make a body go and do something he knew would lead to the worst sort of trouble he could find: teaching her to steal corn.

But that's what I set about to do, trying all the while to make it right. I could steal the corn myself and then share with her and with only one of us stealing it would only make it half as bad if we got caught. And then too, that ought to be better than just plain stealing without intentions of sharing. I knew better. Ma had taught me better long ago. She taught me that the likes of stealing and lying would soon sprout out for the world to see— and worse yet, her. The likes of this would lead to two things: shamefulness and a hickory sprout, the shame worse than the licking.

But it all made no mind to the mule. She stood back to take her lesson, and I put a schoolteacher to shame. I stripped off the ear, leaving the cornhusk empty on the stalk which was the way most muskrats worked it. I dragged that ear back to the creek followed by a willow sprout that covered the tracks of me and the mule and left the trench made by the corn and those little paw tracks that would have made a muskrat wonder how his tracks got there ahead of him.

And while the mule sat there on the creek bank on her haunches like a big overgrown dog wallering that ear of corn in her mouth, I filled her in on the rest.

There's nothing like experience even if it concerns the lowliness of stealing corn. That mule had a weight problem. So after she downed the ear of corn I took her up the creek a piece and we whipped that. We found ourselves a place where the creek, and the bank right up to the edge of the cornfield, were lined with shale rock. And in no time flat she was scooting across the rock with the sureness of a lizard, stopping at the edge of the cornfield and stretching her long neck out to pluck an ear from the field.

Then I took only a moment to show her how if the corn got hard she could soften it in the waters of the creek. And so while she soaked her corn in the creek I flopped down there in the center and thumbed my nose at the sun. That mule stood at the edge of the creek, her front legs straddled like a grasshopper playing a fiddle tune, and she held a big ear of corn in her mouth. She looked up at me sorta sorrylike and wiggled her tail which wiggled the rest of her body up front of it.

"Don't you go getting greedy," I said, seeing all those shucks of corn go floating lazily down the creek. And looking at the water I caught the shadows on it. "I'd better be getting these berries home to ma if I'm intending to make it to the hills tomorrow." I caught the look in the eyes of the mule as she stared toward the cornfield, looking like the world had just come to an end. "We'll wait a few days and come back for another fat mess. If we get to stealing too much and too often, Simm Johns is going to start watching that patch. There's a limit to what even muskrats can steal."

I guess I should have looked closer into the eyes of that mule. I might have seen what was there and found a way to talk her out of it. But I was just too wrapped up in having me a mule about to see what was there all the time, sticking out like a wart on a frog.

But it was then, I think, she set her plans, which included a way to work around me to get to them. She never made a blunder during the days that followed. At least not during the daylight hours when I was with her. I found me an old rope, made a halter, and rode her every place out of seeing distance of ma, pa, and Simm Johns. Outside of them I guess we got a little careless and got ourselves seen by a few people that lived along the creek. But we never figured it mattered a heap about them.

Since there was nothing on my mind but that mule I figured there was nothing on that mule's mind but me. It seemed only natural for me to think that way. We'd gather berries during the day and toward evening we'd work to the top of the mountain and stretch out under a tree for a spell and look out over the lowlands. To the left you could stretch and see Bear Creek trailing through the hills no wider than your little finger, shouldered by the great bottoms of Simm Johns' corn, the greenness tinted by the blue fog that hovered over the valley of the evenings. And here again I had a chance at the mule's plans and let it pass. For she stood pointing that field like it was a covey of quail and like she could land in the center with one jump off the mountain and flush them.

And then it happened. Her orneriness showed through and she got us both caught good and proper.

I had just turned up the slope, toward the last of the week, and she wasn't anywhere about. Well, I didn't give it much thought at first. "She's hiding," I thought. For we had taken to playing hide-and-seek together. So I just stuck my hands in my back pockets and looked around slow and easy-like, fairly expecting to see her big rump sticking out from around a tree. For she was too big and awkward to hide anywhere without help from me—help like my always pretending I couldn't see her.

After about fifteen minutes I got a little worried and stepped up my pace. The next thing I knew I was running through the pine grove, searching behind every bush and calling for her in a voice low enough to die before it reached the foot of the hill. I got to thinking that maybe she had up and left me. Just rogued off to break my heart, knowing I had had time to get used to having the old fool about.

I ran across the hills with the briars scratching my face and picking out the threads of my pants. I made it to the squatter's shack where I had found her. But she was not there.

I searched then until the shadows hovered over the mountains. The birds went to roost and I knew if I didn't get home ma would send pa to look for me. And if the mule was still about maybe he would see her somewhere along the way and she'd be in trouble.

I was just feeling so low that I walked right into the yard, my head down, without seeing Simm Johns standing there talking to ma. The look in ma's eyes told me that something bad had happened and at least half of it was of my doing. I was hemmed in so tight that I wasn't likely to wiggle out.

CHAPTER 3

But Greediness Gets'em Caught

Simm Johns said, "Well, I can't tell for sure just how much corn she et all together." Then he looked toward me and snurled up his lip. "Oh, but she thought she was tricky. Didn't just walk in that field like you'd be expecting a worthless critter to do. Not that mule. Plucked them ears off the stalk slick as a corn knife and drug'em to the creek to make it look like the doings of muskrats."

Ma put her hands on her hips and squinted her eyes.

"Now Mr. Johns," she said. "Surely you don't believe . . ."

"Now bear with me, Mrs. Warfield," Simm Johns said. "I didn't believe it either at first. Fooled me good. But I seen it with my own eyes. Caught her sneaking out of that field like a big overgrown muskrat. Followed her. She waded into the creek, shucked out that ear of corn and stuffed the shucks into a muskrat hole leaving a little out to bobble in the current—just the way a careless muskrat would do. She seen me and took off. I says to myself that glory be if it weren't that mule that once belonged to Ed Riley, man that worked a while for me and lived over in an old shack on my land. A drifter he was. I hired him with the promise he'd shed hisself of a mule being as how I wouldn't have one on the place. 'Shed yourself of her,' I said, 'and you got yourself a roof over your head and fifty cents a day grubbing sprouts.'"

"What's all this got to do with Isaac?" ma said, judging the sun and knowing that pa was due in—hungry.

"Plenty!" Simm Johns said. "I took a run first over to Ed Riley's shack thinking that he just might have come back and fetched that mule with'im. He rogued off about six months ago. The place was up in weeds and not a sign about. Nothing but cattle stompings." Simm Johns took time to scratch his head and cut his eyes at me. "I might have just let it all go at that. But it being a mule I couldn't. Worthless critters, given to meanness and destruction. I wasn't about to be outfoxed by one. I'm a tractor man myself."

He drew down his lower lip and looked off at his tractor which was parked at the edge of the yard. He had a habit of driving that tractor about everywhere he went like most people do automobiles. He'd built him a little shed over the seat to ward off the rain and sun and put him a yellow horn on it that went, if you said it, *uhooooooooga*, drawing out the *ooooooooooo*'s until you were most out of breath.

"Well," Simm Johns said, "thought I'd just do a little inquiring along the creek. At least a dozen people told me your boy Isaac and that mule was thicker than two peas in a pod. Him riding that mule up and down the creek from sunup to sundown. I don't need to tell you, Mrs. Warfield, that possession is more than half of the law. That makes Isaac responsible for the corn, since ownership takes in the innards of that mule as well as her outards."

Well, the hair fairly raised on my head. I was hit right smack in the face with owning that mule, something I had been thinking for a while now anyway. I'd even been bragging about it. Why, I had stood up there on the hillside bucking up to a big white oak that I pretended to be Simm Johns and I said to it: "So you don't want a mule on your pasture! So this mule is on it and she belongs to me. What of it?" Naturally he just stood there trembling. Why he just withered down like frost under a hot sun, knowing he was facing me head on and wanting no truck with me. Answered me meek as a field mouse: "Nothing. Nothing at all." And then just to show him how tough I really was I went around the slope knocking the heads off Queen Anne's lace and daisies, spreading the seed over the pasture so it would sprout and stunt out the grass. And to wrap it all up good and tight I said once more to him: "And furthermore, from this point on keep that tractor of yours at a fair distance. Makes this here mule nervous and I won't have it. Understand?" Meek as a toad frog he said: "Yes sir." Good and proper-like.

Pretending is all right. It can be downright fun. Only trouble is you never really expect the things you pretend to really happen. So here I was faced with it all and squirming like a June bug with a blue jay after him.

"Well," ma said, "I just don't believe it. Isaac and a mule! He'd a-said something to me. He's not a bad boy to lie."

At this point if there had been any good to me I'd a-hung my head in shame, ma standing up and believing in me, and me with a pack of lies hidden from her too big to carry. But glory be if I just didn't just stand there to shame myself worse. Hung my head down for pity and a look on my face that plainly said Simm Johns, the big bully, had no right to even think I would be part of such a thing.

"Why, even if Isaac *was* seen with a mule," ma said, "that surely wouldn't mean the mule belonged to him." Ma gave me a look that I took to mean that I wasn't as well off as I thought I was and she would let me know more about it when we were alone. "If Ed Riley chose to leave a mule alone in the hills you could hardly expect someone else to be responsible for its doings."

I swelled my chest and looked toward Simm Johns like I was saying I was backing ma all the way and that he didn't have a good leg to stand on. I was beginning to feel some better since he hadn't mentioned having the mule up to now and I figured he'd not found her and she was all right wherever she was, with a good chance I'd find her first.

But Simm Johns was not about to be fooled that easy. He was a horse trader and one of the best. I'm not meaning that he traded horses. Calling a man a horse trader here in the hills means a man can outsmart, outsell, outtrade, take advantage of, most people about. Drawing them in close whatever the means and putting the sting to'em for the better part of the bargain. And Simm Johns was the best at it. He knew where my weak point would be.

"Maybe you're right, Mrs. Warfield," he said, keeping one big eye on me, which held the look of doom. "I just wanted to be sure before I caught that mule and hauled it over to the tannery. Wanted to be sure there wouldn't be no hard feelings because of old Kate ... that's what Ed Riley said her name was ... and no one to stand up for her before them skinners slips the hide off that poor critter's back. Old and unwanted she is and ain't apt to bring much. Hardly enough to pay for the corn. Hide is all she's got. They can't render bones down into soap."

Simm Johns knew he was getting somewhere and so he primed me again.

"Just my luck to catch a mule and it be old and skinny. Couldn't a-got a fat one. That makes a difference when it comes to skinning'em out. Hide sticks to them bones. Well, no matter. Who's to care if she dies or not? Maybe she'll fetch enough for a gallon of gasoline."

He grinned from ear to ear. He had me now and he knew it. I swear he was a good one. Make no mistake. Take ma: She had about as much use for a mule as a woodpecker has for a metal clothesline prop, but she just stood there like she had lost her best friend in that old mule. He had gone and tricked me just as bad as I had tricked him in the cornfield. And the thing was you know that Simm Johns was just the sort to maybe do everything he said he would if it meant winning.

It came down now to the little mule. I was up a stump and nowhere to slide off. And it came to me then and there just how much old Kate meant to me. Not caring one particle for my own hide I closed my eyes and said:

"That mule is mine!"

"Your mule!" ma said.

"I found her in the hills," I said.

Ma looked at me with a frown on her face.

That was the way it stood. And then pa came around the side of the house. He spoke to Simm Johns and then kissed ma on the cheek—shaming me there in front of Simm Johns—and stood back listening to ma, her words falling fast and piling up like flakes of snow. And her look all the time saying that the time had come for pa to take a board to me and stop all this foolishness, which I figured pa would do.

But it was one of those times you get yourself a blessing you don't deserve. Or figure on either, for that matter. Pa turned and looked at me with a grin that I'd bet a buckeye said: "Kinda tough sometimes, ain't it, Isaac?" And me trying all the time to keep from crying in front of him.

"I don't say he owns the mule," pa said. "But 'pears to me he had some part in the mule's taking that corn. That so, Issac?"

"Surely did, pa," I said.

"Slick as a muskrat, eh?" pa said. He snickered, reached out and picked a cocklebur out of my hair. Looking now at Simm Johns, he said, "Stuck part of the shucks into a muskrat hole you say?" Pa was laughing out loud now.

"Ain't one particle funny, Jeremiah," Simm said to pa. "Your boy Isaac is to blame for the mule and I got you dead to rights. You know that possession is better than half the law."

"Possession," pa said. "Where's the mule, Isaac?"

"I don't know, pa," I answered.

"Well now, Simm," pa said. "You got a mule?," seeing

he didn't have. "That sorta puts a different light on possession, wouldn't you say?"

"Now look here, Jeremiah," Simm Johns said. "Ain't no need for you to try to go squirming out. I got you in a noose and you know it."

"Ok," pa said, "you go tell your story to the judge in town. Tell him about a mule that ain't there since you can't furnish it for proof." Pa grinned. "Might tell him about the doings of that mule too. Hard telling what she might do next. Or . . . let things ride as they are and we'll settle for the corn since Isaac admits to part of it."

Well, if Simm Johns was leaning pa's way he wouldn't be apt to come right out and say so. That isn't the way a horse trader does things, especially not Simm Johns, proud of being the best about.

"How much you figuring the corn to be worth?" pa said.

Simm dropped his head a mite, put his chin into one of his big hands and bit at his lower lip.

"Kinda hard to tell what corn will fill out to," he said. "Being good weather and all like we had this year I'd say she gobbled down a good four dollars' worth counting ruination of the fodder which I ain't about to feed to my cattle after being wollered around by that mule. They're choicy."

"Take a mighty good mule and a mighty good season to 'count for that much corn," pa said. "But since Isaac admits to a part of it I reckon it's fair to pay the other man's price."

Pa reached in his pocket and counted out the money, pulling it out slowly.

31

"You think it's right, Jeremiah," ma said, "to pay out hard-earned money for Isaac's wrong-doing?"

"I'm willing to stake Isaac," pa said, making me feel as important as I had ever felt. "Once. A man needs someone to stake him. Why, I wouldn't be apt to have my shoe cobbler's shop if my pa hadn't staked me once."

"But there's a heap of difference in—." Ma never got to finish. A mule's bray came tumbling down the mountain:

"*He-haw-e-e-e-e-e-e-e!*"

And there she was. Just popped out up near that pine grove with her legs spraddled out like a sawhorse.

"There's that critter!" Simm Johns yelled. "For the life of me! Spunky enough to steal my corn and come back to mock her doings. I'll have her hide!"

Simm Johns ran to his tractor.

"I'll run her hide off and drag her in!" he said.

Pa turned to me.

"Listen, Isaac," he said. "Answer fast now. You believe that mule done all them things? I mean drug that corn to the creek and stuffed the shucks in a muskrat's hole? That'd take a human-thinking critter."

"I surely do, pa," I said. "I surely do."

"Hold up there, Simm!" pa yelled, walking toward the tractor and stopping to break a long twig off of a low limb of a tree in the yard. "What makes you think you can run that mule down with this here tractor?"

"I've no time for foolishness," Simm said, starting the motor. "I'll run her legs into a nubbin and have nothing but the hide on her back to sell!"

"She looks mighty peart to me," pa said, looking

toward the slope as if he was trying to judge the worth of that mule and then looking back as if he was trying to figure if I had given her too much credit. And then she cried and her braying came rolling down the slope again.

"If you got something on your mind, say it," Simm Johns said.

"She's got a keen voice," pa said. "Longest and loudest I ever heard on just one mule. And according to what you say she must have a head full of sense to go with it."

I knew for sure that Simm Johns wasn't going to stay there long having himself insulted and his tractor along with it. Or having pa poking that stick into the gas tank of the tractor either, though Simm Johns didn't see that. Yet Simm Johns wasn't about to squirm out of a bet he could smell as a winner a mile off.

"Speak your piece," he said, just like he had pa on the hook.

"I got four more dollars that says that little mule will bray you and that tractor right off your own land," pa said.

Ma opened her mouth to say something, but Simm Johns didn't give her a chance. For every word and every second counted now.

"For four dollars I'll run that mule till she's as limp as a milkweed hit by frost," Simm said. "Even throw in two dollars to boot to show that my heart's on the right side about it."

"Do, and I'll back that boot by carrying that mule off the land myself if you run her down," pa said, slapping his long arms against his legs.

Simm Johns stopped his tractor at the fence gate, got

off to open it, then drove through. After he closed the gate and got back on the tractor, that was the last time, as far as I know, that he was off the tractor until the race was over.

Up the slope he went driving with one hand and slinging his hat round and round above his head with the other. Screaming like an Indian after a scalp:

"All right, you flea-bitten critter, I'm coming to wear them legs down to the length of pipestems! Ye-e-e-e!"

Then he was lost in a cloud of smoke and it being late evening, there was just light enough to show that that crazy little mule was standing waiting on him, not making one motion to move.

I touched pa's arm.

"She ain't going to move, pa. He'll flatten that poor little thing out like a skipjack," I said, meaning a flat-sided fish we sometimes caught in Bear Creek.

But pa only slapped his leg again and laughed louder than before, saying in between laughs, "She's a genuine mule for sure." That made no sense to me. Unless she moved soon she was a dead mule for sure.

The land about would be level enough for the tractor except near the top of the ridge where the great roots of the oaks swelled underneath, mounding huge chunks of land into the shapes of bird claws. Here in the rough land grew the sawbriar, scrub timber and bushes, and a fair amount of blackberry vines that could reach out and pluck a man right off the seat of a tractor. They'd plucked me from the back of Kate and I wasn't about to give that tractor more credit than my mule.

This was where Kate would head for, I thought.

She'd lead Simm Johns slowly up the slope of the mountain and bog him down between those big roots and the chase would be over.

That's just what she didn't do. And what pa said next nearly scared me out of my hide:

"I'll be doggone if that mule ain't going to make a race of it!"

She stood next to the pines until Simm Johns was almost close enough to reach out and touch her. Then she lowered her head and blasted him good.

"He-haw-e-e-e-e-e-e-e-e-e!"

Then she turned, flipped her hind legs at the tractor and went stomping around the side of the hill on land level enough for the tractor to follow. Which it did. Simm Johns shook his fist now, madder than ever before, I reckoned.

We stood there in the yard, that is, me and pa did. Ma would have no part of it. I kept hiding my eyes when the tractor got close to the mule and opened them when I heard pa slap his legs and go to laughing, knowing that Kate had got out of the way again. Of a sudden just when it looked like the tractor would roll over her she would make a quick turn. Simm Johns would shake his fist and take thirty feet to make the next turn, having to dodge and cut in between trees to boot.

Up toward the top of the ridge they would go until they got so small that you could have cupped them both in the palm of your hand. And I'd be thinking that Kate had grown tired now and was set to bog the tractor down. Then she would stop, coax the tractor on and bring Simm Johns and it back down the slope.

The shadows moved in fast, quilting the tops of the hills, and darkness came down the slopes. Simm Johns turned the tractor's lights on and the beams stretched out into the night and lit on Kate's back and rested there, making it look as if she was harnessed to the tractor.

Pa fumbled with the stick in his hand and said:

"We might as well grab us a bite to eat and set this one out. They've got a long time to go before the race is over. No doubt now that mule is set on taking him all the way."

As I followed pa to the house I got to thinking about what would happen when the race was over. How much longer could the little mule last? She had to be slowing down now and I wondered if her old joints were popping like they did sometimes whenever we ran along the hills. She had nowhere to call up extra juice to stop the squeaks. Time had taken it away, dried the pools up like heat will do a creek bed.

I wondered if she would just finally have to stop somewhere along the slope. And would Simm Johns hate her so much that he would just keep coming until he had broken every bone in her body?

If I were going to get an answer from pa I had to do it quick. There wouldn't be much talking about it once we faced ma again.

"Will he run over the mule, pa?" I asked.

"Run over her!" Pa looked strangely at me. "He ain't going to get closer than the swish of her tail." Pa held the stick up to the kitchen light and stared at a mark he'd made by chipping the bark away with his fingernail. "He ain't got much gas left to do that with."

I got to thinking about pa and that stick at the supper table and almost choked to keep from laughing about it— which would have been doom for me, being at the table and ma already mad as a hornet. If pa had his measurements right and was right in his judging of that mule, he stood to trick Simm Johns right off his feet, something no one had ever done before. Pa had taken a good look and made his bet, knowing what the little mule would do and her being dead set on doing it.

"Isaac!" ma scolded across the table, I guess seeing the grin on my face. "You're at the table. After you eat you go into your room. Things are bad enough without your having to set in here and watch your pa make a spectacle out of himself!"

Pa did just what I thought he would do. He kept quiet. That's the way it was when ma was mad as a hornet. I tried to stretch out my eating, got caught, and got sent into my room quick. This wasn't a time to be meddling. I listened for ma and pa with my ears and kept my eyes peeled to the window to see the mule and Simm Johns if I could.

It seemed to go on for ages. After a while, I heard ma say:

"You'll have a hard time getting forgiveness for this, Jeremiah. He's going to run that mule right into the Sabbath and a mortal sin."

Just then I heard the clock set in to striking twelve midnight and Saturday ending.

"I ain't wanting to take advantage of the Lord," pa said, "but I've waited years for a square shot at Simm Johns and I don't think I'm about to be begrudged now."

Then the noise of the tractor stopped. Its lights went off. It was all as quiet as if the noise of the hills had been sacked up and thrown in the creek and drowned into nothing.

I pressed my face against the window. I thought of the worst. The little mule squashed flat against the hill. Then I wondered why the tractor had stopped up there on the hill if this were so.

And then I saw a small shadow coming down the slope toward the fence line. I held my breath, and swallowed hard when I saw Simm Johns straddle the fence. But before I could conjure up some mighty sorry thoughts, I heard the little mule bray from along the slope.

"He-haw-e-e-e-e-e-e-e-e!"

She had won!

Simm Johns stopped long enough atop the fence to shake his fist up the hill toward the sound and then got down and walked on his tiptoes across the yard.

I heard the door that led outside open.

"Over here to pay, Simm." It was pa.

I squinted and looked out the window at an angle, so I could see. Simm Johns had a hand in his pocket.

Pa held the stick up and rubbed his hand over it.

"Run out of gas, eh?" he said.

"You tricked me, Jeremiah," Simm Johns said, looking toward the stick.

"Why I'm surprised at you, Simm," pa said, "accusing me of a thing like that on the Sabbath. Four and two makes six. With as good a corn crop as you got that oughten to bother you."

"I'll get the better yet," Simm Johns said. "I'll shoot

39

that critter come daylight!"

"Like to put another two on that?" pa said. "It's a real pleasure to do business with you."

Simm Johns went stomping off around the side of the hill and I went back to thinking of the little mule and pa.

"Ain't you ashamed!" I heard ma say.

"Sure am," pa said. "Easiest money I ever made."

"Evil money, betting money is," ma said. "Won't do no good to spend it."

"Spend it!" pa said. "I'm aiming to frame it and hang it in the shop."

I peeped through the door and saw pa counting the money again.

"That's a smart little critter I tell you," pa said. "You see the way she kept that tractor going uphill? Doggone if I don't believe she did it knowing it took gas that way. She didn't have to make a race of it. Could have gone along the ridge and stopped it all."

"For shame," ma said. "First Isaac, then you."

"Isaac?" pa said.

"Teaching that mule to steal corn," ma said.

"Why, Emmazet," pa said. "You don't think that mule is human enough to learn to poke shucks of corn in a muskrat's hole, do you?"

"Isaac admitted to it," ma said.

"Trying to protect the mule," pa said. "Just trying to protect the mule. Only natural for him to do that. Soft-hearted. Takes that much after you."

"Don't tie me in with that mule!" ma said. "Don't wrap your sin around me! At daylight the mule goes."

"Goes where?" pa said.

"Back," ma said.

"Back where?" pa asked.

"Back —" ma studied for a moment—"well, back far enough where we won't have to worry about it all no more."

"I don't think we'll have to worry about that," pa said. "If I know mules she won't be within gunshot come daylight. She knows Simm Johns will be after her."

That was the way it was left. With loneliness again tucked around me and thinking all sorts of crazy things, I couldn't sleep.

I counted sheep and the first thing you know little mules were jumping the fence. And then an old, tired mule came along. So sore that she just stopped and sat down on the other side. Couldn't jump. That was Kate. Needing help in a bad way.

I opened my eyes and the picture didn't change much. Only thing was instead of the mule sitting there by the fence she was sitting up at the edge of the pine grove, just as stiff and sore. I got to thinking about that and what pa said about her being out of gunshot come daylight.

So I thought I'd help her some.

I'd sneak to the kitchen where ma kept a bottle of liniment handy, slip back to my room and then out the window and up the slope to where the mule ought to be stretched out stiff and sore. She'd have a lot of walking to do when daylight came and she went deep into the hills with no path home. I wasn't wanting her traveling over that rugged land in more pain than she had to have. Our time was running out.

I could hear pa snoring as I tiptoed past their door,

41

and figured ma was asleep since she wasn't quarreling at pa for it and asking him to turn over since she always said he snored only when he slept on his right side.

I made it into the kitchen and fumbled in the dark until I found the liniment. I stopped breathing, and listened to make sure they were still asleep. I tiptoed on.

"That you, Isaac?" ma said.

"Yes'm," I answered. "Just been for a drink of water." I swallowed. The big bottle of liniment felt heavy in my hand.

"You know I had reason to send you to bed," she said.

"Yes'm," I said.

"I just didn't want you to go to sleep without knowing that," she said.

Now I couldn't just go back into my room and then right out the window. I had to wait now for ever so long to be sure that ma was asleep. But finally I crawled out the window and was on my way.

The big moon lighted up the hill and made a wide yellow path that I could have traveled blindfolded. Crickets sang from the grass and a rooster crowed out from a far distance, sending cold chills over me. Not only were me and that rooster at odds, since he was crowing for daylight and I wanted the night to last forever, but his crowing was a bad omen. A rooster crowing long before daylight was a sure sign of bad luck. Maybe the betting had brought it about, I thought.

One thing for sure about that rooster: He would win, for daylight would come. It would be on me, I thought, if I didn't quit standing there listening to him and get on to the pine grove.

I didn't stop again until I felt the soft needles of the pines under my bare feet. The smell of the pines was everywhere.

"Kate," I said, almost in a whisper, no louder than the quarrel of a sleepy bird.

I listened and heard nothing but the wind, it blowing soft and hot against my body. And I got to thinking that this was the first time I had ever known the little mule's name and wondered what she would think of that.

If I had waited for her to come to me I wouldn't have found her at all. For I found her bedded down in a clump of needles and not figuring on moving. She looked up at me with her big, brown eyes blinking like lightning bugs that have fallen to the earth. Just too sore to raise her head much. I saw her wrinkle, drawing in air, then swell, and I stood there frozen, waiting for her to give us both away. But she was too tired for that, too. She just dropped her head and let the air seep out without more than enough strength to blow out a match.

I stood above her with my legs spread and one hand on my hip, trying to look like I was plumb disgusted. "Serves you right, you old fool," I said. "I mean being sore and stiff. You ought to have knowed better than to try to wear a tractor down."

The next thing I knew I was on my knees beside her and her old head was in my lap. She stuck her nose against me and blinked her eyes and she could have up and stolen all the corn that grew in the mountains right then and it wouldn't have changed things one particle. I just wasn't caring at the moment.

I pulled out the bottle of liniment and started at her

broken hoofs, working my way up gentle-like. While I rubbed I talked, starting out by scolding her for stealing the corn since I was afraid that with or without me she might take a notion to go back.

What a foolish trick it was to buck Simm Johns. I told her that. Making him look like a pure fool in front of folks. And I turned my head to hold back my giggling. Just thinking about it and so proud I was next to busting. But she never knew. She never knew that as I rubbed in the liniment the extra pats she got were my way of saying: "You hitched right up to him, old girl, and beat him good and proper."

I'd rub a while and talk a little and then stop to see how they both were setting with her. I took her looks for words and could tell that she was grateful for me being there. Being a mule she couldn't speak a word and didn't have to. And I thought how lonely the world must be not to be near a thing that looked like you. To be almost dependent on something like me and me not knowing how to help but wanting to so bad.

I talked to the mule about leaving come daylight. I took my time about it. But to save me I couldn't think of a place in the big world where she could go and be wanted. That was awful. And she had a sad look in her eyes. She knew where she stood now and what I was trying to say. Like she had been an old fool to ever think me and her would work out.

The next thing I knew I felt something tap me on the shoulder and I looked up at pa.

"Let's go home, Isaac," he said. "Your ma is worried about you."

"All right, pa," I said. "I just thought I'd rub Kate down some before she left come daylight."

"I know, Isaac," he said. "It's all right, boy. It's all right."

He looked down now at the little mule. Straddled his legs and grinned at her. Then he bent down and stroked her nose.

"I don't know how many rounds you've had to fight to get this old here in the hills," pa said, "but you won a good fight today, old girl." Then he looked at me. "You've helped the mule with the liniment, Isaac. It will take out a lot of the soreness."

Ma was waiting for me when we reached the house. She just stood staring at me, not saying a word. That always makes things worse. Just standing and staring at me when I had done something I wasn't supposed to do. It always makes me say something since being quiet will wither me down.

"I just figured to stay a little while, ma," I said. "I fell asleep."

"You should have told me," ma said. "Not just go traipsing off and scaring me that way."

"I had to see the mule, ma," I said, "knowing that she would be gone when daylight comes. Thought I ought to try to let her know why she had to go. Not let her just go without ever knowing why. But to save me I didn't know what to say to her."

"It might have been all right if you had told me," ma said. "Being gone without saying nothing makes a body think all sorts of things, none of them good."

That was about all that was said except that sometime

during the night ma opened the door to my room.

"Isaac," she said, "I didn't want the night to end with my knowing that I had lied to you about letting you go to see about that mule. I wouldn't have let you if you had asked." She came close to the bed. "But I'm glad you went. And to save me I don't know the answer for that mule either. I only know she has got to go. She can bring nothing but trouble."

"Yes, ma," I said.

At the door ma stopped again.

"Don't go to thinking I've softened a heap and go sneaking off again," she said.

"No, ma," I answered.

And that night the softness of ma's words was about the only thing I could think of that was good, though I knew they would not help the mule one particle come daylight.

CHAPTER 4

Being a Hero Kills a Conscience

The sun was up early scooting out the little sparkles of dew that hid under the blades of grass and weeds. But the night hadn't just passed without bringing something. It and pa had worked to soften ma until she had consented to let me go to the pine grove come morning and look for the little mule. If she was there I could take her back into the hills to where I had found her, being some responsible for her being here and all. I could take her and leave her to keep her from being shot outright by Simm Johns, shot at least so close to the house. If she was shot far off we had no way of knowing about it and what you didn't know wasn't bound to hurt near as much as knowing it. I could just think that the mule had wandered farther away than ever, off Simm Johns' land. She would too, if she had any sense, ma reasoned. I wasn't sure about it and pa didn't say.

If the mule did have good sense, she didn't start out with much reasoning to back it up. I found her right there inside the pine grove, flicking her tail and hiding behind a pine tree. She was a kind of stupid mule in many ways, I reckoned. She was just too big a thing to go trying to hide behind a little old pine tree and she ought to have known it. All that pine tree did was cut her in half, her tail around one side and her big eyes peering around the other.

She didn't even know that it was no time to play about. Unless maybe she was taking me seriously and pretending to be right happy about everything until the end came. If so, she was standing up under it all a mite better than I was. We were still close enough to the pine grove to chuck a rock into it when she got after her first butterfly. Jumping around like she hadn't had any race with that tractor at all.

And seeing the old ornery thing trying to stretch out her sore muscles, I got to thinking that maybe she was right after all. Maybe it was best to just be happy about the whole thing and spend her time chasing butterflies and eating blackberries and then sit a spell on the ridge to watch lizards, birds, and snails and look down on the land below. Trying to spot Simm Johns if he came with a big gun. The tractor was gone. Pa said he had seen Bunt Rankins—who owned a little strip of land bordering Simm Johns', couldn't make a living on it being hillside and all, and did a little work for Simm—drive it away just at daybreak. I'd been lazying in the bed past sun-up since my lids hadn't been shut long at the time.

That's what we did. Me and that mule just shuffling along with the world under our feet all the way to that old shack.

It stood old and still as the morning about. I sat down under the forks of that big oak and Kate went to the fence of the shack like she was wanting to start right back at the beginning.

I closed my eyes and all of it seemed like a dream. You know how it is sometimes. You come up on things that sort of tuck tail and twist around until you are right back at the start, and feeling as if you've been here and seen the things yet just can't seem to pull them into place. Like it did happen and then didn't happen at all. That's how it was with me at the moment. If I had had a berry bucket I'd have sworn that there had never been a day of pure joy with that mule. Just the beginning. No ending. Wouldn't have been no stealing of corn. No trouble. No tractor.

This old shack was where I found her in the beginning and where she must have wanted to be since she had had a world to ramble in and had picked this place.

If you looked at it right it had advantages. If she could last out the summer Simm Johns would be using the shack to store hay and fodder in to throw out for cattle to keep from having to haul it all from his own barn. He'd have the little haystacks spread over the hills like pony express stations from the pages of history books. When he had pitched the hay out and gone Kate could sneak in and eat.

Well, the rotted gate was still down. She could have grass from the yard and shelter inside the shack. Dodge rains of the summer if she stayed and snows of the winter if she tarried.

I'd catch her head down eating grass and then leave her there. Thinking about slipping off made me feel pretty small, not tall enough to reach the top of a bull thistle. She walked inside the fence and stood waiting for

49

me to follow.

"Think I'll just mosey around the other side and get myself a heap of shadeberries," I said. "Just help yourself to the grass."

I started and she followed. I stopped, she stopped. I started, she started. I stopped and she stopped, just like she knew something was up.

"Can't I go eat some berries without you tagging along?" I said.

Those eyes again as big as butternuts. I'd have to do something. I pulled a bunch of grass and held it out to her. Doggone if she didn't nudge it out of my hands and let it fall to the ground.

"Ain't no way to be about it," I said.

She shoved her head into my hands now, making me too short to look over a toad stool and knowing I had to do something fast before I dwindled from sight. I stepped back and said:

"What's troubling you, you crazy old fool? Don't you know when you ain't wanted?"

So help me, I got to thinking about Simm Johns sneaking over the hills to gun that mule down and cart her off to the tannery. Then using that tractor to drag her with. And just before the shot, her up and thinking I didn't want her anymore. Thinking that she might be shot if I didn't do something, I took me a switch and swarped her across the rump.

"Git!" I said. "Git far away!"

She quivered from the blow, me knowing full well that I didn't hit her that hard, yet knowing how bad it hurt. It was like it was when ma took a branch to me.

50

Never hit me too hard. It was the thought behind it that hurt. A soft blow that took away a little of her caring for the moment.

Kate caught the softness in my eyes. She took advantage and jumped back like she was twenty years younger and willing to forget that the blow had ever come.

I swarped her again. She looked at me like she was trying to figure out how I could hit her like that with softness in my eyes and she backed into a patch of cockleburs.

I would leave her this way. And so I turned up the slope with full intentions of never looking back. Wouldn't have either if I hadn't lost my footing.

That's not exactly right. I got almost to the top of the ridge and then slipped a little. I was thinking of the swarps I had given her and her maybe thinking I was no better than Simm Johns. So, sort of sliding my foot a little to help me out, I turned to take one last look.

I saw her and then pretended I didn't. But she could no more hide behind a tree than a squirrel could behind a broom straw. She was following, slow and sneaking, with pure intentions of staying the night in the pine grove above the house.

I must have looked as big as the mountain itself to ma as I walked into the yard. She started right off heaping praise on me to no end for what I had done. Been man enough to take that mule off like that and ward trouble away for us all.

I was just human enough to feel guilty about it. I mean just rearing back and letting ma heap praise on me like that for something she thought I had done but hadn't. But the guilty feeling didn't last long. And ma waited on me hand and foot.

"It's all right, ma," I said. "I knowed my job and I did it. That's all."

And then she told the story over and over again with me adding a word here and there whenever she got bogged down or didn't seem to stretch it out far enough until I got to taking the whole tale for gospel truth. Sorta puckering up at the sad edges and swelling out my chest and facing up under it when the last came, leaving the mule.

There was even a difference in pa. He came out to help me with the wood cutting and pointed out the fine points by saying things like, "Be careful how you swing that ax," and such. He looked at me proud-like, as if I was a man now for sure.

"Everything's all right, pa," I said. "Time just comes when you got to make a decision."

Pa grinned and looked at me like he meant to say that bydogs he doubted if he would have been man enough to make the right one like he thought I had.

Pa got to talking about the coming winter. How that old single-barrel gun he called a blunderbuss because it knocked you half out of your senses everytime you fired it just wasn't a suitable enough gun for me. Ought to have an L.C. Smith double barrel. One of those light field grades. And a dog. Purely didn't know how we had got by without one since old Drum had died two years ago of old age.

It wouldn't be one of those little dogs like women

sometimes take to, pa said. One that would be apt to plop over if it came face to face with a good-sized possum. But a real hound. A broad-nosed, thick-chested, long-eared, bugle-voiced dog. One that would just run the dickens out of all game within smelling distance, and that taking in a fair piece of land. And I sat back like I was meaning that would be all right.

But an evening can be an awful long time. And when you are a hero of a story you can be too much of a hero. I mean you can get the ones that are doing the bragging on what you did to be a hero thinking that they just might be adding too much importance to it. It happened to me.

And when it did I was at my worst. Just went around hanging my head down like I was having awful thoughts again about that mule and what I had had to do. Like it was taking my life. I went into periods of silence, shaking my head about, down low, like I was pulling the sorrowful picture of it all up again.

It brought them right back, heaping on the praise higher than ever.

I faked not being hungry, you know, lost my appetite and all, and went to bed early, knowing full well I'd suffer for that before the night was over. But thinking I might get out of that by sneaking up during the night and eating.

I lay in my room flat on my back keeping a pitiful look within calling-up distance just in case ma or pa came in, which I purely figured they would before they turned in. You know, to see if I was still all right and all.

I got to thinking about what I had done and where I stood. Just how shaky the foundation was, being weaker than an ant hill, little red ants at that. Then I got to thinking that it all made no matter. The land was not a solid place to build on in the first place. Just when you worked yourself to the bone to better it all something or someone would come by and outdate you and swat you out like a fly. That's the way it was with Kate. Here she was living in a world that said it was wrong for her to eat corn and go around being a mule and being in the way about it. When that was what she had been put here to do and be and had spent nearly thirty years, which was about her age, pa said, judging by her teeth, proving herself to be a good one. The worn scars of the harness on her shoulders to prove it. She'd come in here and worked out her life pulling a hillside plow to furrow the land for people and then a tractor had come along and swept away her past, present, and future. Now she was just in the way. People's memory was no long than a tadpole's tail.

Mighty queer world. Take me. I went sneaking to Bear Creek for a swim just like pa said he had done a thousand times when he was a boy. And yet whenever ma had me by the ear for the same thing he never spoke a word for me. Shook his head like he was agreeing that the creek was nowhere for me to go alone. And me able to outswim a minnow.

It looked to me like the world had sort of started downhill since pa's day. For both me and that mule. Hard for me to make a man and harder for her to find a place to die in comfort. If I could just be like pa and rear back and say: "Ah, for the good old days."

I'd go back a little farther. I'd have that mule hitched

up to a wagon just as the wild Indians were a-coming over the bluff. She'd pull us to safety and be a hero about it and everyone would want her then. But that's what I mean. Our world had gone downhill. Nothing left to be a hero about. Only room to be in the way. As for the Indians they were all gone. Unless you wanted to include that old Shawnee that came to Tatesburg when the weather was warm to set up a stand and sell snake ointment. And he'd been mixed with the whites for so long that he had to stay in the sun to stay brown, pa said.

About the only good thing left it seemed to me was pretending. And I went after that like it was the next thing on the list to be scratched out. I could sit on the back of that mule and whip more Indians than a thousand-legger bug had legs. Or, I could lean over and wrap my arms around the little mule's neck and know that something belonged to me. I could laugh at the day and mock the night knowing that there was something in between.

I didn't know where to turn come daylight. Any way spelled trouble.

I'd get up in the morning, get myself fattened out with praise while it lasted and get into the hills by telling ma I thought I'd just go to spotting nut trees about now so I wouldn't have to waste all my time when they ripened out with frost just looking for them.

I sure never thought to wake up and be looking Simm Johns square in the eyes. Him big, real and red-faced as the morning sun and set on outtalking the wind.

"Come during the night," Simm Johns said to ma. "Knowed I'd be watching that field during the day and that ornery critter come during the night and shucked out enough corn to fill every muskrat hole within sight."

Ma didn't say a word to me. Just turned into the house and come back out carrying a long-sleeved shirt. She handed it to me.

"What do you figure the corn was worth?" ma asked.

Simm Johns rubbed his chin.

"Six dollars," he said. "Not a cent less. Half of what she took was from my sweet-corn patch. Ripe and ready to come off."

"How much you pay for picking sweet corn?" ma asked.

"Dollar a day from sunup to sundown," Simm Johns said.

"At fifty cents a day, 'lowing time for daydreaming, that would come to twelve days for Isaac," ma said.

And bydogged if Simm Johns didn't have nerve enough to reach over and feel my arm just as if ma was auctioning me off and he was seeing if I was worth the price. Then he curled his nose up at what he felt and looked at ma.

"I'd a heap rather have the six dollars," he said.

"But six dollars wouldn't be near as apt to get shed of the mule," ma said.

"You're so right, Mrs. Warfield," he said. "Yep, you're so right."

I never spent a more miserable day. First it was the sun, big and hot and purely intending to rest the day on my shoulders. And there was the creek. So close that I could have thrown a clod into it. Cool and sweet-looking as a gourd of well water. Not a breeze to stir it.

Me alone and deserted by my own ma and the mule

to boot, which ought to be stretched out on the slopes under the shade with her belly full of corn. Sweet corn at that, choice of the lot.

The corn blades touched me, itched, and turned the skin red as a chigger. And the redbirds and jaybirds jumped around in the willows telling me that they were wild and free and had no one to answer to.

Before that day ended it seemed to me that my whole life had just dwindled down to picking corn. I could close my eyes and see the big, long green walls with the little narrow paths of earth separating them. So close that they squeezed you in where the green arms of the corn could reach out and pick on you. And me looking down those paths thinking that here was where I would walk my life away.

To make it worse Simm Johns was near by, and he came close enough to keep saying:

"Mule worth that much, Isaac?" Then he would laugh louder than the jaybirds.

Pa never knew how much I appreciated him right there, and how happy I was that he had only bet Simm Johns six dollars. If it had been more I would have been working that corn until my skin furrowed with age just like the land about. Just the amount he had lost! That's what Simm Johns had upped his price to. Getting his money back, and getting shed of the mule to boot. And my own ma conniving with him. Pawning me off at half price.

When I got home my back was bowed and I didn't want no truck with nothing. Not even the little mule that had got kind of brazen and had come down to the fence line this side of the house. She stood staring at me, with those big eyes seeming to say, "Where you been all day?"

Well I was tired and mad and figured there wasn't no need taking it all out on the mule. So I thought I'd move on and hope for sympathy from pa.

That's when she brayed and got herself in bad. I just hadn't worked all day in the cornfield to come home and be laughed at. So I sort of edged up to her and said:

"How'd you like to march off to the tannery?"

That didn't set too well and I could see it. Maybe she didn't know what I was saying. Maybe it was the look she saw in my eye. But she came close and stuck her nose in my hands which softened me like a spring violet and I patted her on the nose and said:

"I didn't mean that. I guess I'm wore out and thinking the world is against me."

She tried to follow but I wouldn't have any part of that. I was already sentenced to two weeks in the cornfield and not wanting more than that. So, thinking she might be lonely and knowing how bad that can be, I sat with her a while there along the slope. Didn't say much. Just a-watching the stars come out to blink like lightning bugs along the hills. Wondering what sort of land it was above them and if a man would have to pick corn and try to hide as big a thing as a mule.

She walked back toward the pine grove, her head down and her legs moving slow and quiet. Me telling her that if a chance came I'd sneak out at dinner tomorrow and come to the pine grove. I was sort of begrudging the mule some; I had to go face pa. All she had to face was a soft bed of pine needles with the tops of the trees lit up with stars.

Pa had a lot of chipping away to do—I mean all that praise he had heaped on me. And pa had his special way of doing it. Like he kept asking me to pass the corn at the supper table.

After supper he looked at me sort of easy-like.

"Your ma tells me you found you a job, Isaac," he said. "Proud of you."

And then that night he took his 'taterbug down from the wall and sang:

> "Brown is the color of his true love's hair
> What more is there for me to say?
> She's got four legs and the sneak-e-n-est ways
> She's stole Simm Johns' corn away
> Poor Isaac to pick the corn to pay.
> Poor Isaac to pick the corn to pay."

The corn stayed with me the night. Came to hant me like a booger. One of those boogers brazen enough to win a prize. For it did not run and hide during daylight. It followed me every step right up to the end of the second week.

CHAPTER 5

A Polecat Is the World's Best Shot

The days that followed were just plain nip and tuck. Seemed to me that Kate had learned her lesson about going to the creek to steal corn. I liked to think it was because of me. She valued my being with her of the days along the slopes more than she liked the corn. And it kept Simm Johns at a distance.

Ma had a suspicion the mule was still about but never saw her. For we had sharpened up on staying out of sight. But ma was busy putting up canned goods and getting ready for the coming winter and she didn't say much, or look much.

I thought pa knew and was on my side but just couldn't come out and say so for fear ma might find out.

Simm Johns wasn't about much and Kate had learned to hide from him like a squirrel in a nut tree. She knew how far her braying would carry and only used it whenever she got too excited about something to hold it back.

I even got to spend two nights with her along the slopes but they turned out to be miserable for us both.

It came about the day we were traipsing along the slopes and came face to face with that polecat. Well, you know how that mule was to go chasing things. That it was a polecat made no difference to her. It popped up in front of her, stopped and looked easy-like, then turned to mosey off just as slow and easy. And seeing the mule following, it turned its head up like it was saying "You crazy?"

She was. For you just don't go around chasing polecats that don't want to be chased and willing to let you know it. I guess they know they got you at odds which just doesn't make'em the running kind. Not like a rabbit or a groundhog. So that big black polecat just turned again and looked that mule in the eyes like he was willing to let bygones be bygones and meant for her to just go about her business. She didn't.

Faced with times like this you go to slowing your voice and everything else you got control of since being quick makes excitement and excitement spells doom. So I stretched out my voice and walked as slow as riding down a sapling tree.

"Hold up, Kate," I said. And just like I was egging her on she went at it full charge. And that polecat had no notion of moving one step. I tried to head her off.

The polecat lowered his head and peeked back between his legs as if he was planning to frame us both in. Up went his bushy tail, slow and easy as taking a sight over a rifle—up like opening your hand slow motion.

I caught Kate, threw my arms around her neck and stopped her so fast she bowed in the middle. She looked me in the eyes ever so slow and we both looked at that polecat and closed our eyes. His gun was cocked.

One of the things I purely despise about a polecat is that he never misses. This one did no worse. He fogged up just enough land about to hold me and that mule. And although I couldn't see now, I figured him to be off about his business since they always do, knowing that one shot does it. I was blinded and Kate was on her back rolling over the land like a sawlog, trying to give what she had on her to the leaves and grass. I was close behind, offering the leaves and grass boot if they wanted it.

We rolled, coughed, cried, drew in mountains of air. Hers came out going, "Shooooooo." Mine came out fussing at her for all I was worth.

We tried everything. Tried to walk it off. This didn't work so we slipped to the creek and I scrubbed us both down with sand and water. I couldn't tell if it helped or not, for it's hard to tell how much polecat is around when there's nothing but polecat smell about.

Kate walked around with her head hung down like she was trying to make me believe that the polecat had done her wrong, taken advantage of her, attacked her. That same old trick that I would hope to use on ma a little later on in the evening.

It never worked for me either. I never got past the door. The evening wind was at my back.

"That's close enough," ma said.

That evening I scrubbed with lye soap in a rain barrel in the backyard and ma handed my supper out to me. Later she handed me out a blanket and said she hoped the bugs were kind to me if they made it past the smell.

So thinking I couldn't be worse off and was safe I went to the pine grove and curled up beside the mule. Just drenched in polecat juice both of us. It kept the bugs at a distance and drove the hants away.

CHAPTER 6

Strike Up a Drum and Blow a Flute

Well, the end came a few days later. I thought it was the end. Because a cat only has nine lives and I didn't figure Kate, being a mule, was entitled to more than that.

The summer was growing old. The leaves on the trees were already turning red on the end, curling up to blush at the sun. And me and that mule had already started our talk about school, that was coming up for me soon now. Me talking with words and her with looks and doings. We started each talk slow and pitiful and then in the end decided to forget it all until it really happened.

We began to look more toward the evenings since that would be the time we could mostly be together. I got to teasing her about maybe her even working out at school and all. Like maybe coming in handy to pull a wagon for a hayride and the like. She didn't seem to take much to that, turning up her nose when I got to the part about having a pretty girl up there beside me. Jealous, I figured. And I got to telling her that she sure would be a pretty thing sitting up there on the seat beside me and leaving the girl to pull the wagon. That seemed funny.

To tell the truth I didn't take much to it either, I mean

the talk about the girls. I never put any stock to speak of in girls. They were forever telling the teacher about something you ought not be doing. But I guess I took my joy to kid from pa.

I think that mule knew better and just let on to believe me. For she knew that me and her were as close as bark to a tree and you just don't go peeling that sort of closeness off easy-like.

I guess we had done most everything. Hid out in the hills like tramps, fought cockleburs and sawbriars, and hidden under the shelter of caves to ward off a storm. But always being together, which was what counted most.

We'd traipsed around most of the day when we came to a gulley, cool and quilted with moss and wild fern, and grass so tender that direct sun would have struck it dead but couldn't because of the shade of the big beech trees that hovered over it like a setting hen. And the grass was deep green and spindly and small as strands of hair.

A lightning-struck poplar tree was bowed low to the earth, its tops sprawled out on one side of the bank and its roots on the other. A big poplar log that offered plenty of footing to cross from one bank to the other. As inviting as could be. And over the side of it was a six-foot drop.

Kate was eating grass and I was making my way back and forth across that fallen tree. Paying no attention to anything else. Then of a sudden, halfway out the log, I felt it tremble. I turned and saw the old mule, two feet on the log and two feet on earth, and a look in her eye that said she was dead set on getting those hind hoofs on.

"Whoo," I said. "Now you git back." I was afraid to go to her, afraid that she might think I was coaxing her on. I was afraid to go to the other side, afraid she would surely follow. Talking seemed the only way. That wasn't much. If you've ever tried to talk a mule out of something it is dead set on doing you know what I mean.

"Get back, you old fool," I said. "Logs are not for mules."

She grinned, silly-like, and squeezed a third foot on the log, fighting for balance. And then she brought the last one on.

I scolded her until she was a third-way out the log and then I quit. She was too far now to go back. She couldn't turn on the log and she would never make it backwards. And she would never make it to the other side. She was in a heap of trouble and didn't know it. For there she was, her old legs trembling like four weeds in a windstorm, her broken hoofs slipping on the log, and a look on her face that was pure pleasure. Grinning like a possum in a 'simmon tree.

She edged her way an inch at a time, slipping, getting her footing again. And I guess she thought she had the log whipped. For she shriveled up, drew in a mountain of air.

"Don't do it!" I screamed.

But it was too late. Only the first came out.

"*He-e-e-e-e-e-e-e.*" I closed my eyes, and wished I had closed my ears, too. She hit the ground like a tree falling: THUD!

She was still breathing when I reached her. Deep breaths. Enough to shake the tops of the grass. Her sides moved in and out in great heaves and her head was flat on the ground. Big eyes blinking and looking nowhere.

One leg folded up under her and helpless.

I tried the best I could to scoot the leg out. But she was too heavy and if I even touched it, she groaned. All I could do was scoot her head into my lap and sit beside her as helpless as I ever could be.

I got to thinking about the leg being broken and how animals such as mules with broken legs are mostly shot. And knowing that Kate would be shot anyway if she couldn't hide from Simm Johns, my mind became as mixed up as an old owl's that forgets sometimes and comes out to screech in the daytime.

And then I thought of pa.

I scooted out from under the mule's head as easy as I could. I knelt beside her and wiped away the pain-water that came from her eyes. I said:

"Don't worry none, Kate. I'm going for pa. He'll know what to do."

Down over the hill I went, losing my footing more times than I could count, the sawbriars and blackberry vines whipping me good. They picked out the cuffs of my britches as keen as ma could have done with a needle. Picked my face too. And the cuts burned from the sweat. All this and the evening was late, late enough for pa to be in the house and ma waiting supper on me, and mad as a nest of hornets.

"Pa! Pa!" I yelled from the side of the hill, and I kept yelling as I ran right on into the yard. It was enough to wake the dead.

Pa swung out the door, ma close.

"Pa!" I said, gasping for breath. "You've got to come quick!"

"What's wrong?" pa asked.

"Please, pa!" I said.

Pa turned to ma and seeing her wringing her hands said:

"Don't worry, Emmazet. We'll be all right."

When we got to the gully and pa saw the little mule there, helpless, he just knelt beside her and patted her on the head.

"Easy now, old girl," he said, talking as low as he ever talked to ma. "It's going to be all right. I've come to help."

And trying to pacify the little mule I said:

"Hear that, Kate? Pa says he is going to help."

But she didn't even try to raise her head.

Pa looked up at me and there was a frown on his face. His hands had moved over the mule so fast you could hardly see them.

"Everything seems to be all right but the leg," he said. "I've got to get it out from under her before I can tell how much damage there is to it. How did it happen?"

I hid my face for shame. For what might seem natural enough to me would be strange for pa. It would for anyone that didn't know Kate. "Walking a log," I said.

"Walking a log!" pa said. "Glory be. What next!" But his face held a grin. He broke into a laugh and then got to his feet, took out his pocket knife and whittled down a fairsized limb, trimming the smaller branches off as he went.

Kneeling beside the mule again he scooped out a pocket of earth and stuck the limb under her.

"Get near her now, Isaac," he said. "This old mule is

going to need you about now."

And she did, too. She moaned to high heaven when pa put his shoulder to the limb to raise her up some. And I bit my lip to keep from saying soft words to her. Holding the weight of the mule on his shoulder, pa worked his hands under her side and pulled the leg free.

"She's been laying on it so it's numb," he said. "But it ain't broke. Just out of its joint. We'll have to slip it back and make splints."

Pa straddled the leg now and put his feet against the shoulders of the mule. One hard jerk and it was all over. Kate looked around and I think she was even mad because pa did it so fast she didn't have a chance to cut a shine.

Then pa cut the splints. A long limb to go on the outside of the leg, sticking above her head like a flagpole. The other was shorter to fit the inside, cupping under her breast, near the leg. He bound them with strips of cloth from his shirttail and we hoisted the mule up.

We must have been a sorry-looking sight coming over the ridge toward the pine grove, like the last of a whipped army. Pa with his shirt chewed nearly off, me with cuts and scratches all over me and black as tree bark. And Kate was the pitifulest of all. Hobbling along, bobbing up and down with the big splints on her, mad as ma would be apt to be when we reached home. The only thing I reckon we needed was a white flag on top of the taller splint.

Kate would go no farther than the pine grove. She might have been beholden to pa. But ma was a different matter.

Pa looked at the pine grove.

"Well, you're home, old girl," he said, knowing all along that here was where she had been staying. "The splints won't have to stay on long."

Ma had seen us from the yard, squinting and shaking her head.

"Did Simm Johns shoot the poor thing?" ma asked.

"No," pa said. "Nothing like that. She just fell off a log."

He sorta yawned and looked unconcerned.

"Log!" ma said. "How on earth did a mule fall off a log?" She looked at me. "Look at you, Isaac!"

"Well," pa said, "good thing she wasn't no higher up than she was. Could have fell from the top of a tree."

"Jeremiah!" ma said. "We'd better have a long talk." She got me by the ear just as I was turning to go. "You too, Isaac!"

"After supper?" pa said, bending to give ma a loud peck on the cheek.

I didn't feel like eating. Ma looked at me and said, "Eat up, Isaac. You'll be apt to need a full stomach." That made it worse.

"Emmazet," pa said, pouring a cup of coffee, "I just might save you a lot of time if you hear me out. I know how you feel about the mule. Well, I saw Bunt Rankins today. Said he had enough land to pasture the mule for a spell."

"Jeremiah!" ma said.

"Now," pa said, "I'm not saying that the mule is our responsibility. Ain't saying that she belongs to Isaac. I just don't think she deserves to be shot because she's a mule. And more so now because of that ruckus with that tractor. I feel beholden now."

"Jeremiah!" ma said.

"I'm thinking Isaac could take her over there in the morning and put her in the pasture. Only long enough for either me or Isaac to find a decent home for her," pa said.

"Is she hurt bad?" ma said, surprising me to no end.

"Her leg is mighty sore," pa said. "She couldn't get out of the way of a snail right now."

"And what about the pasture rent?" ma asked.

"Wouldn't be much," pa said. "A dollar a month. Isaac could pay me back after he sells his first load of walnuts. He's agreed to it."

I knew then who I had taken my lying from. Pa hadn't said a thing to me about a pasture. Though I was agreeable to what he said.

I dropped my head to look as sad as I could. And scratched up and all I must have been a sorry-looking sight. Pa edged her on.

"It's a way to get shed of the mule," he said.

"I don't know," ma said. "Seems like a lot of trouble for something that don't belong to us in the first place. That mule is a rogue and nothing but trouble. She just keeps getting closer to the house all the time. First thing you know I'll wake up and find her at the breakfast table."

"The least we can do is find her a home," pa said. "That oughten to take over a few days."

"Well," ma said, "if it means getting shed of the mule once and for all. Isaac can take the money for the pasture rent over in the morning."

"The first month is already paid for," pa said.

"Jeremiah!" ma said. "You fooled me!"

But ma was grinning now and watching us eat.

That night I got to thinking how bad the day had started and how good it had ended. Just showed you that you never had a way of knowing what time would bring. Not any way at all. Who would have thought that the mule would at last have a home for a while? Somewhere where she wouldn't have to run at the snap of a twig.

Strike up a drum and a flute and you've got yourself a fair picture of me and that mule the next morning going over to Bunt Rankins' place.

The tail end of a ragged army, just two of us since pa had gone on to his cobbler's shop in Tatesburg. Over the ridge we went, her limping and that big splint sticking out like a sore thumb to latch onto every briar bush in sight.

Bunt Rankins' pasture was no better than pa said it to be. Not enough grass to pasture the mule long. It had been cropped short and worn thin until you could have shot a game of kimmydike on it, never losing a marble in the grass. Might have in the weeds, though, for weeds covered it. Sagegrass, Queen Anne's lace and bull thistle and a little weed called a cow weed which is blue as the veins in an old woman's leg; the ladybugs like to climb on it.

We found us a tree for Kate to lean on and I took off the splints and rubbed the leg down with liniment to help take away the soreness. Then I fastened the splints back, Kate looking at me with pure disgust. We took a look around.

73

Below we could see the smoke curl from Bunt Rankins' cabin just over the knoll. And then we saw Bunt Rankins pop up around the side of the knoll, limping on a cane.

"Brought the mule I see," he said before he reached us. He wasn't looking at me at all but just at Kate. His bushy hair blew in the wind, long and tobacco-stained, and when he got closer I could see that his right eye twitched about like it was anxious to see what the other one was going to do. He was bowed, older than Simm Johns, and had a grin on his face that I couldn't tell was one he put there or got it natural-like and couldn't let go of it. He stared at Kate close now. "Warn't no need my making apologies to your pa 'bout the pasture. Judging that mule it don't look bad. A dollar for pasture rights is cheap for a varmint like that." He stared at the splints. "I've seen cattle yoked in peculiar ways, but never seed a mule yoked like that. Rogue is she? Bad at jumping fences?"

"That's a splint," I said, thinking that Kate looked better than he did. "She popped her leg out of joint."

"Eh?" he said. "How'd she do that?"

"Walking a log and fell from it," I said.

He twisted his cane in the ground and drew up his mouth like he wasn't putting much stock in a mule being able to walk a log.

"Foxy little booger, ain't you? Guess she runs rabbits, too," he said.

"Yes sir, she does," I said, being as honest as I knew how, and wanting to brag on Kate's doings some. "But she's a silent trailer and you have to watch her ears to know which way the rabbit's going."

"Well," he said, "see this here bum leg? Got that from tripping on a rainbow trying for the pot of gold, too." Then he laughed and showed his crooked teeth, walked up to Kate and pushed her mouth open "Ain't enough of them teeth left to scratch a flea with."

"Don't need'em," I says right back, "since there ain't no fleas on Kate." I figured that ought to set right.

He shook his head.

"Never judged a flea to be that smart," he said, laughing. "If I heerd your pa right he said you'd have a home for that mule time school starts for you end of the month."

"That's right," I said.

"Well," he said, "you don't have to cramp her none over here being you're paying for the grass. Let her have the freedom of the land and eat all she wants."

It wasn't eat all she wanted, I thought, watching him limp off, but what she could get. Maybe a bite or two with me helping her. Grass would have been a plumb fool to grow on land like this.

And while me and that mule grubbed around for a little I got to thinking about her teeth. First off it had been ma saying:

"Keep your distance and don't let that mule bite you!"

And Kate having to soak her corn before she could eat it.

Then pa had looked at them, grinned, and said to save him he didn't know how she could eat grass at all.

Simm Johns had accused her of outeating a muskrat.

Everyone seemed to be picking on her teeth one way or the other.

75

She wouldn't have to worry about using them much here in this pasture.

"This is your home, Kate," I said, closing the old gate. "I'll be back after I get my work done at the house."

And I walked slowly back over the ridge toward home. I turned to look at her, caught her walking the fence line like she was looking for a break. For her home was the pine grove and she would be restless without it. In a few days I would be able to take the splints off and that would help some. She'd get used to the pasture. If she didn't and longed for the pine grove—well, who was to know? After all, the fence wasn't much. About as sorry as my thoughts. School just over the hump and pa searching for a home for her.

CHAPTER 7

Look Out, General Washington

I thought we had it all worked out, me and that mule, when school started. Pa hadn't been able to find a home for her up to this point and I had had the same luck since I wasn't looking.

The pasture bill was going into its second month but the summer had come around to being on my side after all. Walnuts and hickory nuts looked to be plentiful. I'd be able to sell enough to keep from sponging the pasture bill off pa.

Ma wasn't pleased that Kate was still on our hands, but since the last month had been quiet—at least she thought so—she seemed content to wait us out a mite longer.

I had set my sights, given a lot of thought, to the coming winter. Kate would need a shed and all. But school put a damper on it and I had to give it up for a while.

Fact is, I was plumb scared stiff of that city school. Ma saying that they wouldn't be apt to put up with ornery ways and such. Got so scared that I even gave my face an extra scrubbing though I couldn't see to save me where people in the city would be apt to notice dirt any more then they had at the country school. Maybe it would be because the teacher would have fewer of us to stare at, focusing in on the dirt. Out in the country our teacher, old Lila Roots, had nine grades to worry about. They had more teachers in the city, which showed the lopsidedness of it all.

So when I left for school Kate seemed content to wait right there in Bunt Rankins' pasture until evening when I promised to come. She took advantage of the way ma had forced me to dress up. Acted at first like she didn't even know me, not fooling me in the least. Then she curled back her upper lip, which was her way of laughing, and brayed to high heavens, which didn't set well with me. It was all bad enough for me to be prettied up but to have an ornery mule laughing and making fun made me self-conscious. Everything was new and hard to take as it was.

"Just how would you like to have the splints back on?" I said. "You wouldn't look so doggone pretty yourself then." She got straightened out with that and so I says: "Stay in your own pasture where there's less trouble till I get back from school and there just might be enough light left for me and you to take another look at them nut trees before dark sets in."

Kate took a liking to that and she just stood there watching me walk off like her feet were stuck to the ground. Looked as innocent as a broom in the corner.

I got stuck in one room at school with a little puny woman named Miss Canlittle for a teacher. I had got myself a seat by a big window looking out over the hills and was trying to squint out it, without turning my head too much, to see all the freedom taken from me. I was sitting low trying to look out as much as I could with little of me showing. And I still say it was that starched collar on the shirt that singled me out from the start. For Miss Canlittle raised her eyes over her glasses and placed the finger of doom on me. Then she counted down the roll and found my name:

"Isaac," she said. "Isaac Warfield. You are in history class."

"I am?" I said.

"You are," she said. "And since you obviously don't need to listen to what I read suppose you tell the class what you know about General Washington's crossing the Delaware. How it was that decisive battle that brought your country into being. A good place to start."

She sprung it all on me too quickly. Just wiped all I had ever learned about General Washington out with a few words. Not only did I not even know General Washington, I was so scared I didn't even know who I was. I looked straight ahead like a man that has found a hant and is cornered.

"The raging water of the Delaware and makeshift boats to cross in," she was egging me on.

I should have just sat there like a knot on a log. But I got to thinking about that big river roaring on. I was remembering how Bear Creek could get rowdy and out of its banks at times. Wouldn't be anyone apt to cross it. And there was General Washington's makeshift boats at that. With nothing in my head but to please that teacher I said:

79

"He sure never made it."

Laughter and catcalls surrounded me. Came down on me and found me and I felt no bigger than a pignut.

"If he hadn't made it you wouldn't be here today," Miss Canlittle said and quieted the room with her eyes. "Before you leave this class you will know something of the founding of your own country."

Well, small as I felt I wasn't thinking that General Washington had done me much of a favor if he did make it. I mean causing me to be singled out in that class with every face a strange one and all. I sat there glancing out the window at the big sun resting on top of the ridge, thinking how I'd like to lasso it and pull it on over into evening.

That's when I thought I saw something move in the woods above the schoolyard. A brown shadow that was catching specks of the sun.

There it was again! Just about the same path I had come to school on, moving as slow as a hound dog on a cold trail. And then for ever so short a moment into the opening.

Glory be! It was Kate. She stepped out of the edge of the woods.

Well, I sort of edged up in the seat and twisted my head so I could see over the room to see if anyone else had seen her.

There was no fooling that mule. She knew she wasn't supposed to be here. For she didn't come walking in like you'd think a mule ought to. Not Kate. She lifted one front leg as slow as if it had been hooked in a glue pot. Set it down and brought up the other. Came tiptoeing in with her back curved like a whipped hound dog. Just as low and sneaking-like.

I got to worrying about her getting next to the window and seeing me and so I sort of lowered down in the seat trying to make a sawlog out of the top of the desk to peek up over at Miss Canlittle.

Now Kate was in the tall grass of the schoolyard. Just stopping to pick her a bite here and there, then raising her head to give the schoolhouse the once-over. The longing in her eyes fairly took my breath away.

The sun got itself out of the rut and was sliding ever so slow down the slope. Kate sort of stretched out in the heat of it and flopped down like she knew I was about and was set on waiting. And I trembled there in the seat thinking that I was fairly set on breaking her neck if I made it out of the schoolhouse. I'd get her under the cover of the woods and what I'd say to her wasn't worth repeating.

Then I got to thinking: Just how well did I know that trifling mule? Tomorrow, if I lived the day, I'd change my seat, to one away from the window. But just as I thought of my one chance Miss Canlittle snatched it out from under me.

"Remember your seats. They will be yours for the school year. Don't carve on them."

Troubles had just set in.

With school out for the day, Kate made herself as scarce as a bat in the sunlight. Tried to fool me into thinking she was nowhere around. But several times on the path home I thought I heard her in the bushes up ahead.

I'd fool that mule. I stopped, figuring her to be sneaking on. Then I turned myself up a short cut to Bunt Rankins' pasture and hooked myself up in the forks of a black gum tree where I could watch the path I had taken to school.

And there she came, the old fool. Creeping along like a ground squirrel, stopping every few feet and cocking her ears to listen for my footsteps behind. Then she scooted on.

She worked her way up to the end of the path, right under the big gum, looked around and grinned. I grabbed me a handful of gumberries and dropped them on her head. She looked up.

"All right, you sneaking mule!" I said. "Caught you dead to center. Don't try to squirm out. I saw you in the schoolyard."

I scooted down. She hung her head low, caught in the act and no way out. I walked her to the gate and blinked my eyes when I saw the gate wasn't open.

"All right, you troublesome critter," I said. "Where did you get out of the pasture?"

She pawed around in the earth like she didn't know what I was talking about. Biding time just like I did whenever ma asked me a question I didn't want to answer.

"Waiting me out will do you no good!" I said. "Might as well give up."

She stood as quiet as the land about.

"Ok," I said. "Instead of going to look for walnut trees we'll just spend the evening walking the fence line and find that break you came through."

Well, she just stumbled along behind me like she was looking her heart out, sticking her nose into the brush and jumping back out of the way whenever I pulled a clump of vines from around one of the fence posts to see if the break was there.

After a while I gave up and looked Kate in the eyes. Inside her old head was the answer. And it was a good one, written all over her face and not a word of it you could read.

I sat down and put my head in my hands like I was trying to think, which I was. She plopped down beside me like she had a problem that needed figuring out too.

I got to thinking how Miss Canlittle had swept me into nowhere there in the schoolhouse. Stirred me up until she could have got any answer out of me she wanted. Fright did it. That was it. Fright was nothing but trouble and was the lowest state of mind you could be in.

If it worked on me, made a fool of me in front of a whole class, why wouldn't it work just the same on a mule with a bunch of trees looking on? I turned to her quick as a wink, my finger outstretched:

"What do you know about General Washington?" I said.

She perked up her ears and flattened them out to the top of her head.

"So!" I said. "You ain't as smart as you thought you was."

She wrinkled, swelled, brayed.

"*He-haw-e-e-e-e-e-e-e!*"

"Shame!" I said, clicking my tongue and shaking my

head. "Ain't no respect or appreciation left in you. That's all. And old General Washington trying to cross that big Delaware River, even bigger then Bear Creek, so you can have a country to live in."

Her ears shot up and her big eyes scanned the pasture. Then she looked at me like being here wasn't a smart thing to brag about.

But being on my own grounds here in the hills it was all coming on strong. I mean the story of General Washington. Clear as a mountain spring. Especially how he had gone and chopped down a cherry tree and been man enough not to lie about it. That's the part of the story that ma had used on me so many times before whenever she was trying to get the truth out of me. The thing was to try to belittle a fellow till he wasn't fit to polish the General's shoes. Then feeling low as a striped snake you'd come out with it and not be as lucky as the General in the end.

"Well," I said, chewing on a straw, "recollect the time the General chopped down that big cherry tree in his ma's yard. My, but his ma was fit to kill. Snuck right up to him and said: `You cut that tree?'"

Kate curled up her lip and grinned like she knew what the answer was.

"Nope," I said. "You ain't right. Why, faced with the licking of his life he just up and said: `I won't tell you a lie, ma. I cut that tree down.' Yep. Come right out, he did, and owned up to it."

Kate rolled over on her back, covering her eyes with her front legs, peeking out at me, her head sorta turned to one side and looking like she was sure surprised at it all. Halfway believing me.

"Well, his ma was so proud of him that she didn't even give him a licking for what he had done," I said. "Goes to show that it pays to tell the truth."

Kate dropped her eyes like she was ashamed of it all. Like I had touched her heart.

"Now," I said, "where's that break in the fence?"

She covered her eyes again. And I leaned close.

"But you know, Kate," I said, "I ain't so sure about that cherry tree either."

She looked at me now like I was coming around to her way of thinking.

"Nope," I said. "Ain't sure. For they're some folks say his ma had stuck him to the backyard and he had snuck through a hole in the fence and ran off. And it was that hole she was trying to find. I like that story. Don't matter, though. I mean it being a cherry tree or a hole in a fence. He up and told the truth. That's what counts with me."

She got to her feet and started nibbling at the short grass, cutting her eyes up at me just like it all made no difference to her.

Then a thought hit me. Why, I thought, that mule doesn't know a thing about General Washington. I mean what is done and what isn't done. What is past and what is present.

"Well," I said slow and easy, "General sure does have a job ahead of'im this week. Somewhere around page twenty-six in the history book at school as Miss Canlittle sees it." I chewed on a straw. "Got to cross that big Delaware River, bigger than Bear Creek, and fight it out with them British. Every one of them meaner than Simm

Johns." I waited for words like Bear Creek and Simm Johns to take hold. "Got to give'em a good whipping or we ain't got no country at all." Then I snatched at my head like I had been stung by a bee. "Just a minute! I sure am all mixed up. Why, if he ain't there yet then how could we be having a country right now? I mean one with a little patch of land like Bunt Rankins' pasture sticking from it like a sore thumb! Couldn't have! Glory be! No pasture, no mule, since I couldn't even be here."

Well, I fairly set her back. She did every trick in the book. Every one of them set on letting me know she was right there beside me. The last to come was the loudest bray you ever heard.

I stuck my finger in my mouth and held it out to catch the force of the wind. Then I let my eyes wander over the land.

"Wind sure is noisy this evening," I said, stretching to my feet.

She pawed the earth and kicked around.

I yawned and stretched out my arms.

"Guess I'll just be moseying along toward home, being there ain't no pasture or mule around here anywhere."

That's when she started backing. I stood to one side as she whirled past me. Just sailed over that fence like a bird. Hit the ground on the other side, rolled over, and came up grinning like a possum, plainly showing me that there hadn't been a hole in the fence in the first place.

"Bydogs," I said, crossing the fence to reach her, "the General's going to be mighty proud when he hears about this down at the school. Your just coming right out with the truth. Bet he'll sew old Bunt Rankins' pasture onto these United States so tight a buzz saw couldn't loop it out. I sure got myself a truth-telling mule."

I scratched her behind the ears which was what she dearly loved. Not too much though since it caused her to sit back on her haunches and fall asleep. But I was powerful proud of that mule—a little proud of myself, too, being able to tangle her up in a tale as wild as fox grapes and maybe saving us both.

"You git yourself back over that fence," I said, "and soon as I let ma know I shined at the city school today I'll be back and we'll just take a look at some walnut trees."

Feeling proud but with more troubles on my mind, I walked toward home. There was Kate, walking around during the day like she couldn't cross a plantain leaf and then going sailing over the fence like a bird. I had suspected she might search out a break. I could have mended that. But I couldn't clip her legs like the wings of a chicken to keep her on the ground. She was a rogue for sure.

Maybe yoking her would do it. Putting something around one of her legs to keep her off balance so she couldn't jump. But it was dangerous. Fool that she was, she might try to make it over anyway, get caught in the fence and break her old neck.

Being caught with her in the hills was bad enough, or being caught with her near the house. But being caught with her in town was worse. And Miss Canlittle making it sound like General Washington was having trouble! Reading slow along the pages of the history book, raising and softening her voice to add to it. She'd never believe that General Washington never had it so good. I mean I would have traded him jobs at the drop of a hat. That is, the way I felt about it now. I didn't know at the time what Kate was thinking, and that it included the General.

It took Kate three days to set her sights for General Washington. And that's just how long it took Miss Canlittle to pitch General Washington's growing-up days into a doodle and bail'em up tight. Any stretching to be done in the story had to be done right there on the banks of the Delaware. That's where Miss Canlittle had the General now, letting him sit there while she conjured up the job ahead of'im. But it was a pretty day to just sit and wait. You couldn't see a leaf stirring outside the schoolhouse. Looked all the prettier since I couldn't see Kate anywhere about.

But with the sweep of her hand Miss Canlittle stirred up the awfullest mixture you ever saw. That little squeaky voice of hers mocked a roll of thunder and put you in the right setting, which was, of course, the bank of the Delaware where the General was taking it easy waiting on her. She said:

"And the General stood before his troops, darkness and storm around him. The Delaware hiding in the darkness except for the huge floats of drifting ice that caught the meager reflections of the moon." Me sitting back thinking what a pretty sight the General had before him. But not for long. She pulled her mouth into a smirk and squinted her eyes. She said: "And on the other side of the river in far greater numbers, neat and warm, protected from the badness of the night, were the British."

I fairly despised those British. Knowing full well that I was a-going against pa's rule that said you never ought to judge people until you knew them. But it was easy to see that General Washington's truck with those British was all lopsided.

The room was as quiet as a mink sneaking up the creek. Everyone stared at Miss Canlittle, including me, waiting for her to get the General across.

"They slipped into their boats," she said. "Slid beside the big chunks of ice." The class rolled and dodged with her voice. "The General stood majestically in the bow of the boat, facing his men. He looked toward yon bank"— a sweep of the hand nearly knocked me out of my seat, her quivering the yon till it sounded like the whinny of a horse—"toward the British under the command of General Cornwallis. Raised his mighty arm and said—"

"He-haw-e-e-e-e-e-e-e-e!"

It was enough to wake those British. I fairly expected to see them come tumbling from the pages of the history book. It fairly raised the hair on everyone's head in the room until the tops of us looked like a stubble field.

"Run!" Miss Canlittle yelled. "Run for your lives! It's a monster!" She leaped to the top of the desk, which was something I would have given odds against her being able to do. She waved the book she kept the roll in around and around in the air. "Run! I'll hold it off as long as I can!"

Kate, spotting me, stuck her head inside the window. She was a sorry-looking sight. She had been in a patch of cockleburs and they had picked up blades of grass from the schoolyard and the grass hung from her head like the stringy hair of a witch.

She had the silliest grin on her face, and she looked up at me and, right in front of the class and Miss Canlittle, licked me down the side of the face. I swallowed and looked Miss Canlittle as near in the eye as I could. Couldn't very well since she was busy running her finger down the roll book, to get to my name, I think, and said:

"Isaac! . . . Isaac . . ."—she looked back at the roll book—"Isaac Warfield. Run before the monster snaps your head from your shoulders!"

By this time most of the class, being closer than Miss Canlittle, had gotten their bearings, set their eyes on Kate for what she was, and commenced giggling. And I bucked up and said:

"She can't bite me. Her teeth are too short."

The giggling got louder. Miss Canlittle jumped from the desk to the floor, saw Kate poke her head through the window again and jumped back on top of the desk. Then she hopscotched down the room on top of the desks, waving that roll book like a club.

"Stand back!" she screamed. "Just stand back!" And she came on like a charging bull.

I closed my eyes since I thought she would land the first blow right on the end of Kate's nose and me knowing how sensitive she was there.

I didn't have to pop my eyes open to know that Kate was sucking in. You could feel the air leave the room.

"He-haw-e-e-e-e-e-e-e-e-e!"

It straightened Miss Canlittle out like a piece of flannel in a windstorm with one end tied. My ears popped.

"Run for the principal!" Miss Canlittle screamed, her hair as stringy as a wild possum vine.

But no one moved. Instead they were holding their hands over their mouths and giggling under their breath. She turned on them and I took my chance.

"Git!" I said. "On your way or it's the tannery!"

Kate looked at me with a grin, and made no motion that she would go.

"The General ain't across the Delaware yet," I said. "And I ain't said a word to him yet about your telling the truth!"

Well, she turned her heels and hit for tall timber. Miss Canlittle got up her nerve, bent over and peeked around the windowsill. She saw the little brown spot disappear into the woods.

"We'll organize!" she said. "We'll organize a posse and hunt the monster down!"

And figuring she'd be apt to find out sooner or later, and hoping to stop a posse that might go gunning for Kate, I said:

"It ain't no monster, Miss Canlittle. It's a mule. A meaning-no-harm mule . . . I think."

Miss Canlittle stopped in her tracks. And hearing the giggling going on she looked at me with the same eyes she had used on the British.

"A mule!" she said. And then just like she was thinking that she had gone and made a fool out of herself in front of a class, she looked at me like I could be the goat to get her out. "You say meaning no harm," she said. (I guess I might have done the same, I mean being shucked out there in front of these students that've come to learn something) . . . "you say that a mule stopping General Washington from crossing the Delaware is NO trouble?"

Then she puckered her mouth and looked out over the room like she was leaving the decision up to them, having proved her case.

She wasn't anybody's fool, Miss Canlittle. She had gone and hitched me up beside General Washington, making me look mighty puny, and I was even feeling a little guilty about it myself. The only chance I had was to separate myself from the General. Me and that mule were in worse shape than the British on the other side of the Delaware. For I didn't figure the class were fools. I put myself in their shoes. They were all in bad from giggling, and might be punished. But here was a way out. Join Miss Canlittle, help get her off the hook and they were all in solid.

Me knowing the answer and couldn't say it. No doubt about it, it was the name Cornwallis that had caused Kate to bray. The corn more than the wallis. For you see Kate was like that. I mean certain words would cause her to bray every time. Especially when it came to something that spelled eat. And corn was one of them. Hay would do it. Timothy would do it. Fodder, orchard grass, bluegrass. Crabgrass would cause her to stick out her tongue. And tannery would usually make her scoot off same as saying Simm Johns or ma. Lots of words and you had to know them—that is, if you weren't wanting her to bray and you were quick.

The way I figured it, Kate had been near the window listening about the General and started sucking in and wrinkling up when she heard Cornwallis. She got the bray out just at the time Miss Canlittle said, "Washington said."

"Just as if the General doesn't have his hands full as it is," Miss Canlittle said, the class looking on like they had all lost their best friend, glancing at me like I was the cause of it all. Which I was, but they had no way of knowing that. They wouldn't either, if I could help it. Kate was on her own just now. A heap better off than me. She had a running start. I didn't.

Miss Canlittle poured it on me, up one side, and down the other. I hunkered down as far as the desk would let me.

"Well," Miss Canlittle said, "if that mule comes again and bothers my class the principal will have a way of dealing with it. And no more impudence from you"—she looked down the roll sheet—"Isaac Warfield. Is that clear!"

"Yes'm," I said, trying to remember some of her actions and words to use on that mule when I got over to Bunt Rankins' pasture.

What I didn't say to that mule wasn't worth shucking out. I laid it all on with doom riding on every word.

She flinched, hunkered, hid her eyes, and looked sorrowful. But I think she watched me closer for signs than I watched her. And when she saw me easing up she came over and put her nose into my arms just like she was willing to forgive me for it all.

"Doggone it, Kate," I said. "That's the trouble. You just ain't supposed to go sticking your nose into my arms whenever I'm fixing to lay one on you. I couldn't do a thing like that to Miss Canlittle. I mean go putting my head in her lap."

CHAPTER 8

Kate Defeats General Washington

My plan was to get me a good strong rope and stake the mule out. Take her down in the branch that sliced the land in half and tie her there. Give her enough rope to let her graze, turn to the branch for water, or get in the shade of a tree to dodge the hot sun. Maybe after a few days on the end of a rope, freedom gone and all, she'd be content to stay in the pasture while I was at school.

Well, Kate sure didn't take to that rope. She whimpered, stomped, rolled over, and played dead. And then she put a sad look in her eyes to follow me all the way to school, half worrying me to death.

Everywhere I looked I saw the sad eyes of the little mule, a look that plainly said she was trying to figure out what I was punishing her for. She was all mixed up about me. She was used to being punished until I came along. Maybe now she was figuring she had shucked up to me and I had turned out to be just like all the others.

What a heap of problems! Winter coming on. I could feel it in the wind that came down the hill, spinning leaves that had curled at the ends and were set on dying an early death. Blackberries had been gone for ever so long and the banks of Bear Creek were heavy with elderberries.

The little berry of the elderberry bush was a good way to tell when winter came. For at first there were the white blooms, hanging to the bushes like pods of white grapes. But a touch of winter wind and the bloom popped off and left small berries under a thin sky.

Soon the frost would come and quilt the land and the grass would turn brown and be no good for Kate to eat. Kate would be needing shelter and considerable more to eat than we had been able to hide along the hills. She would need some corn for strength and fodder for bulk.

The season, as I said, showed good signs for being a good walnut year, but I only had to close my eyes to see that little mule standing knee-deep in snow, pawing the earth for signs of grass, steam from her nose drifting into the cold sky. I could see her shivering from the cold, hiding in the woods waiting for Simm Johns to throw out food for the cattle, then trying to sneak in and steal a bite. But cattle don't leave much except tough fibers of fodder and with her teeth mostly gone Kate couldn't eat that.

I could have gone into the hills and frozen with her. But it wouldn't make the pain less.

The bargain had been that either me or pa would find a fitting home for her before the winter set in. I didn't lie altogether about looking. I just looked for a different sort of home, that's all. I looked in the hills for a warm cave or something of the sort, making little progress. And if pa was making progress he didn't say.

Where could you find a home for a mule on old legs, one too old to plow an onion patch without coming down with stiffness? Although pa didn't talk much about her either way I was figuring one thing: He didn't want to see harm come to her.

Kate could have made it easier, but not unless she stopped being a mule. And to tell the truth I wouldn't have changed her one particle. She was mine, hide, bones, and what flesh there was. She was the only thing in the world I figured I owned outright. The only thing that had come to depend on me, trust me, and listen to all the dreams that were swimming back and forth in my head. She swelled the days to fullness, put something inside them, more than I ever had had before. Even put purpose to grass without it just being a carpet to walk on. Made me respect and appreciate things.

Well, I worried right into my school seat. Didn't even take notice to see if the class was holding a grudge against me. Passed up all the clouds, the ice, and the darkness of the night along the Delaware. Didn't get my bearings until General Washington was standing up in the boat facing his men.

My hair fairly stood on end, all without reason. Just remembering was doing it. Remembering was doing something to the class too. I heard the rumble go over the room. Miss Canlittle let her eyes fall over the room and it got as quiet as a mountain rock.

I peeked out the window and drew in a big puff of air. I felt good. Real good. Thinking Miss Canlittle could just bring the General right on across. Kate was all tied up to a big beech tree, used to it all by now. Probably swatting flies and resting in the shade. And . . . maybe peeping now and then toward the sun to see how much longer I'd be gone.

That's what I thought!

The first knowledge I had different was a brown nose popping over the windowsill, crawling like a brown bug. Then two eyes. Brown as a sunflower after the redbirds and blue jays have gone with the seeds. Two eyes that weren't even looking at me at all but were set on Miss Canlittle, her being deep now in the General's story.

I squinted my eyes over the room. All the eyes were squinting toward me and toward the window. And little smiles followed, and then straightened out when the class looked toward the front of the room. All was quiet, but all the faces in the class were flushed red. Everyone in the room was waiting for the mountain to fall except Miss Canlittle who was struggling to get the General across and figured the time she was having was putting the quietness to us. She was looking at the book and waving her hand like she was swinging an ox whip.

She quivered her voice and said:

"He looked toward yon bank." Everyone was humped up now like a roomful of bullfrogs on a creek bank. "Toward the British under the command of General . . ."

"*Uh hum-m-m-m-m-m-m-m-m-m-m!*" It was the loudest I had ever cleared my throat in my whole life. Even fooled some into jumping before the shot was off, the shot being the braying of the mule. I even got a few sorry looks. I swear if even the mule didn't look at me with disgust. And then she jerked her eyes away from the window when Miss Canlittle placed the look of disgust on me. Me feeling bad enough as it was. For I had hoped to drown the Cornwallis out by clearing my throat. But do you think Miss Canlittle would just go on and get it over

97

with? Nope. She stopped with pure intentions of back-tracking. The class—or the mule—would not miss a word.

I stopped her as many times as I could, making a race of it, right down to the bitter end. Miss Canlittle had set herself to outdo me, speeding her voice, trying to beat the clearing of my throat. Slowing the words and then speeding up to trick me. She caught me off guard, then spit the words out like a buzz saw spitting sawdust!

"Under General Cornwallis!"

I threw my hands over my ears like everyone else. Miss Canlittle grinned, didn't look up, and went on with the speed of lightning, her victory won. Then she looked up ever so quick, and saw our hands over our ears, but it was too late:

"Shook his mighty hand and s-a-i-d . . ." It tapered off as slow as a wind petering out.

"He-haw-e-e-e-e-e-e-e-e-e!"

Out of the room she went, and before the class could take advantage, she came back in with Mr. Weathers, the principal. She pointed in the direction where the little mule had just scooted off.

"Had teeth two inches long!" she said, gasping for breath. "Tried to come right through the window." Then she did something that women do that has been fooling menfolk for years, pa always said: She cried, hung her head, and sniffled.

And with the weakness that all men have, Mr. Weathers patted her on the shoulder and shook his head. He handed her a handkerchief—something women never seem to carry when they cry, but are always jumping boys for not having—and she blew her nose. He looked at her like saying she had done all the school could have expected her to do.

"It was a bad time to come," he said. "But don't you worry about it. You just go back to the General and leave the monster to me."

And just like pa he had that look on his face—a look that plainly said he was humoring her and not believing.

This was a time, I thought, as I walked to Bunt Rankins' pasture, that talking wouldn't be enough. It had to amount to more. There had to be punishment. Whipping was against my grain, ma being mostly the cause of that, but I had reason right now to think that ma had a point. Fact is, the farther along I was getting the more I was just thinking how many good points ma had. Well, I had grown out of most of the lickings, being tall and spindly and as ma said old enough to reason with, but just now and then when all else failed she took a board to me. All for my own good, she said, and it mostly was.

And yet it wasn't the whipping part I was thinking of now. I was way past that. I was at the forgiving part. The pouting over, and things come back into normal shape. It had always turned out that way with me and ma. Ought to be the same with a mule.

Just like me at times, nothing else had worked. I had talked as long and as hard as I could. And as hard as I knew it would be to hit the mule it seemed better than losing her, which I was going to do unless something happened to change the way we were going. She had to mind what I told her to do. That was all there was to it.

Coming to school was bad all right. But now there was even more. The worst of all was slipping the rope. For she had known what I had tied her for. To stay put. To stay there and wait for me to untie her. There was no amount of reasoning to show different.

I would make it short. Walk up, swarp her good, and leave her alone to know that I was disgusted and wasn't likely to put up with her foolishness. She'd pout around a spell and I'd go back to tell her that it was all for her own good and she'd come around to knowing I was right. Then things would be like they always were with me and that mule.

I guess maybe she knew what was coming. She could have hidden, but she didn't. I could see her standing there under the beech, waiting, looking pitiful. The big rope lay loose and curled at her feet. And she stomped at it and made it all worse. Picked it up and flung it away, twirling it through the air like a brown snake.

"If I had left you loose in the field, Kate," I said, "it might have been partly my fault."

I stepped into the branch and cut me a good-sized sprout. I didn't say much.

She didn't even try to move. Just stood there like an old fool waiting for the blows. She might have even talked me out of it as halfhearted about it all as I was. But she didn't try. Just kept looking toward the rope and shaking her head.

"Why did you do it, Kate?" I asked, looking toward the tree where I had looped the rope. She had twisted on it so hard that she had skinned the bark off. And I could see where she had torn up the earth. "After you knew I was meaning for you to stay tied?" I took another look at the beech and at the smaller tree close, all skinned and bent.

She hunkered up and stood waiting. And I closed my eyes and swarped her hard across the rump. I opened my eyes and saw her quivering. And then I lit into her, each blowing digging into my own hide. I heard her low grunts, and yet couldn't hear her move a foot from where she stood.

"You won't be apt to untie the rope tomorrow," I said. "You'll stay here and be good about it. You don't belong at school. You don't belong in town. You belong here in the hills. And no one even wants you here but me. Can't you get that much through your old head?"

I left her there standing under the tree, her head low and her eyes following me. Me wanting to make amends but knowing that every blow would be wasted if I did. You couldn't whip and pet at the same time. This one had to count. And I didn't believe to save me I could whip her again.

With my head down and my thoughts lower I didn't hear Bunt Rankins until he was almost upon me. I saw him limping up the hill, knocking the weeds out of his path with the cane. He came up puffing and wiped his head.

"Thought you might like to know you almost lost your mule today, boy," he said, setting me back. "Lucky I saw her. She was braying to the sky. Enough to wake the dead." He steadied himself on the cane. "All wropped around one of them little trees, strangling nigh to death. If you aim to tie a critter, son, tie it in the open where

101

it ain't apt to wrop around something and shorten the rope. Keeps'em alive longer."

"I'm obliged to you," I said, wanting to shuck him and get back to that mule.

"It's all right," he said. "Hanging just ain't much of a way for a critter to die."

I hurried back toward the hollow. So close to death, how was she to know I hadn't meant it that way? I got to thinking she had been trying to tell me in the only way she could. Showing me her dislike for the rope, kicking and stomping it, like she thought it was the rope and not me. Bless her old heart. The licking she had took. What was she thinking about that?

Right now I had to get to her. First I walked, and then I ran. But she wasn't at the beech tree.

I caught a glimpse of her walking along the bony ridge. Her head was low and she didn't look to be more than a few inches tall, framed against the sky and the evening sun. A tiny brown speck that meant all the world to me at the moment.

I yelled at the top of my lungs. I saw her stop, look down the slope for ever so spare a moment, and then walk on.

I finally caught up with her and she didn't slow her pace at all. So, I just stuck my hands in my pockets and walked along behind, dodging the bushes and all.

"Where do you think you're going?" I said.

She didn't bother to look back. Just walked ahead, her old hipbones poking up like a set of stilts, looking like they would pop through the hide at every step.

"You can't just walk with no place to go," I said.

She stopped only long enough to look at me with the saddest eyes I ever saw.

And, thinking I might be winning out, I looked at her like I wasn't giving in too much.

"Going to walk yourself into winter and starvation?" I said.

Then I got to thinking that she might have turned against me. The loneliest feeling in the world swept over me.

"And what about all that hay me and you got stored up?" I said.

She never bothered to bray at the mention of hay, which she always did before. Just stopped to tug at a pod of crabgrass, gave up and walked on. Like she was saying she'd be apt to starve.

"Well," I said, "just go on. You never much wanted to stay with me anyway. I been watching you stomp around, restless and raring to go somewhere. You been thinking about it all for a spell now and just now got nerve to do it."

She turned to look at me for the longest time yet. Surely I was reaching her.

"Oh, don't worry about me none," I said. "I'm used to being alone. Lonely as a cricket. And all that work I done, gathering up the hay for winter. That's all right. I'm used to hard work and being alone all the time."

I could tell by the way she was perking her ears that she was catching every word. I was talking as mournful as a winter wind.

But she never stopped. Just listened.

103

"I didn't mean for you to get hurt on the rope, Kate," I said. "Wasn't intending that at all. Don't want you to leave me, either. I just ain't got nothing without you."

Kate stopped. Maybe it was the words, or maybe it was the change in my voice. She had learned to know both. For whatever her reason she stopped under a big, sprawling oak. The last rays of the evening sun were sifting through the limbs, through the yellow leaves until they dropped on her back like patches of gold, settling there old and tarnished, blocked out like a piecework quilt.

And not knowing what else to say I sat down on a log and wiped the sweat from my face.

I felt her push her nose into my hands, and I let my hands ramble until they swung around her neck.

"Let's go home, old girl," I said. "I ain't ever going to whip you again."

And around the ridge we went. We stopped under a big walnut tree. I pulled a low one off the limb and cracked it as if I wanted to test the kernel to see if they were ready to gather. Me knowing full well they weren't since there had been no frost yet to set the kernels. And it took a frost to make a walnut fall free from the tree and keep the winter.

The kernel was soft and watery and needed more time. But I gave it to Kate because I just wanted to give her something. And she wrinkled her face into a grin and took the kernel with her tongue just because she wanted to accept it. And if it wasn't ready to eat she never let on.

CHAPTER 9

There Ain't No Friend Like Elwood

The next morning the little mule swelled me with pride. Not by what she did exactly but by what she *didn't* do. And that was to follow me to school.

Miss Canlittle brought General Washington across the Delaware good and proper-like, took him into a fierce battle with the British and brought him back out clean as a melon rind.

I was happy for the General. I wouldn't want you to think I was trying to take one thing from him. But all the time, from the minute the battle was over, I let my mind wander back to Bunt Rankins' pasture. Simply thinking I'd tell Kate the whole thing. She'd be happy to know he had come out all right and that old Bunt's pasture had been tacked on.

And who was to think it wrong if I shipped a mule into the story somewhere and brought it out a hero? It might just give her something to walk around important-like about. And if anyone ever needed that it was Kate.

To the class it was as if a big weight had been lifted from their backs. They had watched the window as close as Miss Canlittle did. And once the battle was over she placed the book on her desk and sprawled out in her seat like she was as foot-weary as the General.

But the day didn't end that way. The way I see it was that Kate had just overslept. She had waked up, squinted her eyes up through the big beech limbs, seen the sun all balled and big in the sky. Then she had taken off toward school like she was hell bent to election. Just like *she* would be punished for being late.

She was there at noon. I didn't see her. I had stretched out under a tree to eat the sandwich ma had packed for me and had then moseyed out in front of the school to wait for the lunch hour to be over. I usually did this since I feared Kate might be somewhere in the woods and would be apt to see me if I was in the back of the schoolhouse too long and come running.

That's when Elwood Sperry, the one person I'd been palling around with at school, ran up to me.

"Better come quick, Isaac," he said. "Looks like trouble in the back."

I looked to see—and fairly expected—someone chasing him, figuring he'd come to get me to shuck'em off. Which I would have done or tried to, since I liked Elwood. Fact is, he was the only good thing I had found up to now about the school. His being a friend kept me from feeling all lost in the city.

He was one of those little fellows that creep under your skin and raise a welt. His pa was the town banker. Elwood was a tiny thing, puny as a tadpole. Shaded from the sun, pa might have said, though I don't think he would have said that in front of Elwood's pa, since pa had had to go to the bank to borrow money several times when business was slow at the cobbler shop. And he was intending to go again when he got on his feet good and solid, to borrow money to get back on the farm. Back where he belonged and where he said I belonged. He had lost his farm during the depression and since that day had been living, he said, too close to the city to suit him.

Pa said that I would make a good farmer since I loved the land. And he was always telling ma whenever I came in scratched, or even smelling of polecat, "You can take Isaac out of the country, but you can't take the country out of Isaac. Born in him."

But me and Elwood just took up from the beginning. Maybe it was because he was so small and puny and had to take a lot from most of the other boys at school until I came along to take up for him. Or maybe it had been his standing around there at the schoolhouse looking lonely and lost, just like I had felt before the mule came. Or maybe I took my liking for Elwood from ma.

For ma was like that. I mean shucking up to things that seemed to have the least chance. Oh, I know she was sort of soured right now on the mule. But that wasn't ma. She acted like she didn't care one hoot about most things, but never a stray dog or cat got past the house unfed. She took them all in.

But me and Elwood hit it off. I'd even asked him to come with me to gather walnuts after the first frost. And his pa had given him the right. I was figuring that a little time for him in the hills, out in the wind and all, would slip a little color back into his face. He wouldn't be as apt to be picked on when I wasn't around. Might even get him to consider the power of tobacco juice in the eye of the other fellow to ward him off. Not many fellows could wade through that.

The day that Kate had scooted her noggin over the sill of that window, I confided in Elwood. Told him outright about the mule.

"Now don't you go telling, Elwood," I said.

Elwood wanted to swear to it but I told him that pa had always taught me that a fellow's word ought to be enough to put trust in.

Well, Elwood said he thought the mule was all right, and that he bet she was a pretty thing. He said this from seeing her head, all he had been able to see. But if he could have thought that much pretty the way she had looked that day, I knew the rest of her would be a picture to him.

Me and Elwood were a good combination. I mean me the country and him the town. We'd divvy up with each other. And that's where we stood right now.

I hurried around to the back of the schoolhouse—and lost my breath with the first look. There was Kate, not hunkered down in front of all those boys at school but offering free rides and giving them the time of their life.

The boys chattered like jaybirds, arguing.

"Oh, come on now, Pete, it's my turn again." Or, "You had the last ride."

That's it. Believe it or not. She was as gentle as a gun-shy dog, and just yanked everything we ever had together right up by the roots. Even rationed out her distance like she was intending to slight no one before school took up. She was enjoying it no end, and perked up her ears like she had at last found what she had been put here to do:

to be a riding mule for boys. Spry as a fiddle, and soaking up attention like a sponge.

"Ain't that great?" Elwood said.

"Great?" I said, thinking Elwood was out of his mind. "She'll be shot as soon as the principal gets here. Me along with her."

Mr. Withers turned the corner of the schoolhouse. "*Hi, hi, hi-i-i-i-i-i!*" he yelled.

Everything, including Kate, disappeared like rain soaked up by a dry creek bed—Kate into the woods and the boys toward the front of the school.

"I'm finished," I whispered to Elwood.

"As pa would say," he whispered, "you've struck a gold mine. Better put, you're on the edge of enterprise."

Elwood talked like that. He liked to use big words.

"I'm on the edge of being pulled into Mr. Weathers' office," I said, "since I'm the most likely one that a mule might be following to school."

Elwood rubbed his chin, his little bird chest stuck out like he had just bought the world and had given me the right to keep Kate in it.

"The hills are yours," he said. "But business is mine, Isaac."

He wasn't about to get any argument from me there. He wasn't a banker's son for nothing. But Elwood worried me a bit, little like that and just itching for something to do.

"That mule is the end of it all," I said. But if Elwood heard me he never let on. He was walking back and forth in front of me now, pacing like a steer waiting for fodder to be thrown out. Stopping now and then to look me in the eye, and then shaking his head.

"You're worrying about wintering that mule," he said. "That right?"

"You know that Elwood," I said. "I already told you about that."

"I see," he said, just like he was hearing it for the first time. "That ought to take corn. Lots of corn. Maybe more than walnuts will buy even with me helping." He swelled out his chest more. "Besides, walnuts are still on the trees."

"They'll fall when the frost hits'em," I said. "If they don't, I'll shinny up the trees and shake'em off."

"That's well and good," Elwood said. "But a bird in the hand is worth two in the bush."

"And no bird at all makes a zero," I said.

"Ah ha," Elwood said, just like he had caught me up. "But you have a bird. The biggest one you ever felt."

"Must be all feathers," I said. "I can't feel no weight to'im."

"Leave the business end to me," Elwood said.

He turned and pointed his fingers toward the boys straying out around the front of the school.

"What's got into you, Elwood?" I asked.

"Simple," Elwood said. "Just purely simple. You offer rides on that mule at a penny a head. Slip out one penny of their lunch money and Kate gets her winter corn."

"If that mule comes here another day," I said, "about the only thing she'll get is a load of buckshot."

"Not to school, Isaac," Elwood said. "Only behind that rim of trees."

"But what's to keep Mr. Weathers from knowing?" I

110

said, being plumb sweet-talked by Elwood.

"Another business deal, Isaac," Elwood said. "I'll start off at two cents a ride. But them that won't tell and promise will ride for a penny. Of course none of them will tell."

No wonder that little Elwood didn't have too much size to him. All of his strength had gone straight to his head. He put me to spending the rest of the evening thinking about all the money I would make. Why, in no time I'd move Kate to a decent pasture and build her a barn that would cause everyone to sit up and take notice. I'd serve her corn morning, noon, and night. And with all my money no one would bother me about it. I'd buy ma a new dress, drum up a little business for pa—people catering to him to get closer on my side—buy a tractor and destroy it right in front of Simm Johns.

Well, even with my mind swelled up with money I wasn't fool enough to think that I could do all that right off. But I was willing to wait, having Elwood around to handle it all—the business end, that is.

I could just sit back and watch the world go by, and me without a worry.

CHAPTER 10

Biggest Mule Ride in the World

We spent the first day looking over the whole picture. And no matter how we looked, it came out pretty as a catbird.

We spent considerable time on the land where we would set up business. It was a natural. There were close to a dozen acres to the plot. Shaped like the head of a man, bald on top, sloping down toward the schoolhouse and rimmed around the edge with a thick cropping of trees. There was a fence, not much, though it wouldn't have made a particle of difference to Kate since she could have jumped it by taking a notion.

And me and Elwood got to figuring that we ought to be all right as far as Kate's being so near the schoolhouse. For just beyond the border of trees the grass was tall and she would be able to graze until noon when she would go to work. We thought that her being so close to the school, knowing she was near me, might satisfy her to come no closer than the rim of trees. Especially when she knew what we had in store for her.

A little checking on Elwood's part showed that the strip of land belonged to the school and the bank, the school claiming and the bank holding a mortgage. The good thing about it was that from the schoolhouse you couldn't see beyond the rim of trees. For the heavy pines grew thick, forming a green wall that you could step into and disappear. But you could come out in less than fifty feet and be standing in grass and looking up a bald knob.

Of a morning Kate would come to school with me. She would pasture until noon in the grass beyond the rim of the trees. (When cold weather came we'd just throw out a little corn and fodder, which would be no trouble since by then we'd have money to buy. Business matters would be left strictly to Elwood.) And at noon Kate would come to the edge of the woods and wait for us. Then, after the rides, Kate would just lazy around the slopes until I got out of school to take her home and wait for the next day of business.

Being the owner of the mule all I had to do was just sit back and handle the cashbox. Listen to the coins tinkle, and keep some account. No trouble at all. Elwood sure went to work on the business end. By the end of the week he had lined up the works. Set the opening day for Monday of the following week. That would give me the weekend to come up with a good makeshift halter, suitable reins, and get the cockleburs off Kate's back so no one would get stuck, or go carrying them back inside the school to draw attention.

The deal was that they would ride bareback at first. As we went on, we might add a saddle and raise the fee. But for now they would have to settle for hide and hair, which ought to be fair enough, Kate being all bowed down in the back.

Elwood had moved around the boys at school as quick and smooth as the summer wind. The weekend would give him time to iron out the wrinkles. Thinks like making sure every boy held out money, the amount depending on how many rides he wanted.

"We got to get them before they reach the candy machine inside the school," Elwood said.

And it was important to see that everyone got an even chance, since a dissatisfied customer was a likely squealer.

Then, me and Elwood staked off the distance the ride would be. There would be at least thirty boys and less than an hour to ride them in. Some would want to ride more than once, depending a great deal on the candy machine. We decided not to try to give rides in the evening. The boys being late getting home every day might bring parents into the picture.

Elwood had it all planned out. We set the distance, walking it off as we thought the mule might walk it. It would be my job to come back over the weekend with Kate and let her step it off. Then, we could come up with a sign, or saying, that went something like this:

BIGGEST MULE RIDE IN THE WORLD— 150 STEPS FOR 1¢

"The thing to do," Elwood said, "is after we get going good you put your money in the bank and let it draw interest."

It sure sounded good to me. And I was grateful to little Elwood. If the money ever got too heavy I would have Kate to help me carry it home.

114

CHAPTER 11

Girls Can Make You Rich

On Monday I was as fidgety as a squirrel on the opening day of hunting season. I knew that Elwood had everything locked up tight, but I was a born worrier like ma.

I tried to shake it all off. I got to thinking about Elwood telling me that it would be that way with me. He said it always was with them that didn't know much about business. He said that's why there aren't many people who have money. Just afraid to go out on the limb and try for it.

Take his pa: president of the town bank. And would you ever have thought that he had started out being a coal miner! Back in the times when the mines here in the hill country were belly mines, meaning you had to go in them on your belly. Not even enough room to stand. Going into those black mines when he was no bigger than poor little Elwood. Crawled in before the light came up and back out when the wick was off. Chipped all day at the seams of coal and came out with his eyes full of dust.

Just goes to show where you can go in the world if you have the gumption to. I'll give his pa credit.

A pauper when the sun comes up and a rich man when it sets. That sure is a big jump. Sort of hard to get used to. And Elwood figuring far ahead of that. Going into the business of insurance and all later on, just in case one of the riders fell off Kate's back and decided to sue us. Accidents were more likely later on when we brought the girls at school into the picture. I didn't put much stock in that.

"Sue a pauper and get a louse." I thought about that, since I was still a pauper and mighty apt to stay that way if the girls were brought in. I just balked on that. Girls weren't for mules. At least I didn't think so. I just wasn't greedy enough yet.

"Put it this way," Elwood said. "You ain't particular up there in the hills whether a walnut tree is a girl tree or a boy tree. You just shinny right up and shake them nuts down."

"Is there a difference?" I asked. "I mean is there a boy and girl walnut tree?"

"Heard pa say there was with holly trees," Elwood said. "Don't see why it should be any different with walnuts."

"Maybe so," I said. "But there's a heap of difference between trees and people."

"How do you figure that?" Elwood said.

"Well," I said, "for one thing a walnut ain't going to go shouting its head off just because it falls from a tree. That's one big difference I see."

"Girls won't either at two for a penny," Elwood said. "They're lighter than boys and we can ride'em two at a time."

"Well, I don't know, Elwood," I said. "I'll have to size Kate up and see how she takes to it."

Then Elwood said that since I was a little green when it came to seeing a good business deal, I could take time to think it over.

I'd need it. I just didn't have time to get my thinking cleared up, being in town and knowing little about it. And being greedy about a thing spelled trouble, country or town. Like shooting out a covey of birds and leaving none for seed. Things like that. First the boys, next the girls, and next maybe the teacher at a nickel and I'd go right back to being a pauper just when I was taking a liking to being a man of means and money.

If I had any doubt about being in business that Monday, Kate didn't. She was grinning from ear to ear when I slipped the halter on her. And she fairly skipped to school.

Elwood slid in beside me in the schoolyard, twisted his mouth to one side and said:

"Everything all set on your end?"

I nodded my head.

Fats Wallen, who sat beside Elwood and was a good three times Elwood's size, grinned at Elwood right there in class and showed him a big shiny penny.

Elwood changed as quick as a frost-struck hillside. Looked around as low and sneaking as me and Kate coming out of Simm Johns' cornfield. Then he shook his head like he had the rickets, which fairly meant for Fats to get the penny back into his pocket before Miss Canlittle saw it.

Me, I was too busy thinking just how little I looked

to Miss Canlittle at the time, but how big I'd grow before the week was out. I noticed that Elwood was having a time with his end of it. Every boy in the room was trying to show him that he had brought his penny to school and would be ready at noon. Miss Canlittle kept calling him down for twisting in his seat.

Once I saw Elwood counting the boys on his fingers. And doggone it if he didn't even grin at Nellie Tuttle, which was something I never thought Elwood would do, I mean shine up to the girls. I knew what he was up to.

I kept fumbling with my lunch inside the desk. I had brought it in a cloth sack instead of a paper poke today. Used a five-pound sugar sack. It had caused some trouble, I mean getting the sack from ma since she used the sackcloth to make things like dishcloths and the like. But I finally told her that I wanted to use it to bring a few nuts home. And even though the nuts wouldn't be apt to keep yet, they ought to be all right for a batch of brownies.

Maybe I was just jittery and all, it being my first day in business. But it seemed to me things were starting off wrong. The plan had been for all the boys to go around natural-like, eating their lunch as usual and not causing suspicion.

But when the noon bell rang they went out of the school like a herd of cattle. Sacks flew everywhere and most of the food was gobbled down before they reached the back of the schoolhouse. They tromped down the girls. And Fats Wallen had said out loud as we were leaving the room, dead in front of Miss Canlittle:

"Got my penny, Elwood!"

He held it out and the Indian on it looked as tall as

me. Fats was grinning from ear to ear, which was something if you ever saw Fats' face. His little eyes set back in the flesh behind humped jaws like two little elderberries.

Elwood added one more notch. Since I was the owner of the business and all, I had to look and act the part. It went with being the president of something. With his pa it was speaking at the Women's League once a week and things like that. Politics and stump jumping for me could come later on, after we had come a ways up the ladder. But for now I had to look important, like Elwood's pa sitting back in a big, soft chair during business hours, with nothing to do but count money. I didn't have me a chair, so I picked a shady spot over by the tree grove and stretched out and waited for the money to come in.

You'd a-thought I wasn't even there. My own mule didn't notice me. She was in her second childhood, never having so much attention paid to her. And I was happy for the little mule. Last week there had been just me and the mule, working out our own problems and not even knowing if we would make the winter. Things had sure changed.

I got to thinking about Kate getting independent and the like, felt sorry for myself, and just sort of spooned around under that shade tree chewing on a straw and thinking. Sizing myself up. I had no right to hold that mule back and I knew it. I should let her amount to something.

Well, every time I got to feeling right sorry for myself on this point, Elwood ran over, I held open the sack, and he let another penny drop from a high distance. High enough for it to wallow around in the bottom and make a sound that went clink, clink, clink.

And first thing I knew I closed that sack and stretched out in all my greed thinking me and that mule together would skin'em alive. Just wallowed in greed. The money had got hold of me, swallowed me up, shucked me down, tied me tight. It was shameful.

Greed grabbed me like a witch and lured me on. Trouble was run plumb out of the country. I began to hear and see things and I kept a tight grip on the sack. I had visions of someone sneaking though the woods and grabbing the sack of money. And I caught myself grinning at the little sounds the pennies made falling into the sack. Clink, clink, clink. Prettier than a mountain fiddle.

Glory be! I closed my eyes and saw little things pop up before their time. I mean things like me agreeing to bring the girls into the business. Why, I began to think, we've been letting a gold mine slip by. And I got to thinking about Elwood wanting to ride'em two for a penny. Maybe that would be all right to start off with. But only until we got them used to riding Kate and then we'd latch the door on'em. And they'd come up with a penny apiece. They'd be glad to pay that price once the pleasure of riding had set in.

There was just no limit to where it could all lead. Take Miss Canlittle. You'd think Miss Canlittle would want nothing to do with riding a mule. Well, that shows you're not business-minded. Just because what had happened had her down on Kate was no reason to think she would always be figuring that way. For it wasn't every day you got a chance to ride a mule, and Kate was the only mule about.

Yep. She'd come across just like all the rest. She was making good money teaching school, I figured. So she'd pay and pay proper.

She'd humble down and come through them woods like a crawdad in winter water, waving that school check at a fair distance to show me she had the money. And I'd chomp a little on the straw, wiggle around unconcerned-like and say:

"Not so fast, Miss Canlittle. Seems to me there's a little score me and you and that mule have got to settle." And she'd know I was talking about General Washington.

She'd be playing a different tune now. There'd be a mending of ways, including a little less homework for me of the evenings.

I was just about ready to pull the principal, Mr. Weathers, into the picture when Elwood nudged me loose. Fats Wallen stood beside him.

"We got a problem, Mr. President," Elwood said.

I looked at the frown on Fats' face.

"Lost your penny, eh?" I said. "I figured you'd wear it out before you lost it, pulling it in and out of your pocket so much. Serves you right."

"He didn't lose the penny," Elwood said. "But after Fats got astraddle Kate I took a measurement of her from the belly to the ground. She was swaybacked two inches more than when the other boys were on her. It's Fats' weight. I say he's too heavy to ride for a penny. And he won't come across for two cents."

"Fats," I said, pulling the straw from my mouth,

sizing him up which took some doing, and trying all the time to look like it was all a trifling matter to me, "you're as fat as a corn-fed hog." Fats looked at me with his little squinted eyes. He dropped one of his jaws, which he could do anytime he wanted to, shucked up a sad look and said:

"What does that mean?"

"It means," I said, opening up the mouth of the sack slow and easy, "let me hear another clink."

"I ain't got another penny," Fats said.

"What do you mean you ain't got it?" I said. "Didn't you bring money for the candy machine and save some back?"

"I brought the money all right," Fats said. "But I eat it all." He looked sadder than ever. "All but one penny that Elwood said I could ride for."

"Then you've gobbled yourself right out of a mule ride," I said.

That didn't set too well with Fats. He looked right mean.

"Then give me my penny back," he said.

Well, I sure never thought about taking money out of the sack. I didn't intend to think about that now.

"Fats," I said, "that fatness of yours has done out-greedied your wants. You straddled that mule and bowed her down."

"That ain't no ride," Fats said.

"According," I said. "Just according. According to which was the way you were riding. Some go forward and backwards, others go up and down. You went up and down for your penny."

Fats wobbled away just as the school bell rang.

I walked over to Kate and could fairly tell that she wasn't taking lightly to everyone leaving. She wrinkled up and I stuck my finger under her nose and stopped the braying. I had been working on this over the weekend. It stopped her just like a finger under the nose will stop a sneeze. Try it and see if it won't.

I set her to eat and wallow about, stuck the sack in my pocket, and motioned for Elwood to hurry so we wouldn't be late getting back inside the schoolhouse.

"How long do you figure it will take to get the girls corralled?" I said. "I been thinking about expanding my business."

Elwood looked at me and grinned like he was thinking I had already worn off some of my country edges and said:

"Middle of the week."

The world was a wonderful place. I felt my pocket to see if the sack was still there. It was, and me and Elwood stepped out of the trees.

Kate wasn't far behind us. It was all my fault. Take the corn—I had taught her how to steal it. Take that polecat—I had been making a fuss over her for chasing rabbits and butterflies. Take the blackberries—I had picked berries for her to eat. Take the walnuts—I had cracked them for her. Now, take her following us to the school—I had brought her there. How was she to know she wasn't to come all the way?

The first I knew of her being there was when Elwood came back into the room after being excused for a drink of water. His face was as white as skimmed milk.

He took his seat, scribbled a note and passed it over. It read:

Business doomed. Us too!

I didn't have to worry about answering him. Didn't hardly have time to read the note, when I heard,

"He-haw-e-e-e-e-e-e-e-e!"

Kate's bray was coming from the hallway outside the room, toward the front door of the school.

"Get up, you fool!" That was Mr. Weathers' voice.

"He-haw-e-e-e-e-e-e-e-e!"

"Out, you stubborn mule!"

The mistake came with cracking the door. But Miss Canlittle was too curious to do different. And when she did, it was like opening a hole in a dam. Everyone poured out into the hall.

And there square in the center of the hall sat Kate on her haunches, grinning from ear to ear. Like she was a student and belonged there with the rest of us.

Mr. Weathers was in front of her holding the rope halter with both hands and pulling for all he was worth. But it was like hooking up a field mouse to pull over a mountain. All the while Mr. Weathers kept saying:

"Get up! Get up, mule!"

Kate said:

"He-haw-e-e-e-e-e-e-e-e!"

It was plain to see that Kate was getting the better of Mr Weathers. For each time she brayed she fairly straightened him out. His hair stood on end, quivered, and he held to

124

the halter with all his might.

With all of us watching, Kate made it worse. She bowed her head forward and licked him on the cheek. You could hear the scratch. Just like sandpaper over a rough board.

Miss Canlittle brought one arm around in a big circle and covered her eyes.

"Oho-o-o-o-o-o-o-o-o!" she screamed. "The monster has bit Mr. Weathers!" She looked at us to set the terribleness of that and then looked ahead and yelled: "Hold to it, Mr. Weathers! Don't let it reach the children!"

Mr. Weathers, worn thin as a raveling and edged like a razor, said:

"Maybe you would like to try holding this mule, Miss Canlittle?"

Miss Canlittle stiffened and blinked her eyelids as fast as bird wings:

"My only concern is the children."

Mr. Weathers braced himself and took another braying and spraying from Kate. Then he snurled his nose and looked at Miss Canlittle:

"Children, my foot!" he said. "You're looking after your own hide!"

Miss Canlittle drew down her face and looked at us for sympathy. She got it from the girls and motioned for running room.

In the meantime Mr. Weathers had done some studying of that mule. He had learned to watch the wrinkle in her hide, get a better grip at the swelling up, and set himself for the bray.

Then, giving up on being able to pull her up, he just stood back and studied the mule.

He walked into his office and come back with a board. He walked to the rear of the mule and she turned and grinned at him just like an old fool, enjoying it all. I dodged to keep her from seeing me, edging Elwood closer. He fought to get back.

Well, Mr. Weathers stuck the board under Kate and put his shoulder to it, trying to push her up on her hoofs. He took a deep breath. Up Kate went. Back down she came. Up, down, up, down. Just like she was riding a teeter-totter and liking it.

Miss Canlittle said:

"Mr. Weathers, you're getting nowhere. I do believe you are giving that monster pleasure in what you are doing."

Mr. Weathers stopped and stiffened. He turned slowly.

"Miss Canlittle!" he sneered. "If you are so all-fired concerned for the children suppose you put *your* shoulder to this board. And you are old enough to know that we are dealing with a mule, not a monster!"

It was like flipping the spoon of a trap. Miss Canlittle stiffened.

Kate looked a little disgusted when she saw Mr. Weathers giving up with the board. Miss Canlittle sorta puckered a little for sympathy. I had seen ma do the same thing.

Mr. Weathers was back with his hands on his hips studying Kate again. He turned on us. I dodged again. He set his finger squarely on Mutt Rule and said:

"Run out the back door and get me a handful of

126

grass!" Kate straightened him with a bray at the mention of the word grass before he could get his hands over his ears.

Mutt came back with a handful of grass that fairly curled Kate's hair with pleasure.

Mr. Weathers set his legs just right and held the grass out in front of Kate. Just far enough out of reach so she would have to get up to reach it. Kate bowed forward . A smile came to Mr. Weathers' face.

Maybe he was thinking he had won the battle. Maybe he thought that he would take his time now and get back some of the pleasure he had lost.

Mr. Weathers pulled the grass in front of Kate, so close that it touched the end of her nose. You could hear her snap at it. But Mr. Weathers was too fast and Kate missed. He grinned:

"Thought you could outsmart me, eh?" he said.

But Kate was ready for him the second time around. He came around as slow as a butterfly and Kate picked the grass out of his hands. She sat back and started chewing.

"And what, Mr. Weathers," Miss Canlittle said, "will you show us next?" And she looked at us and flipped her head fast like she was putting a period to that.

"I, Miss Canlittle," Mr. Weathers said, "shall go into my office and call the police. And while I'm gone I hope this mule gets you!"

"*Oh-o-o-o-o-o-o-o!*" Miss Canlittle screamed. And she edged Fats Wallen to the front.

"Better do something fast," Elwood said to me.

"Me!" I said. "And get skinned alive?"

"It's you or the mule," he said, just like his hands were clean of the whole thing.

"What about you?" I said. "It was your idea to bring her here in the first place."

"No time for that," Elwood said. "If the police come they'll blow her up like a bank vault. They carry big guns!"

That did it. Elwood knew it would. I stepped to the front with help from Elwood. Kate saw me—

"He-haw-e-e-e-e-e-e-e-e-e!"

I was standing all alone now, just me and that mule and a hall full of people behind. And just then Mr. Weathers looked out of his office, and saw that mule stick her nose into my arms. Mr. Weathers looked so tall I couldn't see the top of his head. But his voice had no trouble rolling down to me:

"Isaac Warfield!" he said. "You've got five minutes to get that mule out of the schoolhouse and be back in my office!"

And out of the school we went. Kate's big hoofs sounded like thunder across the wooden floor of the hall, making it worse than ever.

She knew there was something wrong, too. She walked ever so close, sticking her nose into my arms and nearly knocking me off balance.

"We're in a heap of trouble, Kate," I said. "The worst is yet to come."

I might have dragged it out, and even scolded the mule. But there's no time for much in five minutes with doom looking you in the eyes.

I hurried to the woods and said:

"If ever you minded, mind now. We're so close to the tannery I can hear'em sharpening their knives."

That did it. Into the woods she went, me figuring I'd soon be coming out the schoolhouse just as fast. Shed of the seat of my britches.

And for the first time I left her without worry that she would follow. Mainly because I didn't have time.

"Why, come right in, Isaac," Mr. Weathers said from where he sat in his office, his big hands folded like shovels. "Won't you have a seat? Be with you in just a moment. Elwood and I are just completing some figures."

Can you beat that! I mean just like I was coming to visit of my own free will!

I took a seat beside Elwood, sitting straight as a poker. I tell you I never felt so small in my life. Never figured my time was shorter, for that matter. For me and Elwood had sure come a long way down. Just shows you what a little time can do. I mean here just a short while back we were both giving orders like General Washington, and now here we sat in worse shape than British prisoners.

Mr. Weathers turned around in his swivel chair and looked at Elwood. He held a paper in his hand that sure looked familiar to me. I mean it ought to. It was Elwood's list of the boys that had ridden the mule.

"Twenty-six," Mr. Weathers said. "I get twenty-six cents. Is that right by your count, Elwood?"

"Yes sir," Elwood said.

"Not bad," Mr. Weathers said. "Not bad indeed, Elwood. A good profit. And no more than you had to work with. Quite ingenious, looking at it from the standpoint of a businessman."

Well, it perked Elwood up some. He stuck out his little banty chest like a rooster first learning to crow. But he swallowed instead.

"But I'm a little in doubt about the reputability of the business," Mr. Weathers said. "Now, the money."

I nearly ripped the pocket from my pants getting it out.

"So," Mr. Weathers said, "I see you're the banker, Isaac. You've moved fast your first year in a city school."

My hands trembled and if the money clinked from it I never heard it. Me and Elwood were just sitting there like we were total strangers.

"All here," Mr. Weathers said. He looked at his watch. "Nearly a penny a minute, judging the time you had at lunch." He changed his look completely, and squinted toward the door as if he expected someone to be peeping in. Then he leaned toward Elwood. "Now, since the money was made more or less on school time and on school property, wouldn't you say the school ought to be entitled to a fair share of the profits?"

It was enough to set you back. Elwood glanced at me. He cleared his throat and sat a little more bowed in his chair. Even crossed his legs.

"I'd say so," Elwood said.

"Good," Mr. Weathers said. "And since I represent the school would you see any wrong in my acting on behalf of the school as the administrator?"

Elwood looked at me again.

"Come now, Elwood," Mr. Weathers said. "You're

131

too good a businessman to squabble over this. Or, perhaps you'd like to have time to talk to your partner."

The old business look was back in Elwood's eye. He sort of squirmed around independent-like and winked at me. Got a go-ahead back from me and he says:

"I'd say that's fair, Mr. Weathers."

Well, there it was. Right out in front of our eyes. He was doing no more than asking for a payoff. Can you imagine? A school principal, I mean. The least person you'd ever expect to ask for a payoff.

If you think I minded looking at that big red streak on Mr. Weathers' cheek where Kate had licked him, you are wrong. Oh, I had at first. I thought it might give me a little trouble. But things had changed.

Fact is, my old greediness was coming back some. Fear of punishment was gone. And I got to thinking about Mr. Weathers horning in, maybe getting too big and asking for too much.

"Good, Elwood," Mr. Weathers said. "Let's see. I'd say that sort of makes us all partners. In a way. Tell me. Do you have plans for more?"

I'll tell you Elwood laid it all out.

"The girls are next," he said. "That ought to double our take. And then"—Elwood looked toward the hall, sneaking like—"and next Miss Canlittle."

Mr. Weathers grinned and then chuckled.

"Now, Elwood," he said. "You sure are a greedy little booger." He looked at me. "How about you, Isaac?"

"I got the mule," I said.

"Well let's divvy up," Elwood said. "If we're going to get the girls tomorrow I got to get to work."

132

"You mean keep the money, Elwood?" Mr. Weathers said. That's right. Just what he said. "Why surely you don't think . . ."

"All right then," Elwood said. "You get free rides on the mule to boot."

Mr. Weathers grinned.

"Well," he said, "I couldn't do that. It wouldn't look right to the townspeople, I'm afraid. After all, I am the school principal, obligated to look after the interest of all my students. And nowhere in the curriculum is there a course in riding a mule, much less paying for it."

Elwood swallowed again and I scooted up straight in my seat.

"And under those circumstances," Mr. Weathers said, "the money will have to be refunded. Now, as for the school's share. After all, school property was involved— and used. Well, I was thinking of something . . . say . . . like working interest. Just a little something that's apt to keep the regular curriculum intact in the future." And then he looked at us like we had given him the surprise of his life. "Were we ever talking of anything else?"

He slammed the sack of money down on his desk. I didn't have a bit of trouble hearing it clink. The noise popped Elwood a good foot out of his seat. And the look on Mr. Weathers' face melted Elwood back into it.

Well, it was sure enough working interest. He figured it up on a day-to-day basis since he didn't know just how many days Elwood was going to last in school.

He reached into the corner of his office where the janitor kept his supplies and came out with the biggest mop you ever laid eyes on. He looked at Elwood, sized up his puniness, and figured Elwood out at a week's work oiling down the school floors, which held down the dust and preserved the wood. He set Elwood's work time at the noon hour since he said that Elwood had already demonstrated his ability at this hour and there wasn't any need to change it.

And poor little Elwood walked out of the office behind the biggest mop ever made. And he had to keep it with him everywhere he went from that minute till the end of the seventh day. Carry it to class and all. Come in first thing in the morning and get it at the office and return it when school let out.

It was then that I again noticed the big lick Kate had made across the cheek of Mr. Weathers. So I sat down in the chair, shriveled up into nothing. I figured I'd pass out of this life right there in the schoolhouse. For I was the president.

I figured he'd lay the wood to me right off, since he had got all riled up at Elwood. But there he sat just staring at me with a smile like I was a long-lost cousin. Then he said to me in a friendly sort of way:

"Your first year here at the town school, isn't it, Isaac?"

"Yes sir," I said.

"And how do you like our school?" he asked.

There just wasn't any need for me to lie. I mean he had got Elwood, tricked him into telling everything he knew. I figured my time was coming.

"All right until today," I said.

"I see," he said. He shook his head like he was

knowing the kind of shape I was in now. "The mule."

Knowing that I was in as tight a corner as I had ever been in, with no way to squirm out, I figured there just wasn't any need of laying all the blame on the mule.

"She ain't really a bad mule, Mr. Weathers," I said. "I mean she just don't go around meaning to do harm."

Mr. Weathers looked at me like he was surprised.

"Why of course she isn't," he said. And he started over the list of riders again.

A different look came over that office and Mr. Weathers. The office was a big spider web and Mr. Weathers was the spider. Me, I felt like I was a fly caught in the web.

He had had Elwood thinking he was off the hook. Had him thinking he was going to walk right out of that office with a sack of money and ways to make more. Then he sent him out in the lowest form dragging a big bushy-headed mop. Nothing could be worse. He had laid the mop to Elwood.

"Well," I said, "I won't say it was right for that mule to come right here in the schoolhouse."

Mr. Weathers looked at me now in ever so friendly a way.

"Don't be too hard on the little mule, Isaac," he said. "I mean she had no way of knowing about Henry Ford and the fact that automobiles have been coming to school ever since instead of mules." Then he leaned close and whispered like he thought there might be someone out in the hall listening: "You don't think she came here for learning, do you, Isaac?"

I'd give Kate credit for knowing a lot. She had more sense than to ever be caught inside four walls for a whole day, not when she had the hills and an open sky to get her schooling in. She had come because I was here and that was all. Anyway, even if she had come to learn, I wasn't about to start siding in with him at this point and getting caught.

"No sir, Mr. Weathers," I said. "I sure ain't thinking that. I'm thinking she had no right to come in here at all."

He puckered his mouth.

"Oh, let up a little, Isaac," he said. "Don't be that hard on the little thing. If you're thinking about that ruckus in the hall, forget it. It didn't amount to that much. Why, a principal has to allow for little things like getting his face sanded down by the tongue of a mule."

"Well," I said, "I sure didn't know that. Surely didn't."

"Why yes," Mr. Weathers said, just like there was a lot more to it than that. "I've practically forgotten it already. If it didn't burn now and then I think I would have."

"Well," I said, "she ain't coming back no more. She wasn't supposed to in the first place. I mean come on in the schoolhouse like that. Just as far as the pasture, that was the limit."

Mr. Weathers rubbed his hands together, shaking his head like he was willing and wanting to forget the whole thing now.

"Well, Isaac," he said, "let's not take up all your time visiting today with talk of that mule. Let's talk some about you and this being your first year here. We want to make sure that everything is all right with you, that we are doing our best with you."

"Visiting" crossed my mind. He sure had a way of

twisting things around and making them seem right. But maybe what he was saying was that it being my first year I could sort of be overlooked for a few things, mainly the mule. That made sense.

"I'm happy that your father chose to send you here," he said. "I've known your father for years. He's a fine shoe cobbler, has a fine shop, and is a fine man."

I figured to steer his mind a little farther from the mule if he was set on forgetting it.

"I want to be a shoe cobbler," I said.

"It's a good profession," Mr. Weathers said. He leaned close. "There's good money in it too. A good *return* on your money." He sure dragged out the *return*.

"Ma don't think so," I said, hoping to knock off the edge. "Pa don't make much."

"Well," he said, "*money* isn't everything, is it, Isaac?" He sure dragged out the *money*.

"Sure ain't," I said.

That's when he got me. Right in that web.

"Now how did we ever get on the subject of *money?*" he said.

I frowned and sat there like a June bug with a jaybird on his tail.

"*Money*," he said. "Money, money, money." Like he was trying to make a connection. He was handling the sack now and I could hear the pennies clink. "I have some money to return. Which reminds me, Isaac, that I have something for you, too."

He walked to the closet and came out with the biggest five-gallon can of oil you ever laid eyes on. He stood over me so tall he had to bend to stay inside the schoolhouse.

Seemed that tall, anyway.

"Elwood mops, and you oil!" he said, in a voice that would put a thundercloud to shame. "And if I ever see hide or hair of that mule on school property again, I'll render you, Elwood, and the mule down until there won't be enough left to fill a thimble. And if I see you without that can of oil in your hands for the next seven days you'll be working here at the school until you're an old man!"

And if you think you can sneak down a big school hall and hide as big a thing as a five-gallon can of oil, it sloshing and smelling to boot, you just ought to try it.

CHAPTER 12

Stay Clear of the Mop That Dyes Her Hair

I guess it was about what you might have expected. I mean Elwood carrying that big bushy-headed mop around everywhere he went. Right into class and all.

By the middle of the week the boys had tacked a name onto it. Myrtle, they called it. Sweet Myrtle.

They'd pass him in the hall, look at the mop and say: "Hello, Myrtle." Not bothering in the least to speak to Elwood. Just like he wasn't there. They cautioned him about carrying her all the time with her head hung down, saying it would cause all the blood to run to her head and make her sick. And when the strands of cloth got a little deeper in color from the oil they accused her of dying her hair.

"Blond today and black-headed tomorrow." Poor Elwood.

I could have really felt sorry for Elwood except I was dishing all my sympathy out to myself and that big can of oil. I couldn't hide it but I was working on trying to carry it around without it splashing so loud or smelling so rank.

Maybe I was better off since they couldn't very well

tack a name of a girl onto a can of oil. But I caught it all in another way. They shunned me, sidestepping and holding their noses like the smell of me and that oil was almost enough to knock them down, which it was.

Me and Elwood sort of singled around during the morning since being caught together was the worst of all things. When that happened, the other boys clattered at us like a treeful of starlings. But at noon, since we could do no different, we got together.

We ate a quick lunch, again since we could do no different, and I went to sloshing the oil and Elwood spreading it out.

I had taken to tying Kate again, this time out in the open—since I feared she would come to the schoolhouse again and doom us both, and Elwood spent most of the noon hour saying:

"You sure you got that mule tied?" I peeped around the big handle of the mop and said:

"Good and tight." And Elwood stepped back to keep the oil from splattering on him and said:

"Do you think one rope is enough? I mean, since our lives are at stake?"

Oiling down a dry spot I said:

"She'd have to pull the tree over to get loose."

Elwood peeped out from the mop.

"Think she can?"

Slish, slosh.

"Don't think she can," I said.

Swish, swish.

"Ain't you sure?" Elwood said.

Slosh, slosh.

140

"I wouldn't put anything past that mule," I said.

Swish, swish.

"Me neither," Elwood said.

And time hung big and timeless as the end of a yawn, but it finally scooted along.

At the end of the seventh day we turned in the mop and oil can, figuring the bow in our fingers from holding them would always be there.

We had paid our debt and I turned once more to think about Kate.

She sure didn't have any kind of a life to look forward to. I mean just spending most of the day tied to the end of a rope. A world that was less then twenty feet long. And unless she were to die on the end of a rope I had to come up with something. She had grazed out about all there was to graze, since there wasn't much for her to graze to begin with. And water was even harder to come by. There was one small spring in the whole branch and it bubbled so slow that the wiggly worms had taken most of it over, splashing it out. I came up with one thing: I'd have to untie her and chance that she had learned her lesson not to go near the school again.

I'd pad my thinking a little. I'd change my route to school. I'd put brush over the old route to show her that it wasn't being used anymore and I'd stake me out a new one. Instead of crossing the hill and coming out at the rim of the woods in back of the schoolhouse I'd go by way of Bear Creek, coming out near the center of town and then walking right up the main street to the school. I would let houses, people, and cars be my brush. For Kate

141

wouldn't want any truck with these. Especially automobiles and people. If she took a mind to follow she wouldn't get any farther than the city limits. And then she would head back for the hill country.

To be even a little more certain, I spent time talking to her about the awfulness of people, streets, and cars. And I told her that if she went into town they might just snatch her up and cart her off to the tannery before I could get her away from them. And she put stock in what I said. For when I brought in the tannery it sewed it up. Her ears flipped into the air and stayed for a spell.

We were busy now gathering walnuts. For the first frost had moved in and put brownness to most things about. We worked until darkness crossed the top of the hills and moved in on us—me climbing the trees and shaking the walnuts down, Kate trying to climb the trees, finding she couldn't, and just standing under the tree I was in, swishing her tail and snorting, mad as a hornet. Mad because she couldn't wrap her spindly legs around the tree trunk and shinny up to sit on the limb beside me. Though sometimes if the tree was bowed she could come as far as the first fork and I'd have to stop and run her back. Most times finding it was best to break a limb and tickle her in the ribs which she couldn't stand and would have to slide down.

But she was handy when it came to tromping off the hulls. We'd tromp, fill the sack and sit for a while under the light of the moon to eat a few. Then I would lift the sack to her back and she'd carry it in, going as far as the pine grove and then dropping them off. And from here I'd roll the sack down the hill.

Pa had agreed to take the walnuts to his shop and put up a sign in the window that said they were for sale.

I set about thinking why it was that the most important answer I ever needed in my life just wouldn't come to me. It was always the smaller ones I got. What I needed was to find a way for that little mule to slip into ma's heart like she had mine. Or even as far as she had got into pa's. For he paid attention to the little silly things that I told him Kate did, like trying to climb trees and learning to crack out walnuts. She was a dandy when it came to knocking off the green shell. And she could crack the brown shell too, leaving me to only have to pick the kernels out for her. All of which saved considerable time. And all of which caused pa to kid me.

"That's all right," he would say, grinning. "But watch she don't learn to pick out them kernels or you'll shinny down the tree one day and find nothing but empties."

And them some evening when the hills were quiet as a buzzard circling in the sky pa would look at me with a frown on his face and say:

"I wouldn't be getting too attached to the little mule, Isaac. We both know that things haven't changed much with the mule as close as Bunt Rankins' place. It's only a matter of time."

And he'd stare into nothing and I'd figure he'd be judging the closeness of winter and snow.

I knew it, too. But I'd cross my fingers and hope that nothing would come to shorten it. Something Kate might do. Like another trip to school or the like.

I only hoped. And that wasn't enough. It came quicker than I thought it might.

CHAPTER 13

A Mule Can Make a School Full of Heroes

Reports got to school by way of the boys who lived just inside the city limits. Reports of a big varmint of some kind that had been seen prowling the neighborhoods. A big varmint that walked on its all fours and had ears two feet tall and eyes that burned in the night like two coal embers.

It had been heard to make a scream frightful to the ears. High-pitched to a fine point that caused dogs to howl, mournful and sad.

And the dogs chased it, some bawling into the night and never coming back. People said they had been gulped down by the varmint. Fact is, every dog that strayed off added another notch to the evils of the varmint. The varmint took most delight in anything the frost had left green, and purely rolled in pleasure from eating in flower gardens: little green shoots, and the straw spread out to cover them from the frost.

It had hoofs and a long pointed tail that came to an end and formed an arrow. Everybody knowing full well that this marked it kin to the devil himself. Some said it had little red wings, since it was seen, with dogs close, sailing over fences that were too high for an ordinary creature to jump.

Well, because of pressure being put on them, Rafrel Skaggs and Milton Boggs, the two city policemen, had investigated. With Milton—since he was the captain—giving out reports from Rafrel's investigation at the scene. How Rafrel was trying to do something. He had trailed it once to the woods and lost its tracks in the grass. Milton had put in his report to the public:

"The varmint reached the edge of the woods with Rafrel on its heels and then just sailed off like a bird."

Another time Rafrel had almost caught it. He ran it right to the foot of the hills, and there it stopped and turned on him. In Rafrel's own words:

"It tuck tail till it reached the edge of the woods. Then it turned with its eyes burnin' so bright it hurt my eyes to look. Its tail was circlin' like a hound dog's tail will do when it knows they's a rabbit in the bush. Teeth was as long as a hammer handle, they was. Spliced at the end which made a fork. Might have run, I might. But remembered that I ain't suppose to run since the town is dependin' on me and payin' me not to. I drawed for my gun which Milton had 'lowed me to put bullets in bein' I was apt to be far away and in no danger of hittin' nobody. It moved in on me. Wrinkled up till it warn't no bigger than a inner tube with the air out. Then pumped out and screamed which blowed my hat off and wrapped me around a fence post. I believe they was fire come from its mouth, too. And before I could get unwrapped it had sailed away just like a bird. High into the air then turned and dove into the ground with a big puff of smoke belchin' from the hole it had made. I went to look and thar warn't no hole there atall."

That was the report that Milton gave out. But once Rafrel hit the streets he stretched it considerable. He had stood and fought the varmint, or critter, as he said, with his bare fists, its eyeballs burning his knuckles. And when it saw that here was a man brave enough to stand toe to toe with it, it tucked tail and dived into the ground with Rafrel's arm going in the hole after it like going for a rabbit. But the hole closed on him and he had to dig his arm free with his other hand.

I knew it was Kate the evening me and Elwood went to look at some tracks it was supposed to have left the night before. There were the four hoof marks, little jagged spots in them from the broken hoofs, which helped to make them look less like the track of a mule, or a horse. And there were the little trails between them, furrows like a muskrat will leave by dragging his tail. But made by Kate's walk. Old and slow, shuffling along, dragging her hoofs like she was carrying the world on her back.

And it all came to me. She had followed me part of the way to school. She had gotten as far as the city limits and stopped that first day. She had stayed to look around. She saw the flower gardens with the brown straw stretched over them. And she saw some touches of green where the straw had been able to ward off the frost.

She had just decided to come back in the night and take a better look, liked what she saw, and started eating.

And what followed got worse and worse. I mean, boys have a way of stretching things when the stretching is in their favor.

Each one came to school making brags of how his pa had stood to fight the varmint out of their flower bed. Made it tuck tail and sail off into the woods.

Then they just shucked their pas and stepped into their shoes. Swelled out their chests like banty roosters and drove on to be made heroes by the girls.

Before the week was out I was about the only boy left at the school that hadn't fought with the creature. Even for the ones who lived far inside the city limits, it got to the place where it was either do a little tracking or be thought a coward.

Finally even Elwood pitched in with his tale. I'm not for holding Elwood too much to blame. I mean as much as the rest. He was just so little and puny and never being given credit with being brave enough to stand up to an alley cat. And he had been pulled even lower by having to tote that mop around the school and all. I guess he had a right to big-dog it some.

I guess I just never thought he could get so balled up.

The way it happened was that the evening before Elwood told his tale, me and him and Kate had gone into the hills to gather walnuts. I told Elwood that the limb on that tree wouldn't hold. But he just went scooting out on it like a measuring worm. The wind caught him about halfway out and lifted him like a cotton ball. Sailed him into the air and dumped him to the ground flat on his back. And one of those big walnut roots got in the way and skinned his face up a right smart.

Well, he lay there puffing and blinking his eyes, afraid to feel his face since it was all numb and he figured

147

his nose and one ear were gone. And then the feeling came back and he felt and they were still there. Just his face all red, and it got redder still when he went home that evening and his ma put some poke juice on it. Liked to have burned him up.

Now, that little Elwood turned that skinned face overnight into the biggest yarn you ever heard.

I never saw such a gathering as he had around the drinking fountain. Girls and boys alike. And by the time I reached him there was just barely room to hang on the edge of the circle. But I could see him standing there with his feet spread, little as he was, swinging those arms and fists for all he was worth. Me knowing they hardly had enough force to knock a good-sized horsefly off Kate's back. He was huffing and puffing.

He stopped only long enough to point out the big bruise on his face, taking full advantage of the night's helping make it worse. It was swollen and red.

Now he didn't get that bruise in any ordinary way. He knew that he was the first boy at the schoolhouse to show up with a bruise worth bragging about and he poured it on. Just standing his ground with that varmint wasn't much in itself since there had been several of the boys at school who had done the same. He'd separated himself from them when the varmint had turned to run. Here he had latched on to its forked tail with both hands and had been dragged deep into the woods so far that it had taken him til near daylight to find his way home. And me knowing that Elwood had got lost in an open field.

His first blow had knocked the wind right out of that varmint. And he had gone in like a buzz saw. It had fought. *Oh, how strong and tough it had been!* Caught him a few times on the side of his face with those forked hoofs. But he had wrestled it and flipped it to its back. Got a leg-hold on and squeezed until fire came out its mouth.

Why, if it hadn't a-been a hant of some kind he'd of brought it in. Dragged it as far as he could and then right before his eyes it had disappeared into the ground. Left like a scared rabbit. And Elwood had stood above the hole and dared it to come back out.

It wasn't that the boys believed him. It was just that they knew he had outtold them. He'd latched on to a tale that they wouldn't be apt to top. Worse yet, they knew some of the girls believed him, since they looked on him with, well, you know the look girls get at a time like this.

Well, I got Elwood to one side and I said:

"Elwood, you're a-going too far. You're going to unravel that tale if you keep adding on."

He says:

"You mean fighting that varmint?"

"It ain't no varmint and you know it as well as me. You know that the bruise on your face is from falling from that walnut tree. And you know that those tracks belong to Kate."

"Well," he says, "you just don't know it all, Isaac. You don't live inside the city limits. I got me a chance to be somebody."

"You ain't got nothing but the girls giggling over you," I said. "That ain't being nothing."

Well, Elwood never got a chance to answer that. I saw Mr. Weathers standing outside his door with his finger crooked and wiggling at me like a fishing worm. Motioning me toward the office.

Elwood saw it too and he slid away from me like water from a duck's back. Just like whatever Kate had done this time, he wasn't tied in with it. I couldn't blame him for that. I would have done the same thing, I guess.

So I just turned and walked toward the office. And there I was. Right back inside the big spider web again.

"Well, Isaac," Mr. Weathers said, "I guess you are about the only man left here at the schoolhouse who hasn't had a fight with the varmint that's been prowling the border of town. That is, since I had my first run-in with it last night. I thought you might like to hear about it since surely it doesn't stand to reason that you'll be lucky enough to be left out entirely."

I just kept my eyes peeled to the left side of Mr. Weathers' face. It was smarted and I was sure that Kate had licked him the first time on the right side.

"Caught it out in my wife's flower bed about midnight," Mr. Weathers said. "Why, it wasn't at all like you would imagine it to be: Split-toothed, pointed-tail, red-winged and set for anger like the devil. Fact is, you might say it was just the opposite." He reached his hand up and rubbed his cheek. "Can you ever imagine a creature given to this much meanness just walking up and licking its tongue over my cheek! And instead of fighting, just sitting down in the center of my wife's prize chrysanthemum bed for more than two hours. With me pleading for it to get out before my wife saw it there. Oh, she knew it was out there somewhere. It had the loudest voice. Not a scream exactly, but something that sounded awfully familiar to me. I told her not to call the police, that I could handle it all right. I felt like shooting it myself. But for some strange reason I couldn't. Maybe it just didn't look mean enough."

He looked at me and by George if the hard lines in his face didn't just fade out right before my eyes. I never thought I would ever see a thing like that. Not from the face of a man I had been willing to place beside the meanest hant in the hills.

"Maybe I think that mule has had it tough enough," he said. "You're probably the only thing good she knows, Isaac. Want to talk about her? I thought you deserved a right to talk about it."

Lying was in the bushes. I mean I never had a man level with me like that except pa. I wouldn't shame me or Kate by being dishonest now.

I started as near the beginning of the story as I could. Back when me and the little mule first met. Not taking up for her but just letting her be a mule and all. And I didn't try to be a hero about it since I never figured I had it in me to be a hero. Neither did Kate.

As I talked there were times I thought Mr. Weathers was really understanding me. Like Kate licking his face and meaning no harm. It was her way of saying she liked him. Why, next to me and pa he was the only one she had ever done a thing like that to. And he rubbed his hand again over his cheek and said:

"I don't mean to be ungrateful."

And then I told him how she liked to sneak up and bray in your ear, that is, if she knows you're her friend. That's the way it was with that mule.

Well, it was then that the talk quieted down to where

you could hear my heart beat. I tried to cover up the sound of it by talk. I tried not to leave out a thing, and told both the good and the bad.

He gave me a long look. And I looked right back, trying to show that I was willing to take what was coming to me. It was then that he fooled me good.

"I'd like to help, Isaac," he said. But you and I know that the mule can't come to school. We know too that she can't go around tearing people's flower gardens up. Scaring people and causing them to bolt their doors and sleep uneasy at nights. Leaving their lights on. Now do you know a way to stop all of this?"

"No sir," I said. "But I think I can find one."

"Well, I guess you know what we're facing, Isaac," he said. "Since I know that it is a mule doing the damage it puts a different light on things. It wouldn't be fair to the townspeople for me to allow all this to continue. On the other hand it wouldn't be fair if I were to tell without giving you a chance to work things out. I owe that to you as one of my students. And then too, I think I have some idea of just how much you care for that old critter. I can give you the evening and night. If you find a way by the time you come to school in the morning we'll forget about it. Ok?"

"I reckon it's more than fair," I said. "I'll find a way."

And I was thinking of the saying that the people you meet and think you like the least sometimes turn out to be the best of the lot. I'll put stock in that.

I walked to the door, stopped, and said:

"I'm obliged to you."

"Just wanted you to know that I don't have a pointed

tail either, Isaac," he said. "Just have a school to run. And
... Isaac ... as I have no desire to be a hero, suppose we
just forget about my fight with the creature."

CHAPTER 14

It Ain't Natural to Lock a Mule in Jail

Daylight broke. It came slow, the sun sticking its nose over the rim of the hills and then creeping up to quilt the valley in patches of light and shade.

Ma packed my lunch and I took a different route toward school. For overnight I had decided that I would not go to see Kate before I went to school. I got to thinking that seeing me might encourage her to follow.

And there was another reason, too. The weather was brisk and chilly and Kate had fallen into a habit of sleeping later than usual. I had noticed her tapering off with early rising and some mornings I had had to wake her up.

Sleeping late was the sign of two things: old age, or laziness. With Kate it was age. For the light never peeped on her with her eyes closed during that whole summer. But now the cold was in her old bones and it made them pop and crack like twigs breaking.

The cold worked the opposite for me. Made me feel frisky as a furred-out rabbit, though I'm not denying that this morning part of my friskiness was in thinking of walking into Mr. Weathers' office and telling him that me and that mule could and would work out our problems.

I'd get in his office early and take good care of it all and then I'd have the rest of the day free of it, free as the wind to just sit back and think about that big fence I was going to build all around Kate's pasture. A fence so high a bird would have to rest halfway before he sailed over the top of it. That'd keep Kate out of town and out of mischief, too.

I could see Mr. Weathers sitting at his desk going over some papers. I pecked on the door window ever so light and he turned and motioned for me to come in.

He looked at me and shook his head and sort of scared me. For it was a look that could have said he had just done some more thinking about our talk and had come out with a different thought about it all.

"I'm sorry, Isaac," he said, motioning me to a chair. "I know that isn't much help. But believe me I'm truly sorry you never got a chance to work your problem out."

Well, he knocked the wind out of me. "I just don't believe I follow you, Mr. Weathers," I said, sure now that he wasn't aiming to give me a chance. "I believe I do have it worked out."

He looked at me with a frown on his face.

"You didn't go by to see the mule this morning?" he said.

"I thought it best not to," I said. "Figured it might be encouraging her to follow me."

He was rubbing his hand over his chin now, making his words come out slow, low, and mumbled.

"Then you don't know, Isaac. Of course, you couldn't

know, not living in town. Well, it's bad, Isaac. Mighty bad."

"What's bad?" I asked.

"The mule, Isaac," he said. "The mule. They caught her early this morning. Chased her most of the night and then some. She might have got away, but I guess they chased her so much that she got all turned around and wandered back into town. Got traffic all balled up and then traipsed over to John Naper's feedstore just as he was stacking his feed out in front. Well, they say she made a mess of it before they got her away."

"What did they do with her?" I said.

"She's not hurt," Mr. Weathers said. "They just locked her up in jail." His face broke into a grin. "Fact is, I understand that took no little doing. Took a dozen men, including the police force, to get her there. I can understand that. I mean, taking into account that the mule didn't want to go." He looked out into the hall, just about the spot where Kate had once sat down on him.

"In jail!" I said. "What will they do with her there?"

"I don't know," Mr. Weathers said. "I never knew of a mule being locked up in jail before. Don't think anyone else in this town has. "

There was no more to talk about and so I got up. I felt like nothing, all the wind out of me. Just as I reached for the door Mr. Weathers said:

"I guess there is little I can do, Isaac. But if you should feel like talking about it, if it should just get burdensome, my door is open to you."

"I'm obliged," I said, walking out into the hall with nothing in front of me.

I walked into class numb. I guess I deserved being called down for not paying attention. For I couldn't rightly expect the teacher to know that the whole world had just been slid out from under me.

Kate in jail! Everything gone. Nothing left.

I took the blame for it all on myself. I could just see that little mule sneaking off into the hills toward town. Coming there to the city limits and stopping, and her nose being like it was, her belly ruling her head, she went on. Right across the city limits.

And then it had happened. Everything broke loose. All she knew to do was to run. And although there was no way to know what was going on in her mind I could imagine her running in fear, wondering what sort of a world it was, and where she would go.

Then town. All balled up. Cars coming at her like evil monsters until she couldn't think. Nothing but cars. To the left and to the right. And then—John Naper's store.

I guess her seeing the corn and bales of hay being put out there was the closest thing to the hills she could find. I guess she just couldn't figure she wasn't supposed to eat the feed. It was there. It was all for a mule to eat. She was hungry and didn't know people put a price tag on that.

I could see John Naper screaming his head off. The police coming and other people gathering around her until she couldn't get a good breath of air. And maybe she looked for ever so short a time in the crowd for me.

Then she just sat down. That's what she did when she didn't want to go anywhere. And I could see the men pulling at her and cursing her stubbornness. It must have been awful. I mean looking through all that crowd knowing there could just be one friendly face among them and it not there. It left her nothing. It left her nobody.

Me and Elwood talked about it at noon but it didn't help much.

"Don't just give up, Isaac," Elwood said. "You ain't licked yet. I mean Kate is still alive. I'll ask pa about it tonight. He studied a little law when he was working in the coal mines and studying. He might know something."

Elwood saying he would ask his pa didn't help much either. I knew he was trying to help, to keep me from feeling so bad. But I had never told him that I knew that his pa had never worked in a coal mine. Pa had told me. Elwood had made it up, maybe to make him seem a little closer to my way of life. I don't know. But what could his pa, I mean president of the bank and all, care about a mule?

After school I walked down through town, coming within sight of the city jail which was on the first floor of the city building. A little two-story cinder-block building that looked as gray as a shadow. I stopped.

I felt low, within hollering distance of Kate and not able to make her hear me. The thick sides of the building hid her from me. They held her from the wind and light of the hills and maybe from food and water. For I didn't know whether they would feed her or not.

I thought once of just walking inside the building and asking to see her. Then I'd know. But I gathered my thoughts and figured pa was my best chance right now. And so I crossed the street and walked toward his shoe shop. I would wait and walk home with pa tonight.

Pa was standing beside his shoe last, spitting tacks from his mouth to his hand to tack the sole on a shoe. He didn't have to look to do this, for a good cobbler never misses his hand and never lets his mouth stay idle while a hand does its work. And pa was a good cobbler. He could make a pair of shoes as easy as mending a pair.

He kept a cowbell over the top of the door that clanked whenever someone walked in, since most of his day was spent with his head down, fixed on the shoe last.

When I walked in, he looked up and spit a tack into his hand.

"I'm glad you came to the shop, Isaac," he said. "I been thinking you might stop by here before you went on home. Mule is in a heap of trouble, ain't she?"

"Is she lost, pa?" I asked.

"I don't know, Isaac," he said. "To save me I've thought about it all day. Been trying to figure the way of things. She's got a heap against her, that's for sure."

"You know, pa," I said, "things have surely changed, just in the time and distance it took me to walk here from school."

"How's that?" he asked.

"Things like Kate. And like you and ma." I sort of squinted a little because I was having some trouble with my words. "I mean, well, just this morning I was still thinking how I was going to up and fool you and ma good and proper. Just find a way to keep that mule forever and not give her up. Watch after her and care for her and just let her have a little time to enjoy herself before she dies. She's entitled to that much even if she is a mule. I was willing to sneak and to lie and to even steal to give her

159

this right. But now it just ain't like that anymore. She's in that jail because of me. Maybe if I had let her go she would have found a good home somewhere. Farther away from town. I guess my greediness to keep her has caused her to end up in this fix. Well, that's all over. I mean wanting to keep her. I know it won't work. Never was meant to, just like ma says. And so all I want to do now is to be honest with her and try to save her life."

"Well, it's the right thing you say, Isaac," pa said. "And it's a shame that the right thing is sure to be the hardest." He frowned again. "One thing I do know, though. Giving up ain't the way out for her. Things get tough but generally there's a way out. I've never seen a pair of shoes I couldn't mend or make. And I've seen some shoes in mighty poor fixes and had to make some mighty odd ones. If there's a way to save the mule, we'll find it." He scratched his chin. "You know, I wouldn't be surprised if the thing for us both to do right now ain't just to get your ma on our side."

"How's that?" I asked, not knowing how in the world ma could fit into Kate's being in jail.

"Well," pa said, "ain't no doubt but what your ma knows about that mule being in jail by now. The news has probably spread to three counties. With Rafrel Skaggs hold of it, probably more. Now I'll bet she's just sitting there on the porch waiting for us to come home. And one thing is sure: We've got to save our own hides to save Kate's."

That made good sense to me, since I could see ma fuming there on the porch same as pa could. Maybe better, because it was mostly my doings.

"What've you got in mind, pa?" I said.

"Well," pa said, "we got to look at, and agree on, facts. Legally, you don't own that mule. Now hear me out. Kate's done a lot of damage there in front of John Naper's store and he's sure to place a charge. City might have a charge, too. Now I don't even know that you could lay claim to that mule and make it stick if you wanted to. But I do know if you somehow did, or tried, we wouldn't be apt to get very far with your ma. Not with all that money involved for damages along with your ma being embarrassed in front of the whole town."

"I don't know, pa," I said. "I just don't know about not saying something. Maybe ma and everybody else wouldn't think much about it. But Kate would. Me and that mule are mighty close. And I sure ain't wanting her to think I have just gone and deserted her to save my own skin."

"I don't mean to go that far, Isaac," pa said. "Fact is, I don't even know how far we can go. I just know that right now ain't no time to have your ma against us. We're apt to have more time around the house to think of something to turn her around. And Isaac, if a man knows in his heart he owns something there ain't no taking it away from him. And if this same feeling is shared by something else, say a mule, then there ain't no little thing like doubt and suspicion going to come sneaking in and taking that away. And just who knows what might come from ma? She's got a soft heart when something's in trouble. Maybe even a mule."

"Oh, pa," I said. "It sounds good to me as long as Kate don't think I've deserted her. I don't care what other people think."

"Good," pa said.

"Where do you think we ought to start with ma?" I asked.

Pa looked at the clock on the wall.

"By getting home," he said, taking off his apron. "There's winter wood to cut. And there're some leaks in the roof we might have time to start on tonight. Why, there are just all sorts of things your ma has been trying to get me and you to do for ever so long."

We walked in sight of the jail on our way home and we stopped for a moment. Pa sized up the building and turned to look toward John Naper's feedstore on the opposite corner where the main street made a sharp turn, bowed into an S and then got straightened out to run the length of the town which in all was less than four blocks.

We could see John Naper standing inside a circle of four or five men, swinging his arms, pointing toward the jail. Pa grinned, thinking I guess that John Naper was building the story of the mule bigger and bigger with each gathering.

Pa looked at the jail and grinned again.

"Just hold on in there, old girl," he said. "You might have company before long."

And figuring pa to be with me now most of the way, I grinned for the first time that day.

Well, if ma had heard about Kate's being in jail, which me and pa knew she had, she didn't get a chance to say a word about it. Pa walked in the door, grabbed her by the waist and whirled her about and then kissed her on the cheek with a loud pop.

And I went to the business of washing before supper without having to be told to do it.

And pa sure kept us going at the table. Ma would just look like she was going to say something and pa would come up with a stopper. Maybe the mending of a pair of shoes or someone who had carried a tale in to him. It had to be this way. For pa figured that we would have to have time to get some good deeds done around the house before ma got a chance to tear into us about the mule. Getting things done like looking toward the wood box and saying:

"Hadn't you better be getting some more wood for that box after supper, Isaac? It looks a mite low to me. And I just know you wouldn't be wanting your ma to have to brave the cold after it. Maybe you better check outside while you're out there to see how much wood there is. I wouldn't be surprised if we don't have to bring another cord or two from the hills in the next day or so to last the winter. Snow can't be too far off now."

"I sure had better do just that, pa," I said. "That box is looking low, and I sure wouldn't be wanting ma to have to go out in that cold to do a job that rightfully belongs to me."

Ma took in all such talk with a frown. And in between she reached to rub the spot where pa had planted the kiss on her cheek. Just like pa had smarted it same as Kate had done Mr. Weathers'. Except there was a smile on ma's face the times she touched her cheek.

I even offered to help wash dishes and was told I'd be in the way since men were clumsy around a kitchen. And the next thing I knew I was on the roof with pa. Set to help him mend a leak that had come there long ago. So long ago that ma had told pa if he wasn't going to fix it she would take to putting her flowers under it this winter to keep them watered.

And once when ma came out to the well for water I fairly broke my neck sliding from the roof.

"I'll just get that water, ma," I said. "No need for you to have to go traipsing out into the cold of the evening."

Ma gave me the eagle eye, and started to say something, but never got to. Good old pa. He chattered down like a blue jay from the rooftop:

"Neither of you will have to be coming out in the cold for water much longer, I'm thinking. We been needing an inside pump too long as it is. I think I've located a good secondhand one. All goes well, Lord willing, I ought to beat the snows with it."

The end came just as darkness set into evening. Me and pa were in the back yard trying to talk to each other above the noise of a crosscut saw we were working over a beech log—my arms numb from pulling the saw, but getting strength when I thought of Kate behind those cold jail bars.

Ma reached out, grabbed pa's hand, and the noise stopped. Then she stood back with her hands on her hips and nary a grin showing on her face.

"All right, you two," she said. "This has gone far enough. I ain't had this much attention since the day I was married. I like it but it has got to end. You might as well know that I know all about the doings of that crazy mule. In jail! Disgraceful!" Then she turned to me. "You ain't brought the owning of that mule to roost at our house, have you!"

It wasn't a question. It was a warning. I looked at pa.

"No need turning to your sneaking pa for help!" ma said. "I'm holding him no higher!"

Pa jumped as quick as a cat. He caught ma by the waist and swung her around and around, ma squirming and yelling:

"Put me down, Jeremiah! Put me down! The likes of you thinking you could fool me like this! Me knowing you were sneaking around and up to something. Knowing all along that something has to do with a mule in jail. Put me down this minute! Whatever it is, the answer is no! No! No!"

She broke loose from pa and swished into the house.

"Stack up what wood we've cut, Isaac," pa said. "I won't be long."

And he swung into the house behind ma.

I didn't get much wood stacked. I never heard such a carrying on inside the house. It was like a dog after a rabbit in a fodder shock. I could see ma go past a window with pa close behind. And to save me ma was grinning from ear to ear and she was giggling and trying to straighten out the word NO.

Then I guessed pa would get her trapped since I could hear him planting kisses on her cheek from way out on the back porch. Which wasn't so way out if you came down to it. Just a wall separating me from them. And me with my ear pressed to the side of it to boot.

I'd hear pa come up with something like:

"No claiming the mule honest."

"No!" and that would be ma.

"Smack!" that would be pa, another kiss.

And the giggling would follow.

Then pa again:

"No money." "No!" Ma again.

"Smack, smack." Pa.

More giggling. Past the window. Ma grinning more than before. Then the quietness of the hills. And me mad at myself because I thought I could never hear another word my breathing was so loud. Just then:

"No fooling this time. A home for the mule. Far away. Promise." Pa again.

"Promise!" And bydogged that was ma. Me thinking she had done stuck on that work NO like a cracked phonograph record. Then: "Jeremiah! Stop, you old fool!" Still giggling. "All right!" And ma swung out the door and nearly caught me listening. She was breathing hard, her face red as a beet and her hair loosened out of the bun she kept it in. Ma was awful pretty like that.

"No claiming that mule, Isaac?" she said. She caught me off guard, but I said:

"No, ma."

"No embarrassing me or making a spectacle of yourself in town?" she said.

"No, ma," I answered.

"If the mule gets out of jail you and your pa will have a home for her to go to?"

"Yes, ma," I said.

Then ma put her hands on her hips and looked like she had just thought of something. She looked at pa.

"Wait a minute!" she said. "All this attention. Just where do I fit in?"

Pa saved me.

"Why, Emmazet," pa said, just like ma had gone and shamed herself. "It's nothing like that. We just didn't want you to be against that mule. Since everyone else is, the poor thing has got all she can handle."

"Well," ma said, "I've got sympathy sure enough. But right now it's not for that mule. It's for them poor men at the jail. Penned up with that mule. They'll never be the same again!"

But ma was grinning now and there was a soft look in her eyes. A look that plainly said that me and pa could just go around talking of the mule in front of her, just as long as we didn't talk too much.

I don't know what sort of magic it was that pa had. But it put ma under a bigger spell than I ever reasoned it would. For that night she came into my room, me propped there on the pillow judging the shadows of the tree limbs on the window to be jail bars. She said to me:

"You asleep yet, Isaac?"

"No'm," I answered.

She came closer.

"I sure wouldn't want you to go thinking I had softened a particle again on that mule," she said.

"No'm," I said. "I wouldn't be thinking that."

She bent over me and shoved her hand into mine.

"Well, here," she said. "You can take this money and stop by the feedstore on your way home from school tomorrow and buy a little corn or something and stop at the city building and see if they will let you feed that ornery mule. No need for her to starve even if she is a mule."

Ma stopped again at the door on her way out.

"That's not a gift," she said. "It's a loan. But I reckon it could be paid back with elderberries. You hear?"

"I do, ma," I said, feeling the warmness of the money, knowing that ma had held it outside the door for a while.

And then the world was quiet. One of those nights close to snow when there's no wind and the moon is bright enough to let you see clear to the top of the mountain.

And then I heard ma again. This time from her room. "Put me down, Jeremiah! You old silly fool!"

But ma was giggling again and pa was laughing loud enough to shake the rafters of the house. A house in which it seemed to me that things were all right at the time. And pa! Well, he had the secret. He had whittled ma into nothing. A secret that I was going to have to learn in time.

And then I got to thinking about seeing Kate. And the beating of my heart shook the bed.

CHAPTER 15

If You Can't Get in Jail Try Lying

We ll, whatever I might have gained in the way of ma I lost the next day at school. Everyone was buzzing around with talk of the mule's being in jail.

And most of the talk was against the mule instead of for her. So lopsided against that if Kate had been searching for a blade of sympathy she would have starved to death.

It stood to reason. It wasn't that everyone was just mean at heart. But you can imagine—getting caught and getting in jail, Kate had un-heroed the lot of'em. Running loose she had made them heroes to the girls. Now she made them the laughingstock, with the girls going around in the hall giggling and making fun.

But they hadn't been un-heroed to the point of not talking about the little mule. And everyone had his own story. Bundle them all up and they would have come out gruesome, mournful, and pitiful.

One tale was that Kate had upended cars all over the main street and then broke out that big plate-glass front window of John Naper's feedstore. And the glass was said to be worth fifty dollars, which was more money than any of them at school could reason with at one time.

Elwood said this wasn't true since he had come by the store just this morning on his way to school and had looked and seen himself in the window just like he had been doing all year when he walked past it. And there wasn't nary a crack in it.

Another tale was that Kate had bit John Naper's arm half off but I knew better than this since me and pa had seen him swinging them about in front of his store the evening before.

And seeing that ruled out his being put in the hospital too, which some said he was.

It stood to reason: Since their varmint had turned out to be nothing but a little old mule the next best course was to make her look as mean as they could and that way still have a little strength left to their fight with her.

They got off with some of their tales of her meanness. Elwood went along with them some. He wasn't taking too light to being un-heroed since he had had the biggest fight of all with the varmint and so had fallen the farthest. Yet he stuck with me.

Kate was really in a heap of trouble. Not only had John Naper placed charges against her but everyone who lived just inside the city limits—the petunia belt, as Elwood named it—had filed a claim for the destruction of their flower gardens. Tack to this her trouble with the city. Loitering, tying up traffic, resisting arrest, assault and battery, disturbing the peace, vagrancy, breaking and entering, and Rafrel Skaggs and Milton Boggs searching the books for more violations.

According to Elwood it would take a fortune—and

then some—to free her. For even Simm Johns had entered the picture. He had been talking to John Naper just
this morning when Elwood had stopped like he always
did to see his reflection in the big plate-glass window, and
he overheard them.

Everyone in town knew that Simm Johns hated the
mule, for word had long been out about her beating him
and that tractor in a fair race. And for a while after the
race the old men of the town had kept a path hot to pa's
shop to take a look at the six big one-dollar bills pa had
framed and hung on the wall. This had caused Simm a
heap of ribbing. It had given a lot of old men a chance
to come back on him for past losses. The only chance they
had ever had, or were ever likely to get.

Well, it had always been Simm Johns getting the best
of the other fellow, not the other fellow beating Simm
Johns. Those who were tickled about Pa winning the bet
included some men who had had no chance to get even,
men that either had business dealings with Simm Johns
or rented buildings from him. Many bought produce and
the like from him, and they feared for their business. So
they just chuckled whenever he was not around and never
let it be known. That is, them that had business with him
talked about the race with others that had business with
him. This way none of them could afford to tell on the
others.

Now, John Naper was tied up tight with him. John
Naper owned his own building but he bought his feed
from Simm. Corn, oats, hay and the like. Things like
meat and eggs, too. Simm Johns had most of the wholesale market wrapped up tight. For he could undersell

anyone trucking feed and produce in and you either bought from him or took from a trucker from far off, raised your price to help pay off the trucking charge, and went out of business by being undersold.

It was no secret that Simm Johns had vowed to get even with the mule. But in time, and with Kate not being seen, talk died down and people forgot about it for the time. But now it was all back out in the open and people were talking about the race again.

I got kind of riled up with everyone at school downgrading Kate so much and I figured I'd just up and fight about it. Might have, if Elwood hadn't stepped in.

"Pay no attention, Isaac," he said. "You need more enemies right now like you need a hole in your head."

"They ain't nothing to me!" I said. "Talking about Kate like that and her in the fix she's in."

"They ain't really talking right now," Elwood said. He winked. "But they will be later on."

"How do you mean, Elwood?" I asked.

"Well," he said, "just don't be too hard on 'em, Isaac. After all, what can you expect? I mean, that mule just up and knocking their legs out from under'em. Me too. Look at me now."

And even though it had served Elwood right I couldn't help from thinking how far down he had had to come.

"Well," I said. "I just ain't for taking it lightly. Them going around calling Kate a convict. You know she ain't been in jail long enough to be nothing like that."

"But you got to look at it sensible-like," Elwood said. "I mean they got something to talk about. Why, the whole town has. A mule in jail! Ain't nothing like that ever happened around here before. No one ever thought of locking a mule up. Jails are for people. Pa says that even Judge Clay never heard of a thing like that, and don't even know what to do about it. I mean Rafrel Skaggs and Milton Boggs locked her up and the charges were put and the judge ain't got nothing to do about that but try it." Elwood smacked his mouth. "And that Kate ain't making it any easier. I mean she's big-eyed Rafrel Skaggs, who's on night duty, braying and keeping him awake until he's staggering around the streets during the day like a town drunk. I mean he ain't used to it. Most times it's just sit around down there and sleep the night, the town being quiet and all. And Rafrel is giving Milton so much trouble about not switching off with him for a night or two that Milton is demanding action from Judge Clay."

I leaned close.

"And what does Judge Clay say?" I asked.

"He ain't got much choice," Elwood said. "It's all being blowed up until the judge can't turn loose of it so easy. Scoop Dawson, editor of the Village Sentinel, is doing a write-up on Kate for the Saturday paper. He's mad as a hornet because the mayor won't give him the right to walk in that jail and get a picture of her for the front page. Mayor claiming that the mule being in there and all is setting the town up to look mighty bad to outsiders, since the Village Sentinel goes into three counties. And Scoop Dawson claiming that he's being denied freedom of the press and planning to go to court about it after he writes it up. I tell you that Kate is making a laughingstock of 'em."

"Do you think I can get in to see her this evening?"

I said.

"I don't know," Elwood said. "Been a lot of people down there trying. People just wanting to go in and stare."

"Well," I said, "maybe I ought to try breaking in. I just got to let Kate know I ain't forsaken her. And I don't even know if they are feeding her."

"You try to break in," Elwood said, "and you will end up in the cell next to her. And remember that you ain't got a chance to free her with you locked up in there."

"Then what can I do?" I said, as much to myself as to Elwood. Elwood was rubbing his chin now. And that old business look was in his eyes.

"There just might be a way," Elwood said, right pleased about whatever he was thinking. "If you were to see Judge Clay. If he were to say you could see Kate. Now there ain't nobody could stop you then."

"Judge Clay!" I said. "Is he mean?"

"I don't think so," Elwood said. "He's awful big. But I don't think he's mean."

"But how could I do it, Elwood?" I asked. "I mean I can't just walk right up to him and say I own that mule."

"Nope," Elwood said. "You sure couldn't do that. That's just what he's waiting on. I mean for someone to come by, or show up, and claim that mule. Then he'll tack a fine on to'im that will stand till Doom's Day. Might just throw him in jail to boot. I don't know. I mean the pressure is on him."

"How much you reckon the fine is, Elwood?" I said.

"That's something we need to know," Elwood said. "Maybe you could weasel that out of Judge Clay without causing suspicion."

"And supposing he catches on?" I said. "I mean about that mule belonging to me and all?"

"He ain't apt to," Elwood said. "I mean I hear told that everyone and his brother have laid claim to that mule. Oddballs looking for a little publicity. Wanting to get their picture in the paper. They'd do a heap for that. Then later they'd just have to come out and untie their ownership. And Judge Clay has hardened up with that. I mean whoever lays claim to the mule is going to have to show proof. Bill of sale for her or something."

"But what will I say to him?" I asked. "I mean I got to have something to say when he comes to the door. Can't just stand there and be snatched baldheaded."

"Just tell him that you came to feed that mule," Elwood said. "Look pitiful and sad, and make sure he sees that you already bought that corn. Since everyone that has been there before has come to lay claim he might just take to someone coming to feed. Cry if you have to. And if that don't work, you can lie. Tell him that you are from the Women's League Committee for the Prevention of Cruelty to Animals. Say that they sent you with the corn. There are a lot of them people, women that is, and they sure got a lot of votes on election day."

"But Elwood," I said, "if I have to come to lying do you think he might think something's funny my coming and not one of the women? I mean, you know, there is a heap of difference between me and a woman."

"Well," Elwood said, scratching his head, "that's what I'll be anxious to find out. If you get to school first thing in the morning, I'll know you made it. I got plans."

Judge Clay's house stood within shouting distance of the city building. It was bordered with sugar maples and covered with oak shingles that had turned white with age. I sure didn't want to see him. I was afraid of him. The name Judge scared me enough as it was. But right now I was fearing more for the mule. And I'd figured not to look too brazen and all when I looked up at Judge Clay. The best way to start would be to buy the corn after I had gotten permission. Taking it there with me might make him think that I was taking a little too much for granted. Being too biggety.

I guess the only thing that kept me from just backing out of the whole thing was my thinking of ma giving me the money to buy the corn. I got to thinking that she might know a right smart about the doings of the jail here in town, maybe like knowing that they didn't bother to feed whatever was on the inside and that Kate was bound to be hungry.

Thinking this I took a deep breath, walked up on Judge Clay's porch and knocked on the door. It opened before I even had a chance to think about running.

The judge stood in the door, not leaving enough of that door frame showing to even talk about. Elwood said he was awful big but he could have done better than that. I mean Elwood had a better way of saying things and making you see the picture. Judge Clay was a giant! He had a great crop of hair white as a winter snow, sprinkled some with touches of black. And his face was wrinkled with age and puffed at the jaws. He wore glasses set down low on his nose, toward the end, and you could look over the top of the black rims and see his eyes. I could hear him

176

breathing and could see his great chest heave in and out.

"Judge Clay?" I asked.

"I'm Judge Clay," he answered.

"I've come to see you about that mule," I said. He shook his head, mumbled something, and looked down at me.

"Coming all sizes now I see," he said. He squinted down at me and scratched his head and then said in a lower voice: "You come to claim the mule and try to get your picture in the paper or have you come to try to get permission to go over there and gawk at her?"

I gulped and felt strange for the moment. I didn't know how many had been there before me. I just knew that of them all I was the only one that could lay rightful claim to her. But I wouldn't.

"Neither one, sir," I said. "I've come to see you about the mule, but for another reason."

"Glory be," he said, backing through the door and crooking his finger at me. "Come on in, boy. It's a real pleasure to have a caller these days who hasn't come to lay claim to that mule over there in the jail."

And I walked into the house feeling as out of place as a crawdad on a high, dry bank.

The judge motioned me over to a chair in the living room, a chair so big that it nearly swallowed me up. I had to stretch to see the flames from the open fire grate on the other side of the room. He sat down opposite me and folded his hands together.

"Now," he said, "since you're not interested in claiming, and you're not interested in gawking, what is it about the mule you are interested in?"

"I reckon it's her belly, Judge," I said.

My answer pleased him good enough to red my face. For he grinned and I had the feeling that I had fouled it all up right at the beginning. And I was never more serious in my life. He reared back and laughed loud enough to shake the room. And at the end of the laugh he yelled loud enough to nearly shake me from my hide:

"Marsey!" He tilted his head at the woman who came to the doorway. "The usual for me and milk for my young friend."

He took time now to light his pipe and that was all right with me since I needed time to quiet my knees. Poking his finger around in the bowl of the pipe he said:

"Let's get acquainted first. Your name?"

"Isaac," I said. "Isaac Warfield."

"Jeremiah Warfield's boy?" he asked.

"Yes sir!" I said.

"Well," he said, poking the pipe again, "I've known your pa for many years. Good man, that Jeremiah. Good man." He looked toward my knees. "Now you just feel at home and tell me what it is about the mule you want to talk about . . . uh . . . including her belly."

I just sat there. To tell the truth, those little words hung in my throat like tiny cowards afraid to come out in the open.

"Come now, Isaac," he said. "You're not in a courtroom. You can speak as you please. Freely." He leaned closer. "You *did* want to talk about that mule?"

"Yes sir," I said.

"Good," he said, taking the glasses from Marsey. He handed me the milk. "Then don't leave out a thing you know about that mule, Isaac. Not one word. The shades of mystery are drawn around that poor creature the worst I have ever seen. I've sat on a bench for over forty years and never known less about a defendant." He grinned.

"Course I never had a mule to try before. But—go on, go on, my boy. Be it a mountain or a mite, don't let a word go astray."

"She's got herself in a terrible fix, ain't she, Judge?" I asked.

"Just about as near the end of her life as she can be," he said. "And up till now it looked as though she would pass from the world without a word of kindness spoken in her behalf. You talk, Isaac. I'll listen."

Well here I go, I thought. Just me. This is one time pa, ma, Elwood, or no one else can help me. I've got to go on my own.

"Well, Judge Clay," I said, "I came here to lie if I had to. But I'm thinking that that ain't going to help that mule one particle now. I'm willing to take my chance and level with you."

"Well, Isaac," Judge Clay said, "I'm going to level with you. I like an honest man. And what you say isn't going to hurt that mule one particle. No matter how bad it is."

And so that's how I got started living with that mule all over again. I tried to talk fast but Judge Clay slowed me down. Told me to quit watching the big hands on the clock in the hall, that he had the night. He slowed me to a catwalk when I got to Kate racing that tractor, made me backtrack and tell it again. He kicked his feet into the air and laughed until he was red in the face. Then he cleared his throat and looked at me serious-like.

I reached Mr. Weathers and his run-in with Kate at the schoolhouse. The judge made me backtrack again and tell it over.

"Worth five years of any man's life to have seen it," Judge Clay said. And I had to tell it again.

I hurried now. For I was racing time. John Naper would be closing his feedstore before long. And if just by chance I got to see the mule I would need corn to feed her.

The end came. And Judge Clay was fast to clear his throat and slow to drink his tea. Then he folded his hands and sat back in the chair.

"Well, Isaac," Judge Clay said, "I just don't know what to say. Guess I'm just not used to having that much honesty tossed on me at one time. It's some story, you know." He leaned closer. "You know, Isaac, I could almost envy that mule. Know something? I'm a little mellowed with age myself. And I'm not so sure that many people of this town aren't thinking they know an old worn-out judge that's been around a mite too long. But even so I am the judge. I'm governed by the lawbooks. There's a lot of charges against that mule that just can't be struck out so easily."

"A whopper of a lot?" I asked.

"Well," he said, "the police department has a loitering charge against her, plus resisting arrest and several more. I could be partial since I figure that . . . Kate . . . has done the city a couple of favors and might be entitled to having them go toward payment. She's sobered up every drunk in town and taken care of the loafers that generally wait around for winter boarding in the city jail. Meaning they don't want to be locked up with that mule. Fact is, some of them have taken the first job they ever held. Willing to go to work rather than be in the cell next to her. So, let's say that the city's charges are hanging at about a toss-up." He rubbed his chin. "There's that *malicious wounding with a deadly weapon* charge that Rafrel Skaggs has laid against her. Claimed she used a concealed weapon to take the hide off his cheek. A tongue, I believe." He cleared his throat. "Might get Rafrel to reconsider after a few more nights at the city building with her. That is, if he thought it would get her out of there sooner. But. There are over a dozen people with charges of destruction of property plus the damages John Naper has filed. These charges will have to be settled by law."

I just shook my head. What else could I do? It didn't look like to me there was any need to even search for an answer. But then, hope can come from strange places. For just when I was the lowest, Judge Clay said:

"You know, Isaac, there doesn't look to be a way out. But tell you what: If I ever had a notion to try, tell you where I'd start. I'd get right over there to John Naper's feedstore. His charges are apt to be the most trouble-some. I'd just start right there and try to work down."

"It sure don't look like much of a chance," I said, thinking more to myself than talking to Judge Clay.

"Sure doesn't," he said. "No one is going to come along and pay out the fines for an old mule that the tannery would be apt to turn down." He looked straight at me now. "You know, it isn't easy being an old mule.

I'm not so sure that it's going to be much easier being an old judge come Saturday."

"Do you reckon I could see Kate tonight?" I asked.

"I'd think so, the case being as it is," he said. "People in jail are allowed visitors. Even the meanest get to see their closest of kin. I don't see why it ought to be any different with a mule. Especially with an unordinary mule like Kate. I doubt that anyone could find the opposite in the lawbooks." He grinned.

"I'd sure be obliged," I said. "I ain't seen her for ever so long. I'd like to let her know that someone on the outside is missing her."

Judge Clay scribbled a note on a piece of paper and handed it to me.

"Better give this to Milton Boggs," he said. "It's the only way you will be able to see her. Just says that you have permission to see and feed her. You'll be her first visitor." He stretched out his hand. "Good luck, Isaac. You've got yourself a whopper of a client."

CHAPTER 16

She Just Won't Listen to Love Stories

Before I reached John Naper's store, which was around closing time since he had brought his outside feed that he put along the sidewalk indoors, I had thought to pay Kate's debt by being willing to work evenings and such around the store. But he gave me no chance.

John Naper said that he didn't have enough business to handle help, but I really thought Simm Johns had more to do with it. For about the only thing now that John Naper seemed willing to talk about was what-all Kate had done. He seemed to purely delight in telling the story over and over again, having a listener and all.

It was hard to be mad at John Naper, for he didn't have a face to match his words. You've seen people like that, always sort of happy and jolly, and always with a grin on their faces.

"I ain't got too much agin that mule," he said. "I just got a living to make. I buy all my stuff from Simm Johns. If he don't sell to me then he puts me out of business by selling cheaper to someone else and then they undersell me. It's just that simple. What's between him and that mule is between him and that mule. I just can't afford to get too mixed up in this thing. If Simm Johns says hold the charges then I ain't hurt none if I do. If I don't I'm a ruined man."

So I took my corn and walked over to see Kate.

I walked through a door that led into the police office. Milton Boggs was sitting behind a desk, his head back against the wall and his eyes closed.

The first words I said roused him some. He opened his eyes and looked right over me.

"I've come to visit the mule," I said.

"You've come to do nothing of the sort," he said.

Just then Rafrel Skaggs rushed through the door and looked up at the big clock over the desk.

"You're late again, Rafrel," Milton said, without even bothering to look at the clock.

Rafrel shook his head and took a deep breath.

"Lucky I'm here a-tall," he said. "I'm dead on my feet." He looked down at me and then stared at the sack, an ear of corn bulging from the top. "What's that you got in that sack, boy?"

"He's come to visit the mule," Milton said.

"That's corn to feed the mule," I said.

And then I pulled the ear of corn halfway out so he could see the bottom of the poke if he wanted to. To see that I didn't have anything like a saw or such in it to try to cut the mule out with. That was the way people were always getting prisoners out of jail in stories.

"You'll feed that mule nothin'!" Rafrel said. "Ain't no one addin' one more particle of strength to that critter in there. She can beller like a boat whistle now. Gettin' stronger all the time. I'm on duty here tonight!"

Rafrel had the reddest eyes I ever saw on a man and he seemed to have trouble keeping 'em open.

"I got a note from Judge Clay that says I can," I said, pulling the note from my shirt pocket.

Rafrel was the first to see it. He stared at it and drew up his mouth.

"Bydogged, Milton, it looks like the Jedge's handwritin' sure enough."

Milton frowned and took the note from Rafrel, fairly snatching it away from him.

"I'll do the identifyin' around here!" he said.

And he stared at the note for ever so long. Then he reached in the desk drawer and pulled out another piece of paper with some scribbling on it and placed it beside the one he got from me. He studied them both.

"Ask me tomorrow and I couldn't tell you," Rafrel said. "I won't have eyes to see with no more. But right now I tell you, Milton, that note is the Jedge's handwritin'."

"Yep," Milton said. "It's the Jedge's all right. No mistake." He reached in a drawer and pulled out a ring of keys. "We ain't got no choice. Blame my hide if I know why he would up and write a thing like that, things like they are around here."

"That ain't hard to figure," Rafrel said. Milton was in front, I was behind, and Rafrel was bringing up the rear, all going in the direction of the jail. "He ain't got to stay over here. That's why. Just curls up over there in that big, high-backed horsechair of his'n and snoozes while I sit over here with that mule every night. Only holding court on Saturdays. Says he wants to try the week's gatherin'. Just like waitin' for beans to fill out before he picks 'em.

185

I tell you, Milton, I've been around. I've talked to people. Important people. They ain't no one of them in earshot that ever heard of a mule bein' locked up and kept in jail before. Hit's makin' us the laughin'stock in all the counties around. Me havin' to go around town as red-eyed as a screech owl in a roomful of lanterns."

"Only thing I can see in our favor, Rafrel," Milton said, "is the Jedge ain't put no time limit on this here note." He looked down at me. "You got two minutes, boy. And you'll be watched ever second of that time. No foolishness! Hit's a desperate criminal in there."

Well, Kate saw me then and charged toward me, hit the bars, and fell back with an awful thud. Poor thing, I guess she didn't even think about the bars at all. She just lay there like her head was swimming in stars, then got her bearings and wobbled to her feet.

She funneled up about all the air there was inside the jailhouse, shriveled up into an old gray-haired sack of hair and then swelled and went down just like someone had pulled a cork out.

"He-haw-e-e-e-e-e-e-e-e-e!"

Then she just sat down on her rear end like a dog and not being able to do anything else just looked square at Rafrel, not me, and grinned.

"Dag nab your ornery hide!" Rafrel said. "She knows my ears is poppin'."

"Rafrel!" Milton said. "Control yourself, boy!"

And then Kate just looked at me with her old silly grin and a look in her eye that plainly said that since there was nothing else she could do from over there she'd just sit to please me a little, and show me the place. It was

something the little mule always did to let me know that things were just all right between us. Went to showing off and the sort.

She looked toward Rafrel again and grinned, watching his expressions as close as she would watch a cornfield. Then quick as a wink Kate pulled her hoof over the bars of the cell just like you would pull a stick over a fence paling. It sounded as if the jailhouse was falling in.

Rafrel jumped back like he had been hit between the eyes with a broadax. "See that, Milton!" he yelled.

"See thar now! I told you that mule is a-hantin' me. Told you there was more to it than her bein' a mule. You never saw a mule do the likes of that. It ain't natural for a mule. She done it half one night and all the other, knowin' full well she was a-poppin' my eyes out! Plumb set to keep me from sleepin'."

Milton looked over at Rafrel. "You ain't supposed to be sleepin'," he said. "You're supposed to be out there lively, with the town dependin' on you."

"Well," Rafrel said, puckering up his mouth, "I sure never heard that one before. You always slept when we used to trade shifts, which was right up to the time this here mule come. Still don't seem right to me that you had to go messin' with the schedule just when the mule got to hollerin' the loudest. You'd think you was the high sheriff."

"Rafrel!" Milton said, pointing to a badge on his coat, so big that it pulled his pocket down in front. "See that badge?"

"Reckon I can," Rafrel said. "My eyes ain't that bad that I can't see a badge big as a garbage can lid."

"A heap bigger than the one you're a-wearin'," Milton said—telling the truth since I could hardly see the one pinned to Rafrel—"means I got a right to have a shake-up in the force anytime I like. I'm the captain around here and don't you forget that. The mule had nothin' to do with it. No good captain would let a mule do his schedulin'."

"Well, I sure wish the city council would go ahead and hire that patrolman like you said they was a-goin' to do. Sure would help a heap. I ain't got a soul under me and it don't seem right, me a sergeant and all."

"Don't let the stripes go to your head," Milton said. "I told you once it was the only way the council could give you a pay raise."

Maybe it was because for the first time in her life the old mule had had a warm place to stay. Four walls and a roof over her head. And maybe since no harm had come to her up to this point, and me finally coming, she was thinking that everything was all right. She whirled around, fairly showing off her cell to me.

She backed to one side of the cell, took a run, stopped on a dime, and flopped over on a small cot against the wall, her four legs sticking straight up in the air. Then she brought her two front legs down, crossed her eyes and looked over toward Rafrel and grinned.

"Glory be, Milton!" Rafrel said. "Ain't you seen enough? It's frightenin', I'll tell you. They's spirits in that critter! I'm most afraid to stay here by myself, I tell you!"

"You big coward!" Milton said. "Wouldn't you be a purty-lookin' thing if'n I told the council you was afraid to stay here at nights? What you after anyway? Tryin' to make a laughin'stock of the whole force? Just because you saw a little simple thing like a mule stretched out on a cot!"

I reached through the bars and touched the little mule on the nose. She scooted close and tried her best to shove her nose into my arms. We were so close, but she just couldn't do it. All I could do was rub her head and whisper in her ear:

"I brought you some corn," I said. "And you know what! Ma loaned me the money to buy it with. What do you think of that?" Then I rubbed her nose again and whispered ever so low: "And we're all missing you." Just thinking that I missed her and no one else was not enough to make up for the big bars in front of her.

Kate took the corn and wallowed it around in her mouth. It was too hard and dry for her to bite. I looked up at Milton.

"Could she have some water?" I asked. "Her teeth are awful short and water would soften the corn a little."

Rafrel stepped up. "Nothin' doin'," he said. "I give her a bucket last night and she sprayed the walls and me down. If I hadn't got Lem Tuttler out of that cell next to her he'd a-laid a corpse today, plumb drowned on dry land."

"Lem ain't in his cell?" Milton said, glancing around the shadows to see through the smaller cell in the corner. "Well, it don't seem right. I been here goin' on thirty years now and Lem's been here longer than me. Drunk, loiterin' or somethin' or the other. He's always found a way to git in. Specially of the winter. What went wrong?"

"I took the water in," Rafrel said. "Give it to that mule. Lem, he sees me going in and takin' somethin' in another cell and he says: 'Rafrel, you brung someone else in here fer the night, he's my company and I demand to be put in the cell with 'im. I'm lonely as a bedbug.' Well, my nerves was all on edge and so I thought it would just be good fer old Lem to be fooled like that. So I jest snuck him in and hid here by the door to take a peek.

"Well, old Lem he spies that big tub of water and he eyes that mule drinking and he says: 'You're the thirstiest jailbird they ever had in here. Tell you somethin' else too: You're about the hairiest and got the longest nose and the biggest ears.' Then he drew back his lip. 'But don't you worry none about that, buddy. I'm the pickilediest. Uh, uh, what a nose! No matter. Let's me and you sing.' 'Bout then that mule wrinkled up and brayed right in his ear. It would have kilt me. But Lem, he sorta shook his head and said: 'Uh, uh, you've hit on a sad tune, which reminds me of the night I lost my gal.' And you know Lem. He starts right in tellin' that mule all his troubles just like he's been tormentin' drunks with here for all these years. Got to cryin' around and that mule givin' him the big-eye. You'd think it wouldn't make a particle of difference to a mule what a feller is talkin' about. But I could see that mule wasn't takin' to being withered down listenin' to a common drunk's talk. She sucked in that water and straightened old Lem out like a minner fightin' its way upstream.

"I took Lem out at his askin'. He says to me: 'Rafrel, take note. I've seen all kinds of'em during my life. I've seen'em turn into snakes right before my eyes. Saw one man turn into a tadpole and then a lizard. I've seen'em with ears `bout as big and eyes a-bulgin'. But I never had one git mad at my talkin' 'bout my girl friend. Hit's time to sober up. I'm goin' straight. The time has come when I'm unwanted by my own kind.' Poor old Lem."

I looked back at Milton, thinking he might want to show Rafrel again who was boss.

"Just a little water," I asked. "Just enough to roll the corn in."

It worked.

Milton said: "Enough water to wet the corn, Rafrel."

I took the time to hurry words to Kate. I told her again that I missed her powerful, that things were all right with me and such. I asked if she was hungry, and told her me and pa were a-looking for a way out and for her not to worry. I thought this pleased her.

Rafrel came in with a small pail of water and squeezed it in to the cell and then he stepped back. Kate bowed down and slurped out the water so fast you couldn't see it, and me looking on. Just dried up the pail and then stared at Rafrel. Just like there had never been anything in the pail for her. She was so good at it that Milton stepped closer and looked down.

"Why, they ain't a drop of water in that pail!" Milton said. "You tryin' to fool me, Rafrel!"

Rafrel frowned and bent over. Kate looked him square in the eye and let him have it. Rafrel grabbed his eyes and jumped back.

"Great Scot, Milton!" Rafrel yelled. "She's done put my eyes out! She's a hant. She's after me!"

"What you're a-needin' is a little sleep," Milton said,

looking toward Rafrel like he was purely intending to put the full blame for his not getting any on his shoulders. Rafrel's shoulders, that is.

And Kate lifted her leg again and drug it over the bars.

"You ornery critter!" Rafrel said, shaking his fist.

"Rafrel!" Milton said. "You're fussin' with the prisoner and that's against the code!"

Any fear I had of the little mule not missing me left when I turned to go. She tried to follow, with a sad look in her eyes. A look sad enough to make me see it for a lifetime.

"Could I come by tomorrow?" I asked.

"That's up to the Jedge," Milton said.

And I walked on home.

That night me and pa had a long talk.

"It's bad, pa," I said. "Even worse than I thought. Simm Johns has took away any chance I might have had with John Naper."

"That's not all," pa said. "He got hold of Bunt Rankins too. Bunt came by the shop today to tell me that if the mule got out he couldn't pasture her any longer. If he did he had worked his last day for Simm, and his bum leg kept him from getting work anywhere else. I guess I can't blame him too much."

"It's been a bad day all the way around," I said.

"Well," pa said, "not all bad. I don't know that this helps the mule much, but I saw Moses Hewlett from over on Hurricane Creek. That shoe I made for his clubfoot had worn thin and he wanted to get it fixed with winter coming on." Pa scratched his head and took his time. "Well, we talked about the mule. Me laying it on about that mule being old and lonely and no one wanting her now that she's got old. I could see that Moses was pulling that mule right up beside his heart so I throwed in a little free shoe work—that your ma don't know about—and we struck a bargain. He will take the mule if she gets free. And it will be the best of all places for her, Isaac. He is a fine man. Lives alone. Has been alone now for twenty years."

"Sure would be," I said. "If she could ever get there."

But pa was wrapped up with Moses Hewlett now.

"No more than a five-mile walk to his place from here. She'd be like a pet to him. Wouldn't surprise me if he didn't give her the run of the house as well as the parcel of hill around. She'd be good for an old man like him. And he'd be good for her. Your ma even agreed to that without one word of fuss. She always was fond of Moses, him with a clubfoot."

CHAPTER 17

Practicing Law Without a License

Well, Kate only had three days to go. That would boil her old life down till Saturday. Three days and my thoughts swirling around in my head like a muddy stream. Not settling on one thing long enough to clear.

But it was different with Elwood. He was like that. Quick as a cat. Never seemed to run out of whatever it was that made him run.

Maybe that's why me and Elwood hit it off. He handled the town, teaching me the ways of it. And I handled the country, teaching him its ways. Together we thought we ought to end up with a heap of sense if we had a notion to.

And that's where Elwood came in now. I mean, the city jail was in town and Elwood felt a responsibility for it. And when Elwood heard me talk of my visit to Judge Clay, his eyes fairly bulged. I never saw a hound dog any happier jumping its first rabbit. He moved around just that quick.

"We ain't got much time, Isaac," he said.

"Reckon I know that," I said.

And then Elwood nearly knocked the wind out of me.

He laid it all out to me.

"I got a plan, like I told you," he said. "Not a business deal like the first one. That is, not hardly. But either way it's better than no plan at all. And the first part of it is finished with you getting to see that mule. Now. You got to go back again this evening and see Judge Clay. That's the only way it will work."

"I was planning to do that anyway," I said. "I spent half the money ma gave me for corn yesterday and I'll spend the rest of it today if I can see her again."

Elwood stuck out his hand.

"Shake, Isaac," he said. "Things are looking up. I tell you it seems like to me that Judge Clay has done gone and made you a sort of lawyer for that mule. That's more than I had planned on." Elwood looked around and pulled me against the wall. "That being so, you ask that Judge this evening to hold a court hearing for that mule. Right upstairs on the second floor of the city building in that big police courtroom where the public can see it all if it wants. Let 'em see old Kate on trial for her life."

"Oh, I don't know about that, Elwood," I said. "Judge Clay is powerful smart about law and all. I ain't about to fool him none. I can't just go in and ask him to do something for that mule when as far as the law is concerned I ain't got no right to her anyway."

"That's where you don't know nothing about law and I do, Isaac," Elwood said.

"Where did you ever learn anything about law?" I said.

"I got it from pa," Elwood said. "Now don't you go forgetting about pa studying them lawbooks when he was working in the mines. Well, he ought to know and he told me once that everybody is entitled to a public trial or hearing or something."

"But Kate ain't everybody," I said. "She ain't nobody. She is a mule."

"That's why you've got to see Judge Clay," Elwood said.

"You've got to find out if somewhere inside them big lawbooks it don't say a mule has got the same rights as a person. Being a mule oughten to make one particle of difference the way I see it. And if I'm right we'll start plan number three."

It made no sense to me. So I said:

"Say them lawbooks do give her a right to a trial before the Judge and the people come. She ain't going to be no better off, maybe worse. They ain't a soul in this town cares one bit about that mule, I mean whether she gets a decent break or not. It's just more eyes to see her marched to the tannery."

"But say there were some people on the side of the mule," Elwood said. "Lots of people. More than is against. Then there might be a switching of ways."

"Glory be," I said. "It couldn't never be!"

Elwood just sorta swelled up and waited for me to wallow in the thought that it could.

"Oh, couldn't it?" he said, slipping in a thread of hope just when I was at my weakest. "You go to Judge Clay's and leave the rest to me. Meet me in the morning early. Plan three will take some time—and doing."

But I walked away not feeling a heap better. Oh, I did at the time. For Elwood could swell you out, make you think you could roll the world up in a ball no bigger than those that hang on a sycamore tree and it wasn't until you got away and thought about it that you knew your pocket had a hole in it. The last time I had seen that look in his eyes it had cost us seven days of hard labor. I couldn't imagine where this one would make us end up. That is, if it came to pass.

But I was hungry for help. Elwood making me feel good at a time like this for ever so short a time was worth it. And Elwood had something else, too. He had that something that made you wonder if maybe there wasn't the tiniest chance for whatever he planned to do to work. It followed you like a shadow and gave you hope where there had once been nothing but darkness. And so I rolled plan three over in my head. Whatever plan three was, and figured I'd see the Judge.

The first surprise I got was that Judge Clay was expecting me.

"Come in, Isaac," he said. "I was sort of looking for you. Got to thinking after you left last night that I ought to have made that note read til Saturday, knowing the boys over there at the city building. Tell me, how did it go?"

"Kate sure did look mighty lonely in that big cell," I said.

"I guess so," he said. "It's not a place to be. Even for a mule. But this will get you in until Saturday." He handed me the scribbled note. "Maybe you can comfort her some until then."

I just got to thinking about Saturday coming quick as

a wink. I got to thinking about plan three, whatever it could be, and I got all balled up.

"I'd like to ask a question, Judge Clay," I said.

Judge Clay looked at me and scratched his cheek.

"What sort of a question, Isaac?" he asked.

"Sort of a legal one I reckon," I said.

Judge Clay grinned, which made me uneasy since I figured him to be taking me lightly and I was never more serious or scared.

"All right," he said.

"I want to know if Kate is entitled to a court trial just like everybody else," I said.

He stared me square in the eye.

"Would you mind to repeat that?" he said. "I want to make sure I heard you right, Isaac."

"I want to know if Kate ain't entitled to a trial like everybody else," I said, having a harder time getting it out than the first time.

"A mule entitled to a trial?" he said. "In a court of law ... me presiding over it?" He rubbed his forehead. Then he sat down in the big chair, folded his arms crisscross over his chest and reared back. He stared at me in a way that said if I had a head on my shoulders and left the house with enough of me to be recognized I would be lucky. "I never heard such a fool question in over forty years on the bench!" But his eyes softened. "But, by golly, I don't rightly know. What made you ask that question, Isaac?"

"I was just thinking that maybe everybody is entitled to a trial," I said.

"Well," he said, "I can answer that for you: They are. But remember, the lawbooks refer to people."

"Not mules too?" I asked.

"Well," Judge Clay said, "if they do, I haven't found it in over forty years of reading."

I guess he could see that it all wasn't setting too well with me. I mean law in general. I mean, I was thinking what sort of a country was I living in? Where you could be hemmed in and have your insides torn out without a streak of law to help you.

"Then if it ain't there," I said, "I don't believe in law no more than I believe you can gather walnuts in the summertime."

"Now hold up, Isaac," Judge Clay said. "The law might not always suit me or you. But law is what the majority of the people want. That's democracy. Equality. And it's the best. It's guaranteed under the Constitution, which is the greatest document ever written."

"If all that writing was done without ever putting a mule in it," I said, "it's sort of lopsided and hard for me to put stock in."

Well Judge Clay sat for eternity and then some.

"You've got to remember, Isaac," Judge Clay said, "that men like Madison, Franklin, Hamilton, and Jefferson were busy men. They had a lot to do. If they had had to put, just spell out, every living thing under God's sun in that document it would never have been written. And yet, in my long years of reading it I haven't come across a thing they left out. I have no doubt but what a mule crossed one of their minds."

"Why didn't they just write it in then?" I said.

"Maybe they did," he said. "But they didn't spell it out to read mule.

Maybe the rights of a mule went under a law that covered a host of things."

"How would you ever know?" I said.

"Well," he said, "we have a Supreme Court that interprets the law of the land. But they are a long way off from here."

"Could we write them?" I asked.

"Yes," Judge Clay said. "That's part of our rights. But I wouldn't be surprised if there aren't many requests for laws to be interpreted ahead of us. And we don't have that much time." He grinned. "I'm sure our request would be an interesting one to them."

"Then, Judge Clay," I said, "how can Kate be tried Saturday if you don't know whether she's in a lawbook or not?"

"I didn't say anything about trying the mule Saturday, Isaac," he said. "I plan to make a decision Saturday. There are charges against the mule. Damages. If there is no one to pay for the damages then I'll have to turn the mule over to the people that have filed these charges if they want her. And they can use her as property to get back their money for their loss the best way they can."

"But that will only mean the tannery," I said. "She ain't good for nothing else. She's too old to plow with now."

"I have no choice, Isaac," Judge Clay said. "She isn't a human being."

"She's got feelings," I said. "She can be hurt."

"But there is more to a human being than that, Isaac," he said.

"Nothing more important," I said.

201

"Well, you've got me there," he said. "I have to agree with you. But I'll have to interpret the law to the best of my judgment."

"And if you're wrong?" I asked.

"Well, I could be," he said. "It's no fun to be a judge. It's a duty, and not recommended to make you sleep well at night."

"Then I guess I got till Saturday before the mule is taken away," I said.

"It looks that way, Isaac," he said. "I'm sorry." I just sat for a moment. For you don't pop up and go into anything knowing that the end has finally come. I wanted to say something powerful bad but didn't have a thing to say.

But as I turned to go, Judge Clay looked at me in a strange way. He said:

"What would you have me do, Isaac?" He popped to his feet and walked toward the fireplace. "Would you have me leave the bench after over forty years of service to be remembered as a serious and honest judge? Or, would you have me throw away these years and be remembered as the only judge in all creation to try a mule—in the flesh—in a court of law?"

I couldn't answer, for my love for the mule was too deep in my heart. And my respect for the judge too great to lie. He just paced up and down the floor like a snorting bull waiting for someone to hoist out something he could charge into. And he kept mumbling and swinging those big hands behind him. The light from the wood fire streaked his face, seeping into the wrinkles of his skin and settling into his great crop of hair like a ball of sun being swallowed by a white cloud.

"You got any idea what would happen!" he shouted. And by his eyes I got the feeling that he wasn't talking to me at all. He paced up and down in front of the fire, twisting his body and smacking his hands as if he were wrestling something mighty powerful. "I'll tell you. This old town would come alive. Some would laugh; some would criticize; and in the end they'd ostracize. The mule-trying judge!" He threw his big hands up and laughed so weirdly that it scared me. Then he leaned close and squinted an eye at me. "In other words, boy, they'd have me on a log headed toward the bughouse. They'd say I blew my top, went off my rocker, went haywire." He stopped and took a deep breath and grinned in a friendly way. "Now. Let's just set all that right over here." And he took that handful of nothing toward the mantel over the fireplace as carefully as carrying a soft-shelled egg. And he placed it ever so carefully on the right side of the mantel.

It gave me time to gulp.

"Now!" He was pacing again, twisting and turning like he had a bear hug on whatever it was he was wrestling. "What do you think a judge does after over forty years on the bench? I'll tell you. He closes his eyes at night and sees people. All of the people that have ever stood before his bench to wait sentence. And he thinks. How many times was he right; how many times could he have been wrong? What more could he have done and remained in the realm of law? Now. Let's just place this on this side." And he carried it just as carefully to the mantel. Then he pulled his big hands together and churned them over and over. "Let's just mix the two and see what comes out."

I gulped again. I watched him pull a closed fist up to his eyes, squeezing it open just like he had caught a fly and was afraid it would get away. Then he looked at me and smiled.

"You're lucky, Isaac," he said. "The mule gets a hearing."

"Well," Rafrel said, "here's the little booger with more corn, Milton. Got another note from the Jedge. That mule was twice as rowdy last night. You tole me you'd speak to the Jedge about it."

Milton yawned and read the note slowly, taking ever so long about it.

"You want to know what I git to thinkin' sometimes, Milton?" Rafrel said.

"What's that, Rafrel?" Milton asked, pulling the jail keys from the drawer.

"That you ain't carin' none about the rowdiness of that critter of nights," Rafrel said. "Like maybe you're a-knowin' the rowdier she is at nights the tireder she'll be durin' the day when you're on duty."

"I told you a thousand times, Rafrel," Milton said, "a captain ain't ever off duty. I'm on twenty-four-hour call and don't you ever let the council hear you say different. Now, you big thing, if you let a little critter like a mule git you down where, oh where, would the town be if a desperate criminal like a bank robber come in? The town havin' to depend on you till I got there?"

"Milton," Rafrel said, "it'd be a snap. 'Cause they

ain't no bank robber dumb enough to git hisself locked up tight with this critter."

Kate was up to her old tricks, along with learning some new ones. Kate was like that. I mean if she found out she could rib you she'd pour it on. And she had sized Rafrel up. She liked Rafrel.

The minute she saw Rafrel she popped beside the bars, ran her hoof over them and grinned at him with all that was in her to grin. Then she curled her lip at him.

"Don't you be makin' faces at me, you ornery critter!" Rafrel said, shaking his fist.

"Don't be tauntin' the prisoner, Rafrel," Milton said. "You know it's agin regulations. I'll not have you breakin' a rule of the force."

"Me tauntin' her!" Rafrel said. "And me with two more nights to go. Not on your life! You know it's the other way around! I tell you, Milton, you got no way of knowin', since that critter sleeps most of the day. You don't have to go in and water and feed her. I tell you she can pick up them grains of corn and spew 'em against the walls like machine gun bullets. Or, she can plink them bars with 'em one at a time."

"You've been sleepin' on the job again, Rafrel," Milton said. "I've warned you time and agin about that."

"Well," Rafrel said, "I only wish the council would go ahead and hire that patrolman like you said they was goin' to. Don't seem like to me you've been pushin 'em like you claim. Been five years now or thereabouts since you mentioned it, as I recollect."

"That's the trouble with you young whippersnappers," Milton said. "You got no patience. You want everything right this minute."

Rafrel drew up his lips.

"Well," he said, "they'd be in a pickle if I just up and quit one day. They'd do somethin' then."

"And where would you git another job?" Milton said, snurling his nose and looking sideways at Rafrel.

"With my experience as a lawman I wouldn't have to worry none about that," Rafrel said.

"Your experience!" Milton said. "In fifteen years to my certain knowledge you ain't brought in a man 'ceptin' of his own free will. Most of them just lookin' for winter lodgin'. You've made one rescue that I recollect. That was getting Mrs. Shackle's cat down from a tree and it ripped the seat out of your britches or else you done it sliding down that big sugar maple and the city had to buy you another pair after all that fuss you caused about it. You remember that, Rafrel?"

"Reckon I do," Rafrel said, "seeing as how you been throwin' that up to me most ever 'day for the past five years. And the council didn't do a thing until after I had wore them britches with a big patch in the back not matchin' the uniform for nearly two years and disgraced 'em. Not countin' the embarrassment to me. You goin' around sayin' I had to wait till the council voted in betterfits fer the force. And then them new britches not fittin' after all the fuss."

"*Benefits*, Rafrel," Milton said, "is not the brand name of a pair of britches. Cain't you git that through your head? It means the council was good enough to buy you somethin' extra."

"Enough extra material for two more pair of britches

is all I can see," Rafrel said. "Only took a tiny wind to make me look a hundred pounds heavier. Just at the time I was sparkin' Talley Marcum and gettin' along so well about it. Always will say them britches bein' that big was the reason she took Albie Dobbins over me. People starin' at me along the streets, crossin' over when I come by like they figured I'd be apt to blow up from the waist down."

"Now look here, Rafrel," Milton said. "You got no call to be goin' around blamin' the council and the town for your sorry love affair. You lost that gal long before them britches got into the picture. You want my thinkin', it was that little music box old Albie was always a-carryin' around the streets under his arm. Plus her old man wantin' to cross that bluetick of his'n with that redbone dog of Wilbur Dobbins, Albie's pa. You never had a chance after that redbone treed them seven coons over in Bocook Holler. Oh, I seen 'em go by here enough. Arm in arm, lollygaggin'. I've heerd Albie pick 'Old Joe Clark' fer blocks on end and that Talley moonin' like a bayed hound dog. Just all wrapped up in that little pickin' box. That's how it was. Face up to it. And face up to another thing, Rafrel, before it's too late. That mule has got the better of you. Done gone and let the town know that it was a mule instead of a fearless creature you fit that night. Me givin' out reports of a varmint wild as the wind." Milton put his hand on Rafrel's shoulder. "Don't take your spite out on me, Rafrel. I'm your friend."

Well, Rafrel sorta humped up and looked mournful. He rubbed his head and stared at the floor.

"I reckon I *have* let the mule git the better of me,

Milton," he said. "My nerves is whittled down to a twig. I'm needin' relief. If they'd go ahead and git a patrolman then I'd have someone around here to let my fire out on. A sergeant ought to have that."

"I'll speak to the council about it agin, Rafrel," Milton said. While they were talking, I was making a little more progress with Kate. Milton let me go in the cell this time and pick the cockleburs from her since I was afraid the hard concrete might rub them in and make sores on her. Then she'd be apt to cut more shines than before. Even Rafrel was for my getting them off. But the hide was already sore around the cockleburs, for she flinched when I pulled them off. She made little sounds that were uncommon for her, little sounds that made me think she felt lonely and lost.

The little mule was wanting to go home. When I left the cell she tried to block me. I hugged her neck and whispered a lie in her ear:

"I'll be back," I told her. "I'll come tomorrow and the next day and Saturday we'll go home."

The mention of home pleased her. I could tell it made her feel good.

But on my way home my promise made me feel worse. I felt just plain miserable lying to her that way, knowing what was ahead for her. But then I got to thinking that since she had so little time, why shouldn't I make it as happy as I could? Why not just let her lie back in that cell and think good things? Two days wasn't long. But then, we had crammed a lifetime into a summer, and been happy about it.

Well, there'd be one happy person: Elwood. I could

just see his face when I told him that Kate was going to get a trial. Me, I didn't know. Looked to me like we were still in the same boat. I'd be pulling for the mule. And Pa would and Elwood would. That made three. Ma, I didn't know about. But I didn't feel any grudge toward ma.

For some things in the world belong to men. It's just the nature of things. Mules, hound dogs, a pocketful of buckeyes and the like. Women take no shine to these things. They're embarrassed by a skinny hound, not figuring that he has to be that way to run good. Just get mad as fire with a skinny hound following them around. And heaven knows what they'd do if an old shaggy mule was behind them. Ma said if she ever saw a thing like that mule hanging around our house, she'd never be able to hold her head up in public.

Well, Kate wasn't much to look at.

And right now I'd lose a night's sleep wondering what Elwood's plan number three might be. But it didn't matter much. I'd not have slept anyway thinking about poor old Kate behind those bars.

CHAPTER 18

The Committee for Prevention of Cruelty to Animals

Elwood fairly clicked his heels together.

"That's just great!" he shouted. "See you at noon!"

And he left me there in front of the school.

"But plan number three!" I yelled. If he heard me, he never let on. He was already through the door.

Me and Elwood never talked during class. Oh, we had for a while, but Miss Canlittle put a stop to that. She moved Elwood to the far end of the room. 'Course, we had another way of talking now. Silent. I mean, you've got to have a way to get your thinking—that can't wait until class lets out—to your buddy. So we used the long-tried method: note writing. You know, those little notes that you scribble on paper and pass from person to person with some wise fellow along the line always reading'em before they reach the one they're sent to. Him knowing he's got you dead to rights, if he wants to nail you.

But I got no notes that day. And that was the day I needed them the most.

Oh, Elwood wrote notes all right. Fact is, he did little else but scribble notes. And me thinking that each one of them was intended for me. Yet not one note ever reached me. They all stopped along the way. I'd watch one of the boys read one. He'd shake his head at Elwood and the note would go back. Then another note would come and the fellow would nod ok.

And Elwood sure picked odd boys to be writing to. I mean boys that you wouldn't think he would have reason to write to. There was Fats Wallen, the biggest tattletale in the school; Sif Adkins, always combing his hair and looking pretty at the girls; Tom Dinkle, nicknamed Tearbaby since he could cry anytime he wanted to and did if you did no more than stick your tongue out at him; and Rouse Sparks, who got to drive his pa's car to school sometimes and had most everyone at the schoolhouse eating out of his hand.

Notes went back and forth between them all the morning. And just before noon one came to me. It read:

Plan number three ok. Will explain at noon.
QR7

Well, the note was from Elwood all right. QR7 was the way he signed his notes, because a note always stood a chance of being ambushed by Miss Canlittle. If you signed your name you were a dead duck. By using a code, you had a chance to get by.

I thought about plan number three until I couldn't see straight. Then at noon me and Elwood went behind the schoolhouse, up next to the grove of trees where we could talk. While munching on a sandwich, Elwood said:

"This is it. The mule goes up in the courtroom. Right?"

211

"Yep," I said.

Elwood took a sprout and scribbled in the ground with it, like he was drawing it all out. And him not making one mark in the earth since it was covered with grass. But it did look sort of businesslike.

"Now," he said. "We go chippin' away like this."

"At what?" I asked.

"People," Elwood said. "We get the courtroom full. People that will be on the side of the mule."

"Can't be done," I said.

Elwood never even paid attention to what I said. He was all wound up and going full steam.

"People that don't necessarily favor a mule, but that ain't about to stand by and see an animal mistreated. Like the Women's League. They've got a whole committee just to see that things like that don't happen. And they sure ain't going to stand around and see a little old grayheaded mule being beat to death in the city jail."

"Why, Elwood," I said, "they ain't laid a hand on Kate down there. I tell you that mule is having the time of her life."

"Say that until it gets out of your system," Elwood said. "Say it all you want. But once me and you walk away from here, don't mention that again. Plan number three depends on that."

"Depends on what?" I asked. "On that mule being beat to death down there. Being starved nearly to death. We'll put out the story that she'd be apt to be dead if a nearly total stranger—that's you—hadn't sneaked in with a little corn to keep her alive. We'll spread the word. We've got two days to do it all in. We've got to get the word to everyone in town, especially around the petunia belt. We've got Fats Wallen, to make sure that everyone knows about them beating that mule out of her hide; Sif Adkins, to bring the girls in to help us; Tom Dinkle, to make it too sad to listen to; and Rouse Sparks to furnish transportation."

"I ain't following you, Elwood," I said.

"Simple, my country friend," he said. "We're going to get the word out about the torment Kate's getting. People will rise up against that. The people in the petunia belt will feel they are some to blame for her being there where she's getting her brains beat out and they'll drop their charges. Many of them are on the Women's League Committee for the Prevention of Cruelty to Animals. The police department and John Naper will become the biggest villains the town has ever known. Pressure will be brought on them by decent people who ain't going to just sit back at a time like this."

"Elwood," I said, "you ought to be teaching school." Then we both clicked our heels together and shook hands. Elwood said:

"I sent Fats Wallen and Sif Adkins downtown during noon hour to see how the word of Judge Clay's plan to hold a trial for the mule is catching on and to spread it out more. The town ought to be buzzing by now."

I was laughing to high heavens. Maybe it was a slim chance. But it was a chance. I never thought there was one.

"How did you do it, Elwood?" I said. "I mean how did you ever get them boys together?"

"No trouble," Elwood said. "Just told'em they could ride that mule all winter free. And then I throwed in

213

things like going on sleigh rides with their girl friends and things like that."

My eyes popped open as big as walnuts.

"Elwood," I said, "you know we can't do anything like that. I told you pa had found a home for that mule if she gets free."

Elwood looked at me unconcerned-like and said:

"That falls outside the city limits, Isaac. In the country. You figure that one out. I got tales to think up right now. Gruesome tales."

He left me standing there still trying to put plan number three together.

Well, ten minutes after Fats and Sif had come back from town the school was buzzing. It was a stir like you never heard.

Scoop Dawson was pinning headlines for a special edition of his paper, this making only the second special edition anyone could remember. The first was about Rafrel's rescue of Mrs. Shackle's cat from the sugar maple tree, and the fuss over that. Now the city council had called a special meeting for the night and the Women's League was trying to save the town from disgrace.

I could just see the word spreading out like a woods afire. Worst of all, I could see ma. She would be in town today since Thursday was her day to shop—her claiming she didn't like to wait until Saturday which was when most of the other people shopped. She said she just got lost in the crowd and had too many picked-overs to choose from. I could just see her sneaking about even though I had kept my word and hadn't tied her in with the mule.

I feared Mr. Weathers since every time he stuck his head into the hall he looked over a gathering of us. But he went right on as if he never noticed us at all. That made me sort of wonder if he wasn't aiming to do his part.

And then the Committee for the Saving of Mules—which is the title Elwood had given to the boys he had picked at the schoolhouse—went to work, Elwood claiming that the title made it all more businesslike and important. I caught little bits of their talking in the hall. I overheard Reny Jackson say to Mary Lewis:

"And Sif said that they had beat that poor mule until one of its eyes popped out. That's awful!"

The tales were gruesome, as Elwood promised. One said she had lost both eyes, and that Rafrel Skaggs had beat her down until she couldn't get up. Rafrel was the worst of the lot since he had stretched a tale about having his hat knocked off by a varmint, claiming he stood toe to toe fighting it and then had it turn out to be nothing but a little mule. A little mule just starving away in the hills and found wandering the streets of town for a little bite to eat. He had taken his spite out on the poor creature, defenseless critter that she was. He had got her down by blows from a billy club until she was too weak now to make a noise. Then he had laid corn just outside the bars and struck her across the nose every time she lifted her tired old head to reach it.

Milton Boggs had ordered all fires turned off in the jail—an order that had the approval of the city council—thinking that the mule might freeze before Saturday.

But Elwood had made sure to stay on the good side

of Judge Clay—partly to make up for spreading the tales and stretching what might have been just a simple case with the Judge just having the mule face her accusers. But now the Judge was bound to hold a real trial, with little chance to back out even if he wanted to. Elwood passed on the story that Judge Clay was standing firm against mistreatment of the mule the best he could, poring over lawbooks day and night to try to find relief for her, looking for a way to get a restraining order against the city officials to keep them from killing the mule. But he was being blocked by John Naper and Simm Johns, both wanting to see the mule dead.

Elwood had set it up so that Simm Johns and John Naper would suffer the worst of the lot. The story was enough to curl your hair.

When the little mule had wandered off the street to keep from being run down by cars, she had sought shelter in front of John Naper's store. Being half-starved to death, she had nibbled at a little ear of corn that had rolled off the top of a basket and fallen to the concrete. And among the facts that John Naper had kept out of the story he was telling about his run-in with the mule had been the way he had run out in front of his store and tried to coat the old frost-bitten ear of corn with rat poison. And seeing this didn't work he had tried to force it down the throat of the mule. Even now, flat on her back in the city jail, the mule was foaming some at the mouth which, as everyone knew, a critter will do when poison has reached its belly.

The little mule hadn't stood toe to toe to fight him but had hunkered against the side of the building while he beat her with an ax handle that he kept in that big wooden barrel of ax handles in the front of his store. It was thought that he'd broke one of her legs. But there was no way of knowing since they wouldn't let anyone in to see her and she was too weak to stand anyway.

The tales were so mournful I got to thinking that I would probably be in trouble when I went down there to see Kate when school was out. I was glad I didn't have to go back to Judge Clay's house to get permission. For once these tales fermented, they were sure to spew over our county and the neighbor counties, too.

"You got to get down there," Elwood said, "but a little later than usual. You got to allow time for everybody to get home from school and get the tales told. Then we'll know if our plan is working."

"How's that, Elwood?" I asked.

"You'll know," he said. "You'll see a crowd like you never saw before coming around the corner of the street and heading toward the city building. People riled up over the mistreatment of that mule." Elwood scratched around on the floor right there in the school hall. "You got to watch for them and time your going in to see that mule just right. Remember, they got to see you going in that city building with that sack of corn. The plan depends on it. Once they see that, you can make your break. Kate's chances are depending on you."

That put a clincher on it and Elwood knew it would. Though I'd a-done it anyway. Elwood judged this part of it to be so important that on second thought he decided he would go with me and stand watch for the Women's League Committee for the Prevention of Cruelty to

Animals to come to the jail. He would watch around the corner from the jail, which was the way they would come since they had their office in the Baptist Church, which stood farther down the street. He'd head them off, having plenty of time since the Baptist Church was almost at the other end of the block. He'd meet me then across the street from the jail.

"Now go over that while I spread some more tales," he said.

When evening came, Elwood hardly gave me time to get out of John Naper's store. I saw him down at the far end of the street waving me on toward the jail. I hurried over, carrying the poke containing the two ears of corn I'd bought in John Naper's store, hid myself behind a big sugar maple, and waited.

I thought I heard Kate bray once, but couldn't be sure. Could have, though. It was time for me to visit. Or maybe Rafrel had taken a peek inside her cell.

I got to thinking about how I believed the little mule liked old Rafrel. All those tricks and all. I got so wrapped up thinking of her and Rafrel that I hardly heard Elwood when he came around the corner of the building like he was being swept by a wind, shouting at me:

"Get ready! Get ready!" When he reached me, he was almost out of breath. "We've hit the jackpot! They're coming! And glory be if Felicia Borders ain't leading the pack! I was depending on her."

Felicia Borders was head of the Women's League Committee for the Prevention of Cruelty to Animals. She had formed the committee the same day that Rafrel

Skaggs had pulled Mrs. Shackle's cat from the sugar maple tree.

Mrs. Borders turned the corner holding up the bottom of her ankle-low dress so she could walk faster. And behind her were more women than I could count.

"Now!" Elwood said, nudging me in the side. "Now! Get going!"

My feet were frozen to the ground.

"I'm scared!" I said.

"So is Kate!" Elwood said, coming up with something to get me to moving and in trouble, like always.

I ran as hard as I could across the street. Ran according to plan, which was to break right in front of the women just as they reached the front of the city building. Then, according to plan, I tripped and fell in front of them so they would have to stop to keep from tromping me. And as I fell the poke with the corn busted open and the corn went rolling out for all of them to see.

I had torn a hole in the poke to make sure the corn rolled out.

The next thing I knew Felicia Borders was looking down at me. She looked at the corn and then back at me.

"Young man," she said, "where are you going in such a hurry with that corn?"

And just like rehearsing a line out of a school play I looked up at her and said:

"Oh! Oh! I am trying to sneak into the jailhouse and feed the poor little mule, flat on her back, helpless and starving to death!"

Felicia Borders stomped her foot, not missing me more than an inch, looked around at the others and said:

"Hear that, girls? They were telling the truth!"

"I told you my Reny wouldn't lie!" I took that to be coming from Reny Jackson's ma.

"Tom wouldn't come home crying his heart out for nothing." That was Tearbaby's ma. I could just see Tearbaby squinting his eyes and the tears rolling like water over a cliff.

"And the boy sneaking to feed her!" Felicia Borders said. "It all fits! I've seen and heard enough! March!"

If I hadn't rolled to one side I would have been tromped flatter than a skipjack fish.

I didn't even bother to pick up the corn. Kate would get none from me tonight. But I figured there was a good chance she would be getting a double helping before the night was over.

I went one way and Elwood the other.

I reached home and found ma just stomping. She had a copy of Scoop Dawson's extra in her hand. It was so fresh that he had picked up the latest rumors, and he had had the papers delivered special, the Committee for the Saving of Mules doing the delivering.

I glanced over ma's shoulder at the big headlines:

MULE TO BE TRIED IN POLICE COURT,
JUDGE DECLARES!

But it was a bulletin blocked off in the center of the page that held my eyes:

MULE REPORTED MAULED
BEYOND RECOGNITION!

CHAPTER 19

You Can't Beat a Rumor in a Race

Nothing beats a rumor in a race. Take Rafrel Skaggs and his run-in with that cat. Mrs. Shackle's cat that Rafrel skinned out of the sugar maple tree. Well, talk of that cat scrape stayed in town at a dead run for more than a year, slowed to a trot the next two, walked two more, and still could be heard anytime things got slow around the town. Pa said it had been the tastiest morsel of gossip the Women's League had ever latched on to.

The *Village Sentinel* had carried the "Cat and Rafrel Story," as it had come to be known, on the front page. Talk had been that Scoop Dawson had taken a picture of Rafrel squeezing the cat until its eyeballs were popping, and hadn't used it. Scoop claimed that someone had broken into his office overnight, taken the film, and made off with it. He said (in print) that the film had been stolen by "forces unknown." But town folk divided the loss of the picture three ways: number one said that Scoop had forgotten to put film in the camera (he had been known to do this before) and didn't have the guts to come out and say it; number two said that he had been paid off by Rafrel, with Milton Boggs helping Rafrel raise the money;

number three said that Scoop hadn't taken a picture at all but was short of print and in trouble since he was running the same old news over and over again and had built himself a new story, printing the loss of the film as headlines.

Rafrel had claimed—at the time—that Scoop had got his eyes mixed up: It was not the eyes of the cat that had nearly popped out, but his eyes, and that cat had nearly scratched them out, his right eye particularly. He said the cat showed its gratitude for his saving its life by putting a streak down his right eyeball as broad as a darning needle. And for over two months, which was the time the "Cat and Rafrel Story" remained the strongest, Rafrel wore sunglasses because he claimed the tiniest ray of sun, or any kind of light, hurt his injured eye.

Rafrel's story got the Women's League all stirred up and they got a committee together to look into his wearing of those sunglasses. They put out a report a week later that there was just nothing to the tale. When Rafrel still wore his dark glasses, even at night, they brought pressure on the council to make him take them off and quit walking around the streets so all-fired biggety and let the public see the scratch.

Well, the council pressured Rafrel until he had to take the glasses off. But he covered his right eye with a black patch, claiming that he had gone to an eye doctor— out of town—and had been told that he might lose his eye if the light hit it just right and rolled around some. But the Women's League claimed they had had a watch on Rafrel and that he hadn't left town at all, and they said that the black patch was scaring children along the streets, since it made Rafrel look like a pirate.

Then Rafrel got mad and said that Mrs. Shackle's cat could just dry away on a limb before he would climb for it again. This made the council begin to boil because Rafrel had taken it on himself to set the laws, and to say what he would and would not do.

Rumor followed that there was about to be a shake-up in the force since it was part of a policeman's job to rescue cats from trees. And the council even went so far as to figure distance. Any cat more than six feet off the ground was said to be in a bad way, and entitled to help.

Rafrel made a public statement then, and Scoop Dawson headlined it in the *Village Sentinel*. Rafrel said he didn't mind getting a cat down out of a tree if it wasn't too high up, and wasn't mean and given to scratch. But he claimed that if the cat was up very high he got dizzy spells on the limbs and his sight blurred.

It was Milton Boggs who was said to have saved Rafrel's job. He had a basket, lid and all, made and placed in the police office purposely to take cats from trees.

But it was still said to this day that if you stared Rafrel square in the eyes he would close his right one out of habit.

Well, Kate was a heap bigger than any cat.

The rumors first reached me at school. Rumors that said Kate had been fed a fine meal. The Women's League committee had stormed into the police office and caught Rafrel snoozing behind the desk where he got to sit when Milton was out of the building.

They had demanded to see the mule and been refused by Rafrel since he said visitors made the mule rowdy and mean, and hard to manage. About that time Kate brayed and Felicia Borders heard her for the first time. You can just imagine how it must have sounded to her.

"That poor creature," Felicia Borders said. "She must be suffering something terrible."

Whereby she demanded to again see the mule. But Rafrel held out, saying that he had orders from Milton not to let anyone through the jail door without either his ok or written permission from Judge Clay.

That was all the Women's League needed. They stitched the rest of it up. Kate had been mauled so badly that Rafrel was trying to keep her from sight.

About that time, to make it worse, Kate was heard raking her hoofs across the bars.

"What's that?" Felicia screamed. "The poor thing is flat on her back in there!"

"Ain't nothing of the sort," Rafrel said. "She's perched on her rear end in there like no mule oughten to be just set on tormentin' me."

"That's all we need to hear, girls!" Felicia Borders said. "He's beat that mule flat on her back and still seeking revenge!"

The women demanded to see Kate again and when Rafrel refused, one of them whopped him on the side of the head with a pocketbook.

Their next move was to Judge Clay's house where they were told (by a member of the Committee for the Saving of Mules who just happened to be around when he left and had overheard him tell the maid Marsey) that Judge Clay had gone to the county seat, ten miles away. No doubt to study their collection of lawbooks, still trying to help the mule.

Then they stormed the mayor's house and were told he was out of town too. But they didn't believe this since he had no reason to be out of town (and were told by a member of the Committee for the Saving of Mules, who just happened to be there, that he had seen the mayor come out on the porch no more than ten minutes ago) and so they left two of the women to watch the windows and doors. Then Felicia Borders marched them on to Milton Boggs' house.

They caught Milton home all right. But he wouldn't open the door since he said it was an unruly mob. He said for them to go home and he would see either the Judge or the mayor in the morning and talk it over with them.

This sewed it all up good and tight. The Women said Milton and Rafrel were hoping to use the night to try to patch the mule up enough to let people see her. No matter how good a job they did, the damage had been done.

And then word came from the two women left at the mayor's house that they thought they had seen the mayor go sneaking past a window.

Only Judge Clay rested from a good bawling-out that night, just the way Elwood had planned it all.

By noon Friday, Elwood was able to report that the petunia belt had surrendered. They had dropped all their charges against the mule and most of them had offered to help, feeling partly responsible, by taking their turn at standing guard on the city building. For Felicia Borders had no intention of leaving the building unguarded.

John Naper was the hardest hit. Not one customer

had been in his store Friday morning. Simm Johns had. But not to buy. Only to let John Naper know that he would help him stand the loss if business didn't pick up.

It didn't by afternoon and John Naper posted the front of his store with special bargain signs since he had lots of items that couldn't stay around over the weekend. But the signs didn't lure anyone in town, just a couple of people out of town who stopped while passing through.

The Women's League took even them into consideration and decided to keep the store watched for outsiders. If too many came, then the women planned to picket the place. But since strangers seldom came into town they didn't figure this would be much of a problem.

Elwood was high on the hog now. He had drawn everything out and was going over it again and again to make sure there were no leaks. He had the groundhog in the hole and wanted to make sure he didn't have more than one entrance.

He even looked at the little skinned place on my elbow I had gotten from falling in front of the Women's League and said:

"Let's bandage that up and pass the word that you were mauled by Rafrel Skaggs while trying to get in to feed the mule."

I like to have never talked him out of this, but I knew I had to. For I was afraid I might be called up in court to tell about it and that would have been hard enough to do with the truth, let alone a lie. I told Elwood I feared pa would seek revenge on Rafrel for fighting me. Elwood said he didn't want that but that I *could* say I just skinned it while trying to sneak inside the jail, scraping it on the bars or something. But I wouldn't go for that either.

"Well," Elwood said, "no need for me to load you down, I reckon. You got enough to do as it is."

"Like what?" I asked.

"Like when the Judge says, 'Is there anyone who will speak in defense of the mule?', you pop up and tell your story," he said.

Shoot me with a gun! I couldn't have been any deader.

"I can't do it, Elwood," I said.

"Why not?" he asked. "You've got to. You are the only one who can."

"I'd drop dead in front of all them people," I said.

"The mule will drop dead if you don't," he said.

"Now look here, Elwood," I said. "Ain't there some other way?"

"Nope," he said. "You've got nothing to worry about."

"Why not?" I said.

"We'll rehearse it out before the trial. And you've got time. It ain't like it was happening to you now."

That wasn't much, but it did help some. You know, as long as you can stick something out in front of you, giving yourself just ever so little a bit of time before it happens, it always helps some. You get to thinking that something just might come along to knock it out altogether. I was planning on something like that to happen. Like maybe Elwood sewing it all up so tight there wouldn't be any need of anyone talking in behalf of the mule.

School let out and everyone went home with a new batch of rumors. Elwood had booked the whole school up solid. He had made it a point to see that everyone intended to be at the trial tomorrow, which was Saturday morning, Doom's Day. He didn't have to do much work here, though, since he couldn't have held'em away with a shotgun.

But to Elwood everything had to be according to schedule. He was like a ball of fire—his shirt sleeves rolled up, and in between he just kept making more promises to the Committee for the Saving of Mules. Things they could do when the mule got free. I couldn't stop him. No need to try. Well, it made no difference. I didn't see how I could keep the first ones. Piling on more wouldn't make it any worse. Nothing else mattered now but saving Kate.

Me and Elwood took a walk through town to check on the doings of the Women's League. Checking their sentry posts and all. Elwood walked from post to post, strutting like he was a general and they were all taking orders from him. He frowned and said:

"They ought to have another woman here at this alley. Rafrel uses it sometimes."

Then he moseyed on, disgusted, for he couldn't say a word, and him a general!

We broke up and I went home to face ma, figuring that it was past time for her to light into me. For by now she should have been able to piece most of it together. She never failed to catch on whenever I was in the middle of something.

And then there would be pa after he came home from work. Ma would be through with me by then. They'd get me one at a time.

I couldn't have been more wrong about ma, I mean about her being there at the house. I did all that worrying for nothing. She wasn't even there. Pa was bent over the stove fixing supper. Imagine that!

"Where's ma?" I asked.

"Oh, in town," pa said, humming and acting just like it was the usual thing for me to come home and find him fixing supper like that.

"What for?" I asked.

"Oh, duty," pa said, still humming, and stirring a pot of soup on the stove. He looked up at the clock on the wall. "Nope. She got off duty five minutes ago. Ought to be home soon now."

What he said didn't make any sense to me.

"On duty for what?" I asked.

"Why for Kate, of course," he said. "I thought you might have seen her."

Like that. Just like it was as common as a cold. "For Kate!" I said.

"That's right," pa said. He looked at me, raised his eyebrows and shook his head. "I don't know exactly how you did it, Isaac—been too long since I was a boy, I guess. But you did it. Yep. If there is one thing your mother will fight over it's something being mistreated. Birds, dogs, cats, wild animals, and now mules. And that mule being mauled made her hit the ceiling. I've been married to her for twenty-five years and I never saw her in such a rage before. She was just storming when she came in the shop early this afternoon and told me to fix your supper."

"By golly!" I said. "I sure never counted on that!"

"Didn't you now?" pa said, setting a bowl of soup in front of me. "Now if you don't feel like eating, Isaac, I won't force you. You must be awful upset the way poor

229

Kate has been mauled. Probably took your appetite clean away. She might not even be alive by now. But don't wait for ma, if you have a mind to eat. She might not eat either, feeling a heap to blame for it all. Talking about how she wasn't kind to the poor critter. Boy, the town looks like it's under martial law the way them women are walking about!"

I could tell by the fire and all in the stove that pa had been home for some time. Longer than he needed to fix my supper.

"What brings you home so early, pa?" I asked. "Oh, nothing in particular," pa said. "I just didn't have a place to work. Your ma opened up a coffee stand in my shop for the Women's League. You know, coffee for the change of shifts. Talked'em into moving their headquarters from the Baptist Church up to the shop so they would be located more in the center of it all. Poor Kate."

"Sure is awful, ain't it, pa?" I said, trying to look as sad as I could.

Pa pulled up a chair and sat down beside me.

"Ok, Isaac," he said. "Let's have it. The whole story. Me and you been on the same side too long now to hold out on one another, ain't we? The town ain't never going to be the same again and I want to know how it all came about. You start with Elwood. That's the beginning, ain't it?"

There was no fooling pa. He had it all pegged right. Even down to Elwood.

CHAPTER 20

Kate Goes to Court

Trial was set for ten o'clock. Ma would be in town by eight since she was to have hot coffee ready to serve by eight-thirty. Yep—ma! Still going strong. She fumed around a little about it all. I mean she was mad that she ever had to get mixed up in such a thing, but I knew good and well that nothing could keep her from going to the trial. Pa said that was because of a woman's nature. Just plain born that way. Curious. Ma wasn't about to miss the biggest event the town might ever have.

'Course, pa didn't tack the same curiousness onto his not opening the shop today. He just claimed that ma and the Women's League wanted to use the cobbler shop again today.

It might have worked—I mean pa telling me that—except that I had overheard ma tell him that if he wanted to keep the shop running the Women's League had the promise of using a tent set up by the Pentecostal Church in that vacant lot down from the business district.

Pa said:

"Nope. You ladies just go ahead and use my shop. It's the least I can do for the mule."

Ma winked at me, giving me the first friendly sign I had had out of her in a spell and we headed for town.

People were coming from all sides. Women with shawls pulled over their heads to ward off a little wind. And lots of small kids running along behind looking rowdy. And everywhere along the streets, mostly close to the corners, men gathered in groups and talked.

Pa peeled off when we reached the shop and wasn't any time at all mixing with a group of men up by the corner. I headed out and looked for Elwood.

It was hard to find him with so many people about. Near the corner, close to the city building, the crowds were thicker still. Sy Mullins, who pa said was the best hoedown fiddler in the country, was already set up on the rear of a flatbed truck and was bearing down on "Arkansas Traveler," the air being so chilly you could see his breath. Simon Baker was on the banjo and Albie Dobbins on the guitar. And Albie's wife Talley was below him still sitting like a moonstruck hound, which made you think that Milton had been right about that little pick box taking her from Rafrel.

Allen Roundhead, the Shawnee Indian I talked about earlier, was up next to the truck since the biggest crowd was there. He was trying to sell his snake oil remedies, which he said would cure everything from a cold to a dose of rat poison.

I found Elwood just as he was giving Fats Wallen some further orders to spread to the gang.

"Remember, Fats," Elwood said, "everyone at school in the same corner of the courtroom, just inside the door. When the mule is led in I want it to sound like a funeral march. Tell Tearbaby he's to lead that part of it." Then Elwood looked at him and winked. "You've done a good job, Fats."

Fats grinned and bydogged if he didn't salute Elwood. Just like they do in the army. Dogged if Elwood didn't salute back.

"How's it going, Elwood?" I asked. "Details!" Elwood said, like the weight of the world was on him.

"Details are getting me down. Now. Let's get your end of it straightened up."

We scooted across the street and into an alley. Then Elwood faced me and pulled his coat high on his shoulders. He said:

"I'm Judge Clay. Now. Ready. *Is there one among you to speak in behalf of the little mule?*"

I raised my hand, swallowing hard, still thinking something would happen to deliver me.

"Me! Me, your Honor," I said. "I'll speak for the little mule since the poor little critter can't speak for herself."

"Nope!" Elwood said. "That won't do it. It's a shame Tearbaby can't take your place. We ought to have a tear when you face that crowd. You might pucker and rub your fingers into your eyes. If you can make them smart you might get a tear. Now, let's go over it again."

We worked on my part fifteen minutes and then went back to the city building so we could make a run for it and be sure we got a place in the corner of the room. It was a cinch some people were going to be standing in the hall.

When Judge Clay left his house, all eyes were on him. He crossed the street and turned up the steps of the city building toward the courtroom. Under his arm he carried a large book that rumor (by way of the Committee for the Saving of Mules) said was the Constitution of the United States. When word spread that the Judge had reached his courtroom, the crowd broke loose and rushed to the stairs.

"Charge!" Elwood screamed in my ear. I heard a fox horn blow from the corner, then I saw boys coming from everywhere, girls at their heels. It was the whole school. Anyone older than them didn't have a chance. They were clearing the steps two and three at a time, moving even faster than I had ever seen them leave the school building when school let out. And that was always a wild race.

Older people fought for footing and you could hear things like, "*Ouch!* Oh—you little heathen!"

I saw Fats huffing and puffing about middle way up the steps and I passed him.

We met in the courtroom, all of us in the right corner where Elwood had told us to gather. The older people got in and scattered over the rest of the room, fighting for seats. Some gave up and hurried to the hall, willing to settle for a peek through the door.

John Naper was up front by Judge Clay's bench, just like Elwood said, since he was the key plaintiff and would take the stand. His charges hung in the balance along with the police charges and a personal charge brought by Rafrel for bodily injury.

I looked over the crowd for ma and pa. I found ma sitting with the Women's League Committee for the Prevention of Cruelty to Animals. Pa had got him a decent seat near the front, not far from Simm Johns, who kept his eyes fastened to John Naper. He was smiling whenever he caught John Naper's eye, reassuring him.

The Judge not being in the courtroom yet, John Naper was the center of attention. He sat with his head down, glancing up only now and then to catch the eyes of the gathering. You could have struck a match on the eyeballs of the women. I never saw such mean looks and I hope I never do again. They were enough to melt you down and dry you up.

Air blew in a crack in a window and the flag by the side of Judge Clay's seat caught it and waved about. And you could hear old men trying for the spittoons and hitting them dead ringer. They were clinking like little bells and the sounds were being sucked out of the room through the open door.

Then Judge Clay walked in. He looked as big as a mountain, with his big black robe dragging the floor.

He sat down slowly, looked over the court, popped his gavel on top of the desk and said:

"This court is in session. A court that many of you are thinking irregular, to say the least. And yet it is my honest opinion and conviction that if there is not justice for all of God's creatures then there is no justice at all." He paused and his words echoed through the room. "Standing at the mercy of this court today is a mule. A little cockleburred critter like those that carried us into this rugged country so many years ago that only the older of us here today can remember those days. You, John Simon"—and his finger pointed at a man sitting on the second row—"you rode on the back of a mule for over twenty miles back when you were courting your wife Pearly. You, Tom—that old slate-colored mule you used to own snaked enough logs down Sourwood Mountain to almost build a town. But that was all before we got progress and got ashamed of how we started. Back then, we were humble and proud and praised that little critter here on the mountains as a godsend. I could go on and on. But I won't. For my duty is to hear the evidence and pass sentence, not to defend the mule. I just wanted to say to you that surely this critter deserves a better fate today than to be excluded from the fold of justice; a better fate than to be snuffed out by a country that has forgotten it. Progress is no good unless the heart goes with it. It is my decision to hold this trial. And if it be the will of the people, it will be my final one. For maybe a mule-trying judge is too old-fashioned, too. But right now this is still my court." He looked toward the door and motioned to Rafrel. "Will you bring the defendant to the courtroom where she will stand without defense and be so judged."

The courtroom was so quiet that you could hear every step Rafrel took down the stairs. *Clip, clip, clop, clip.*

Elwood eased to the door and stood ready to pass the signal back to us.

Then Kate broke the silence. You could hear her clattering hoofs. *Plop, plop, plop, plop.* And then quiet. Then Rafrel:

"Git up! Git up, you ornery critter! Torment me to the end!"

Milton, sizing up the crowd and seeing how they stood, stuck his head through the door and said:

"Rafrel! Be kind to the prisoner now. Remember that's our policy. Let's always live up to it."

You could see Judge Clay frowning on the talk taking

place in his court.

Rafrel made it to the top of the steps with Kate. It looked like he might make it all the way. But no one had paid attention to Scoop Dawson's setting up his big camera near the top of the steps.

First there was a puff of smoke. And then a flash like a streak of lightning. And a loud KERPOP!

Kate wrinkled, swelled, and fairly blew Scoop's camera over. And to boot she raised everyone inside the courtroom out of their seats, including Judge Clay. Which caused Judge Clay to yell out and demand that no more pictures be taken.

And Kate, maybe thinking she had just been shot at and luckily missed, walked along quiet.

As she stepped inside the door, Elwood dropped his hand, and the wailing and sniffling began. It raised like a storm, with only the banging of Judge Clay's gavel finally restoring quiet.

"Another outburst like that," he said, "and I'll clear the court!"

Rafrel led Kate up near the Judge, on the opposite side from John Naper, and she just plopped down there on her haunches, grinned and looked the crowd over. I hunkered down in my seat, since I was afraid she might see me and bray again.

"Read the charges, Mr. Rakes," Judge Clay said. (Syrus Rakes was a well-known man in town who drove the city dump truck and acted as court clerk.) "And face the mule while you read."

Well, Syrus Rakes read the charges, facing that mule and her yawning a couple of times in his face and trying

238

to reach out and lick him.

It was easy to see that the crowd wasn't taking lightly to the charges but was getting tickled from the way Kate was holding up. Brazen as could be.

"She's a brave little thing," someone said, and everyone nodded their heads, saw Judge Clay looking for the noise, and then went to clearing their throats.

"All right, John Naper." Judge Clay leaned over his desk. "Let the court hear your story."

I got to thinking about myself being there in his shoes, facing the crowd and all. I figured he'd be shaking like a leaf in a windstorm. But, by golly, he lowered his head until he got wrapped up a little in that story and then raised his eyes and came on. Just like he was getting the attention he deserved at long last. Just popped his heels together, stuck out his chest and doubled up his fist. He sparred out a few times and faced the Judge and said:

"She was a-coming on, Judge!"

Maybe what gave John Naper the encouragement was the way the crowd had been grinning and looking to be taking him to heart. He had no way of knowing that as he talked Kate had rolled over on her back, pulled her front legs over her eyes and fairly stuck out her tongue at him. Just doing all kinds of tricks. That is, until John Naper turned to face the Judge. Then Kate sat up and her ears perked up. And when John Naper turned his back and looked out over the crowd, Kate made her first move.

John Naper saw the crowd raising from their seats, and maybe thinking he was pulling them up with his talk of his bravery, he yelled,

"She was a-coming on, I tell you. Me standing my

ground knowing that if she reached me she was set to snap my head off like a clover top. She was mean, ornery, and fit to skin me. Me! I can whip an alligator, tie two wildcats' tails together, spit in the eye of a mountain lion! I can tame gorillas or charge bulls! 'Come on!', I said. 'Come on!'"

Kate was coming. Everyone could see her but John Naper, whose back was to her. She came sneaking like a cat after a mouse, setting her hoofs down like they were padded with cotton.

You could hear Simm Johns hissing like a snake trying for John Naper's attention and pointing at the mule behind him. But there was no stopping John Naper now. He thought he had built himself into a hero and had no intention of stopping now. Even Judge Clay sat frozen to his seat, his eyes fixed on the mule and his mouth open.

"Come on, I said!" John Naper jumped up in the air and clicked his heels together. "I can whittle down the teeth of a buzz saw going full speed with my little finger. I can drop a snake with a look in the eye. I use spikes for toothpicks and clean my nails with my meat cleaver. Come on, you varmint, strike your blow!"

Kate crept slower now. She was close and grinning from ear to ear. Everyone in the courtroom bent forward and rose a little out of their seats.

"Eh, she was wicked, I tell you!" John Naper said. "Fire was in her eyes. 'I'm man enough to take it,' I shouted. 'Strike your wicked blow!'"

Kate plopped her head over his shoulder, dropped out her tongue, and sandpapered down the side of his cheek.

"*Ye-o-o-o-o-o-o-o!*" John Naper yelled as he fell flat on his back.

Your ears would have fairly rung from the laughter about. And the laughter of Judge Clay rolled over it all. Then he pounded the gavel for quiet.

Kate sat down on her haunches now and had John Naper pinned to the floor with her tongue.

"Save me!" John Naper yelled.

Simm Johns was on his feet.

"Do something! Do something!" he shouted. "That mule is killing John Naper in front of us all."

Kate spotted him and got to her feet and turned his way. And Simm Johns went over the tops of the people and benches to get out.

"*Who-e-e-e-e-e!*" he shouted.

The laughing was louder than ever.

"Rafrel!" Judge Clay said. "Take that mule back to its rightful place! I'll not have these interruptions in my court!"

Rafrel turned toward Kate and she grinned and stuck our her tongue at him. Rafrel turned to Milton.

"You git that mule, Milton," he said. "She already got me once coming up the steps."

"The Jedge said you, Rafrel," Milton said. "I ain't going over his head. Go on. I'm right behind you."

Well, Kate had sat down again and she wouldn't budge. Rafrel pulled and the crowd laughed and Judge Clay rubbed his chin and studied.

"Tell you what, Rafrel," he said. "Suppose you just have John Naper come to the other side and let the mule have this side."

And that took care of it.

Judge Clay bent over and spoke to Syrus Rakes:

"Let it be entered in the record that John Naper holds a fifteen-dollar charge against the defendant. Let it be entered along side the charges on record, and read by you earlier, from the police department." Then he looked long over the crowd. "Now," he said. "Is there anyone who will speak for the mule?"

Elwood nudged me. I didn't feel it, I saw him do it. I was waiting to faint away. I closed my eyes, just hoping to pass out.

Some said I walked, some said Elwood shoved me. I don't rightly know. All I know is that when I opened my eyes I wasn't in another place where I wanted to be, but right there with all that crowd looking on. Ma and pa had nothing to do with it. I couldn't have seen them anyway. I heard Judge Clay mumbling at me, saw his eyes staring and his lips moving. I couldn't hear.

And then I felt the softness touch the back of my neck. I felt the old head go into my arms. It was Kate, looking at me like I had come at last to take her home to the hills. Like it had been a long wait. I looked her in the eyes and I got to thinking about her old shabby coat being peeled off by a skinning knife. It was terrible and frightening. And then, I just threw my arms around her neck and everything seemed all right.

I wasn't a storyteller. I knew I was no good at that. I guess I wasn't too good at anything. But I just talked to the little mule. Just took her through it all again. The hills, the creek, the school and all.

I remember how quiet the room seemed. I thought I saw people reaching for handkerchiefs. I saw an old man in the corner pull a red bandanna from his pocket and blow his nose. I was sure of that.

And with nothing more to say I said:

"Don't be afraid, Kate. I ain't afraid no more. Me and you are together."

Judge Clay had his glasses off. Remember, I said those glasses looked too heavy.

He looked out over the court. Then he looked down at Syrus Rakes. He motioned for Milton Boggs and whispered something and Milton shook his head.

"Let the city charges be stricken from the record," he said.

Then he looked at Rafrel.

"All right, Rafrel," he said. "Come forward and state your charges against the mule."

"Ain't no need to do that," Rafrel said. "I mean there ain't no need fer me to come nowhere. She's free as a bird as fer as the police department is concerned."

And he got a hand from the crowd that fairly swelled his chest.

And Milton, seeing Rafrel set high with the crowd, whispered ever so low:

"You ain't got authority to speak for the force. I'm in charge around here and I ought to have said that."

But Milton was too late. Rafrel was getting a hand now from the crowd and by George if Felicia Borders wasn't giving him the big-eye. She was a widow woman, you know.

"Then strike them from the record," Judge Clay said

to Syrus Rakes. "And leave only the charges of John Naper to show." He turned now to John Naper. "You got anything you'd like to add at this time?" he asked.

John Naper swallowed and then caught the eye of Simm Johns, who had crept back to his seat.

"Nope," he said. "My charges have got to stand."

"I see," Judge Clay said.

A boo went up from the crowd and Judge Clay pounded for order.

"It's somewhat irregular to bring one case in with another," he said, looking over the courtroom. "But I believe this one to be important to the trial now at hand." He looked at John Naper. "How long have you been setting your feed and the sort out on the sidewalk in front of your store, and on city property?" Judge Clay asked.

John Naper opened his eyes wide.

"Nigh onto twenty years, I reckon," he said.

"And have you always had the city's permission to use their property for your store purposes?" Judge Clay asked.

"Well, no," John Naper said. "Never figured I had to."

"Well, that's a shame," Judge Clay said. "I mean it could be if there were say . . . twenty years' back rent facing you, and due the city."

John Naper drew up his lip.

"Now shucks, Judge," he said. "You know I just been doing some thinking. Yes sir, just doing some thinking while you were talking. Thinking about that little critter over there getting all lost and mixed up good and proper in front of my store. Says I, she's probably hungry and needing help. And it done me plumb good to see her fill her craw with some corn from my place. I felt good knowing that I could help that poor little defenseless mule in some sort of way. Just made me feel good in here by my ticker and my thinking about it right now makes me feel all the better. Now, says I, I ain't holding no grudge or charges either."

"Let the charges of John Naper be stricken from the record," Judge Clay said. And let it also be entered that this court stands adjourned."

The crowd was up whooping and hollering and everyone was shaking hands with everyone else. Elwood said that next to Kate I was the best actor he ever saw. I didn't bother to tell him that I wasn't acting at all. I was just trying to scream in Kate's ear and tell her that she was free. And I was turning to shake a few hands myself. Then I felt the big hands on my shoulders. I looked up into the eyes of Judge Clay.

"Isaac," he said, "the mule is let to your custody. You got fifteen minutes to get her out of the city limits." He frowned at me and then broke into a laugh. "And I ought to get you for practicing law without a license."

I led the little mule out of the courtroom, and we headed home with a warning from ma that we were both to keep a fair distance behind her. For the mule was out of trouble now, and ma had that old look in her eye. Not so positive anymore but enough for me not to be caring about pressing my luck.

And pa? Well, he never did get his pipe lit up. But the wind had come up strong.

CHAPTER 21

Saying Good-Bye Still Takes Time

Ma said that if I would get up early she would let the little mule spend the night in the yard. But she didn't want people coming by, maybe on their way to church, and seeing the little mule come around the house. She'd been embarrassed enough as it was. And she would pay no mind to pa saying that people passing our house were about as scarce as a rooster laying an egg.

For ma reasoned that Kate was a curiosity now and people might just wander out our way to stare at her.

And yet, it was ma who fed her that night. But that was like ma. Bending in the snow to scratch a piece of earth for the lowly sparrow to find food.

She judged my trip to Moses Hewlett's to be a long one. Long enough to maybe keep me from making it back in time for morning church. So, she told me to get up at six, read the Scripture for an hour, and be off by seven.

Well, pa said that since everyone else was rousing early he'd just get up, too.

So at six o'clock we were all up and about, pa fidgeting around in his chair waiting for his coffee and trying to hurry ma in her reading of the Scripture, which she had decided to read since she figured I might be apt to skip over it too lightly.

"A little listening won't do you any harm, Jeremiah," ma said, scolding pa. "Since you first set eyes on that mule you've been stacking up sin."

"Well," pa said, "I sure don't see where helping that mule out some is piling sin on me. 'Pears to me like I ought to be getting a little credit for it. Me knowing that the Good Lord thinks highly of a mule."

"How do you know that?" ma asked.

"Well, it was a mule that carried Mary to Bethlehem," pa said.

"Was not," ma said. "That was a donkey."

"Mite close to a mule though," pa said. "Now how can you get around that?"

Ma studied.

"Well," she said. "It wasn't no sneaking mule like that one out there." But a smile was on her face now and when she poured pa's coffee I knew that things were all right. "I guess you're right, Jeremiah. I guess the Good Lord did have His eyes on that mule after all. She didn't get out of all that with any earthly doings."

Pa sorta gave me the eagle eye but I settled for it.

And then after breakfast I went out to feed the mule a little of pa's chicken corn. I didn't make much fuss over her. You know how it is.

But I fed and watered her and rubbed her down, petting her along the way without her knowing about it. It would be a rough walk. Our last one together.

Pa walked out into the yard. He studied Kate, walked over and patted her on the nose. Then he looked over at me.

"If you'd rather, Isaac," he said. "I mean . . . if maybe you don't feel like making the trip over to Moses Hewlett's I'd be glad to take her for you."

"I appreciate that, pa," I said.

"But me and this mule have been together a right smart now. And it wouldn't be fitting for me to leave her before the ending. I mean I just wouldn't be much of a fellow to not be going with her all the way. Kate would expect that. I would, too, if you turned things around."

I hopped up on the little mule's back and waved at pa.

"I'll be back as soon as I can," I said.

"Take your time, Isaac," he said. "Take all day if you have a mind to. It's a long trip."

And we did. We took the long way. Just loafing along the slopes. We went to most of the places we had been before, like stopping on the ridge and looking out over the lowlands. We snubbed our nose at Simm Johns' cornfield below, stretched out to nothing but a stubble field now that the corn had been cut. The creek was up some, rolling over the bottoms, making the land rich as a miser.

A few walnuts, some possum grapes, and the chasing of a handful of crows. The sun was getting low and we reached Moses Hewlett's place late. Moses stood out in the yard waving his hand as we came down the slope.

He was old and wrinkled and squinteyed. But his eyes were as soft-looking as a pool of spring water. And his heart was just as soft. I could tell by the way he rubbed his shriveled hands over Kate's hide.

"Growed old like me, ain't you, old girl?" he said as he rubbed. "Not a lot of time left." Then he looked at me.

"She's been a good mule, Isaac. I can tell that."

He was rubbing his hands now over the worn harness marks on her shoulder. And then he bent low, raised a hoof and stared at the bottom. He looked at her teeth. Then he came back to her sides. He saw the marks there and stared. And I thought he must have been thinking the same thing as me: They were whip marks, had to be.

"Yep," Moses said, "she's been a working little mule in her day. Been a little mistreated in her time, too. But that's all over now. Ain't it, old girl?" He rubbed her nose. "Me and you will just have the run of this place until our legs run down." He looked at me. "Won't you come in and set a spell, Isaac?"

"Reckon not," I said. "It's a long ways home."

"Welcome to stay the night," he said.

"Ma would worry," I said.

"Ain't that like a woman?" he said. "Well, I got a few things to be done around the old barn. 'Spect you want to say good-bye to the mule. Just remember she's got a good home and you're welcome to come when you like."

"I know she has, Mr. Hewlett," I said. "And Kate likes you. I can tell it."

"Well, Isaac," Moses said, "I guess we got a lot in common. Just looking for a little rest."

I turned to Kate now.

"I guess we done made it, Kate," I said. "Got you a fine home now. Won't be like sleeping alone on the hill somewhere under a rock cliff, being afraid to stick your nose out and you too stiff to run." I patted her on the nose. "Now don't you go to worrying none about me. I'll come to visit. Why, we won't just shuck everything off like that."

That was all I could say if I was intending to leave. And somehow I think she knew. She turned to follow me once. And then she just stood and watched me to the top of the hill. And from the top of the hill I stood to watch her turn and limp toward the barn, toward where she knew old Moses was, looking as tired and gray as the evening clouds.

CHAPTER 22

Kate Didn't Like the Ending

It might have all ended here. Winter set in and I went to visit her once a week. She seemed happy. And Moses was good to her. Everything was all wrapped up. That is, everything but the ending. The ending that the little mule wanted. That's the only way I can figure it.

February came to the mountains. Cold winds and rain, lots of rain. More than pa had seen here in the hills since he was a boy.

At first it came in short downpours and the creeks were able to carry it away. But pa kept a watchful eye since he knew that February is a flood month here in the hills of Kentucky.

He reasoned that the rain itself wasn't so bad. It was the frozen earth, covered most of the winter with snow, that worried him. For the water had not been able to run off, just stayed there in the ground. And the ground was full and there just wasn't any place for the coming rains to go.

And then it was the last of February and the weather broke. It turned warm enough to fool the trees into trying to bud out. The earth loosed the water and the creeks swelled out of their banks. Everything seemed all right.

But the clouds gathered on the first day of March. By evening they had opened, and you couldn't see past the length of your hand.

Pa stayed up late, pacing the floor. He feared a flash flood.He knew they could come quick as a wink, fast enough to catch you sleeping in bed.

We didn't have to worry. Our house was high and dry. But pa knew that there were a lot of houses along Bear Creek that weren't. All friends of his. He just paced the floor, saying things like:

"Another hour of this and it will reach the Hatchers' house."

Ma was worried, too. She knew that pa was seldom wrong in his judgment of the hill country. And she judged the danger by the worry in his face now.

I stood by the window trying to see to the hills. But the rain blinded me. It came in sheets, like a wind blowing over a sagegrass field. It hit and rattled the windows, running down the glass like a thousand rivers. And in between the great waves of rain that came from the hills I could only see to the fence.

That's how I saw it. Something being knocked against the fence, fighting for footing. Too blurred for me to make it out and not enough time in between the waves of rain.

"Someone's coming, pa!" I said. "

Might be Will Hatcher!" pa said, grabbing his hat. "'Spect the water's about reached him and he's needing help!"

Pa swung open the door. There she stood. Soaking

252

wet and her hair parted down the middle of her back.

"It's Kate!" pa yelled.

I jumped a good foot. Ma squinted to make sure and then caught me just as I headed out the door.

"Not in the rain!" she shouted.

"But she'll drown, ma!" I shouted.

"No she won't," ma said. "She's got sense enough to keep her head down."

"Glory be!" pa said. "What could be the reason?"

"Trouble, trouble, trouble!" ma said. "And at a time like this!"

"Well, she can't stay there in the rain," pa said. "I'll have to try to shield her under the house until the rain stops."

I looked for ma to say no. But it would never come. The softness was in her eyes that said the mule was in trouble again. Needing help.

"Well," ma said. Just don't stand there! The poor thing *might* drown."

Me and pa tried to squeeze out the door at the same time. As we stepped out into the rain, we heard a shout:

"Jeremiah!" The voice came from the direction of the fence. We could see a man's shadow in the rain, fighting along the fence for footing. Pa went to the fence to meet the man.

"Will!" he said. "Will Hatcher?"

"Flash flood!" Mr. Hatcher said, reaching pa, and fighting the rain from his face. "All along the creek! Needing help! Every man we can get!"

"You can count on me!" pa said. He looked at me. "Count on Isaac, too!"

"Knew I could!" Mr. Hatcher said. "Can't stay! Got to get more help!"

And it looked like the wind and rain blew him on up the path.

Pa turned back to the door.

"You heard?" he said to ma.

"Yes," she said. "Watch after Isaac."

Pa stepped into the house and came back with a rope in his hand.

"Bring the mule," he said. "And I'll make a rigging on the way."

When we reached Will Hatcher's, the back of his house was under water. His wife and four kids were trying to get as much out of the house as they could.

"Got a sled?" pa asked.

"Wood sled in the barn," Mrs. Hatcher said.

Bear Creek was muddy and swollen. All the prettiness of summer was gone. It was filled now with heaps of brush and corn stubble, boiling against the back of the house into white foam.

Pa yelled at me for help and I went to the barn and helped him hitch the sled to Kate. She stood still and quiet with little puffs of steam rising from her hide.

Pa turned her as close to the house as he could get. And then he left me to hold her and he went to help.

"Just what you value most," pa said. "We got to get on up the creek."

They piled the sled high with their plunder, everything from an old dresser to a rag doll.

"Lead the mule away, Isaac," pa said.

"Gitup, old girl," I said. And she walked away.

We worked into the night, going from house to house. No words passing between us, just now and then patting the little mule on the head and bragging on her. She stood under the rain with her head down, just like she was biding time.

And the time came at the last house. I could see the light of a lantern in the field below, the long row of bottoms that belonged to Simm Johns. The water was swirling high into them now.

Just as we hauled the last load to high land, Simm Johns came up to us. Pa looked at him and wiped his face, then went to his job of unloading the sled.

"You got to bring the mule!" Simm Johns said.

"You live on high land!" pa said.

"It ain't me," Simm Johns said. "It's that tractor of mine. That dumb Bunt Rankins left it down at the head of the bottom this evening. Said it stalled on him and he figured it would be all right to leave it there till morning."

Pa said, "The mud is a foot deep along that bottom. Has to be."

"You can hook that mule to the tractor," Simm Johns said.

"She'll never pull it," pa said.

"Maybe not," Simm said. "But right now it's the only chance I got."

Pa looked at me. He looked at the mule. He rubbed her legs and unhooked the sled.

"You might not have a chance there," he said. "I know," Simm Johns said.

"I know you got me flat. You got me over a barrel. But you ain't a man to set back and watch a valuable piece of machinery like this be ruined over a grudge."

"The mule is tired," pa said. "I can't ask her to go into mud a foot deep even if she would." Simm Johns said, "I'll pay. I'll pay a fair price."

"It ain't money," pa said. "I won't ask the mule to go. It's up to Isaac. She's his mule."

And there it was thrown right in my lap.

I looked at Simm Johns. And to save me I couldn't strike up much hate for him.

"What do you say, Kate?" I said.

But she was already gone, walking toward the bottom.

The tractor was bogged a foot deep in the mud, water almost reaching the seat.

"Not a chance to start it," Simm Johns said. "Gas tank is full of water. If Bunt Rankins had only told me earlier he left it here!"

"He never figured on a flash flood," pa said.

I stood looking. The tractor looked as big as a mountain and the mule was so tired and little.

"What should I do, pa?" I asked.

Pa looked at me and studied for a moment.

"Don't ask me," he said. "I staked you once. You bargain on your own from now on."

The word "bargain" stuck with me. And then a strange thing happened. Right there in all that rain I thought of Elwood. I just kept thinking what he would have made of all this. Bargain, bargain, bargain. I thought of the pastureland above the house. So close to my room I could look out my window and see across it to the pine grove.

I hitched Kate up to the tractor.

"Gitup! Gitup!" Simm Johns yelled.

But Kate never moved.

"Pa," I said, "do you reckon ma would ever let me keep the little mule if I had a pasture for her?"

"How could she help it, Isaac?" pa said. "She don't own the pasture. What could your ma have against a mule after what Kate's done tonight?"

"Gitup! Gitup! What's wrong with that crazy mule!" Simm Johns was screaming now.

"How would you like to bargain?" I said, looking at Simm Johns.

"Like to what?" he asked.

"Just bargain," I said.

"This ain't no time to bargain," he said.

"Best time in the world," I said.

"Bargain for what?" he said.

"For the pasture rights to that field above my house," I said.

"Not on your life," he said. "There'll be no mule on my place."

I stepped down to unhitch the rope from the tractor.

"What are you doing?" Simm Johns asked.

"Taking my mule home," I said.

Well, he looked at me and then he looked at pa. He looked at the creek and wrung his hands.

"You little horse trader," he said. "Worse than your pa."

"Bargain or no bargain?" I asked.

"If you think she can do it, it's a bargain," he said, and his face broke into a grin.

It rested on the shoulders of the little mule now. I stepped up and whispered in her ear.

"You heard. Think you can do it, Kate?" I asked.

And she walked off. Just dug in, grunted, sank into the mud, got footing and pulled the tractor slowly to the high ground.

"Bydoggies," Simm Johns said, "she did it!"

He was too close to the old mule now and must not have seen her. She turned her old head, fairly fixing, I thought, to bite his head from his shoulders. The she grinned that silly grin and sandpapered the side of his jaw.

He jumped back. "Eh doggies!" he said. "Friendly little thing, ain't she?"

CHAPTER 23

Go Tell It on the Mountain

And that was the way it ended. She stayed in the pasture above the house and paid off my debt to the Committee for the Saving of Mules that summer. Slept in the pine grove, after giving rides most of the day.

Then, toward the fall when the leaves turned on the trees and the wild ducks circled the land, she just seemed to grow tired from it all. Closed her eyes there inside the pine grove and went to sleep, with her head in my lap. Just looked up at me like saying: "Guess I showed some of 'em there is still a place for a mule after all, didn't I, Isaac? But it's a big mountain with lots of people. I've surely missed some of them. And I ain't got time to tell 'em all. You know, I'm just plumb tuckered out. I guess it's up to you now to go tell it on the mountain."

And sure enough, just like ma said, time has come and mellowed the little mule into something good called a memory. And I ain't quit telling it yet.

GLOSSARY

The following glossary is arranged alphabetically. It lists and defines words or phrases in *Goodbye Kate* that may be unfamiliar to readers today. Though some may have other meanings, they are defined as used in the book.

banty; banty rooster: This is the folk pronunciation of bantam, a small breed of chicken that is very spunky. A "banty hen" or a "banty rooster" will defend itself aggressively. In America's country districts, a small but brave man was often compared to a banty rooster. Boxing's bantamweight division is for fighters weighing between 112 and 118 pounds.

boot: Something given in addition, as in a trade: "I swapped my old pickup for one that was a little newer, and gave $500 boot.", to boot means "in addition to; also."

damper, as in "put a damper on it": To hold down, or tone down. It can mean that something disappointing has happened and this "puts a damper" on one's feelings or enthusiasm.

egging, as in "egging me on"—encouraging someone to do something; talking in such a way as to push a person into an action.

gumption: Shrewdness, especially in combination with initiative and boldness in getting something done. A person with gumption is an enterprising person.

hant, a: A "haunt" or ghost; a spirit.

kimmydike: A schoolyard marble game popular in the Appalachian country at the time of the story.

light, as in "to light into": Isaac at one point thinks it is time for him "to face Ma, figuring that it was past time for her to light into me." The phrase means to be confronted verbally and given a tongue-lashing. It can also mean a physical attack: "He said something ugly to me, and it made me light into him." The meaning can also be milder: "I was getting ready to light into that cherry pie." The word is sometimes lit, as in, "I thought I was about to be lit into."

lye soap: A strong soap made with water that has been made alkaline by being poured through wood ashes. The soap was used to wash clothes by boiling them. This was often done in an iron kettle set over an open fire in the yard.

obliged, as in the phrase, "much obliged": An old-fashioned way of saying "thanks." The person who says this is expressing appreciation for a favor or a service.

ornery; also onery (adjective): In milder usage, as in Kate's case, the word means something like this: "given to aggravating mischievousness." In more extreme cases, it can mean "full of devilment; mean as hell." The noun form is orneriness or oneriness. The *American Heritage*

Dictionary defines "ornery" as "having an ugly disposition; specifically, stubborn and mean-spirited."

peart—as in "mighty peart": Active, alert. Something or someone described as "mighty peart" is very active, very alert.

pignut: A small, bitter hickory nut. Its kernel is too bitter for humans to eat, but in the days of the early settlement of America, when pigs were allowed to roam the woods to fatten up, the pigs ate them. This may be the source of the name.

poke: A bag or sack. According to The *American Heritage Dictionary*, the word came into the English language from an Old French word, "poche," meaning a pocket.

poke juice: The juice obtained by boiling the roots of the plant known as pokeweed or "poke"; it can be used as a remedy for skin abrasions, but it is very harsh, the cure being almost worse than the injury it is used to remedy. The phrase may also refer to the juice of the berries on the plant; they are called pokeberries, and turn a dark blackish red when ripe. The juice stains a deep red, and the name "poke," The *American Heritage Dictionary* says, comes from a Virginia Algonquian Indian word, "pakon, 'bloody,' from pak, blood." The juice of the berries can be used as a crude ink.

render: To boil down into grease. At a hog-killing, the hog fat was cut into pieces and rendered into lard by being cooked over a hot fire.

rogued off: To "rogue off" is to run away; to wander out of the vicinity. The phrase carries an overtone of carelessness. A person or animal who just "rogues off" does so without any thought of obligation or loyalty to those left behind.

shed, as in "getting shed of" or "to get shed of": To get rid of. This often appears in the form "shut," as in "to get shut of" something: "I want to get shut of this old rattletrap car." (A "rattletrap" was a car that had been used on gravel roads so long that it had loosened up at every joint and rattled all over. Such a car was embarrassing to drive.)

shine, as in "to take a shine to": To take a liking to something or someone.

shines, as in "cutting shines": Acting up; behaving mischievously or in an odd, silly way. Sometimes the capers are involuntary: "After he got the red pepper in his eyes, he cut all kinds of shines."

shoe last: A foot-shaped form (often made of iron) used by a shoemaker—or "cobbler"—to hold the shoe he is repairing. When the sole or heel is being attached or replaced, the shoe is placed over the last, sole upward.

shucked up: Hid.

'simmon tree: The persimmon tree. This small tree— older specimens may get about 40 or 50 feet tall—is best known for its fruit, a plum-like berry with 4 to 8 large seeds in it. The green fruit is so bitter it puckers the mouth, but after a frost, it is sweet and edible. Raccoons, foxes, coyotes, dogs, and even deer and turkeys eat the fruit and scatter the seeds. According to the *Encyclopedia Americana*, Indians used the fruit for food, and pioneer settlers sometimes made persimmon bread from it.

skipjack: *McClane's New Standard Fishing Encyclopedia* identifies this as the skipjack herring, a relatively small (12-16 inches), large-eyed marine and freshwater fish with a very flat, compressed, torpedo-shaped body and a sharply forked tail. The lower jaw projects beyond the upper jaw. It is a very fast swimmer and when played on light tackle leaps from the water like a tiny tarpon, with its silver scales flashing in the sun. The iridescent bluish-green color of the back and the silvery sides make it remarkably beautiful. *McClane's* describes it as "found from the marine waters of the Gulf Coast from Texas to Florida, [and] up the Mississippi River and its larger tributaries, north to Minnesota and Pennsylvania." Billy Clark knew it in the Ohio and Big Sandy Rivers.

The skipjack is often caught or netted in the tailwaters below giant hydroelectric dams and used as bait for large gamefish like the striped bass or rockfish, an ocean fish which has been introduced into America's freshwater lakes and rivers. Too bony for human consumption, it is also used as cut bait for trotlines or jug lines put out for catfish.

snaking logs, as in "snaked enough logs down Sour-wood Mountain": Dragging logs out of the woods with a horse or mule—or a team of horses or mules—hitched to a log chain hooked around a log. The logs are usually dragged one at a time. This was a necessary task in cutting off a tract of timber.

snurled, as in (1) "snurled up his lip": Curling or lifting the lip as an expression of contempt—it seems to be a combination of sneered and snarled; **(2) "snurled up his nose":** Wrinkling the nose.

spooned around: Loafed around.

studied: "Thought hard," as in, for instance, "He put his chin in his hand and studied about it." This is sometimes used this way: "He was in a deep study about something." Someone "in a deep study" is thinking so hard he is paying no attention to anything or anyone around him.

stump jumping: Jumping up on a stump in a new clearing to deliver an off-the-cuff political speech; this phrase, and the more common version, "stump speaking," was used to describe frontier politicians who moved through the backwoods areas to deliver political speeches while running for office. Later on, the term "stump speaking" came to mean simply going from place to place to give political speeches from outdoor platforms or in public halls. As the country's towns and cities developed, it was no longer necessary to jump onto the stump of a recently felled tree to speak; and in the rural areas, schools and churches were available for political "speechifying."

taterbug: An 8-stringed musical instrument resembling the mandolin, but with a slightly deeper tone, due to its rounded back or lute shape. The back was constructed with different-colored strips of wood, giving it the appearance of a potato bug. It was a very popular instrument in the Appalachian country. The term "taterbug" was also sometimes applied to the mandolin itself.

ticker: A colloquial term for the human heart. The term suggests a comparison with a watch or clock: How long one lives depends on how long one's "ticker" keeps ticking.

OTHER BOOKS BY
BILLY C. CLARK

A Long Row to Hoe. By Billy C. Clark. (Ashland, Ky.: Jesse Stuart Foundation, 1992 Pp. 285. Illustrations. $20.00.)

Song of the River. By Billy C. Clark. (Ashland, Ky.: Jesse Stuart Foundation, 1993. Pp. 176. Illustrations. $15.00.)

These two autobiographical books—one fiction and one nonfiction—recount Kentucky author Billy C. Clark's growing up years in Catlettsburg in the 1930s and '40s. Reading them is like entering an enchanted, sometimes threatening, world of myth and folklore, with characters and tales larger than life, with places where houses lean toward rivers, and rivers give and sustain life and then take it back. Here is the story of a man who owns the city, the rivers, and the countryside of his youth in a way deedholders never can—in his heart and memory.

A Long Row to Hoe begins in 1947 with the 19-year-old Clark leaving home, "where hunger was my most vivid memory; and an education was my greatest desire" (p. 27) to study at the University of Kentucky. Because of heavy rains, the Big Sandy and Ohio rivers are rising to flood stage at Catlettsburg, where they form a junction; but

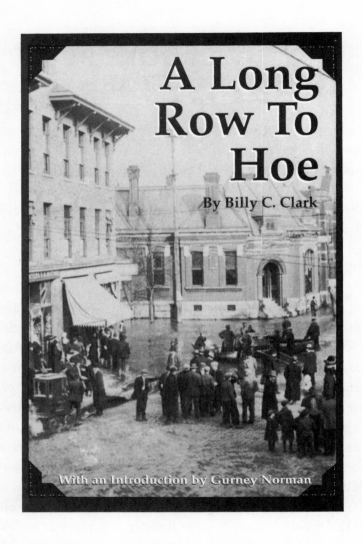

A Long Row To Hoe

By Billy C. Clark

With an Introduction by Gurney Norman

Billy assures a nervous merchant that there will be no flooding. The young man should know. He has spent his boyhood learning to read the rivers, just as he has learned to read the town and its people. Indeed, he has been close to the rivers all his life, from the beginning: "And with a foot of water in the house, the bed where Mom lay surrounded by the waters of the two rivers, I was born, in the rivers of the valley." (p. 71)

It was not a very auspicious start. He was born into a large and desperately poor family. His whiskey-loving father was a hard-luck cobbler and fiddler. At times, his mother had to take in washing. He remembers poignantly when she "washed the clothes over a washboard until her hands would turn as red as the feathers of the redbird that roosted in the willows along the rivers at night." (p. 80) He grew up in a ramshackle house furnished with "drift furniture" salvaged from the rivers. In school he was ridiculed for his long hair (which sometimes was host to lice), his patched clothes, and other embarrassments of the poor. He soon learned that he must hustle to survive. He steals corn and watermelons. He earns skinflint sums of money in various ways: selling animal skins, scrap metal, crawdads, frogs, catfish, walnuts, herb roots, and berries. For a while he even works in the pits where men bet money as gamecocks fight to the death.

Clark recalls a gallery of colorful characters, including grandparents, siblings, and other relatives. His almost mythical Grandpa Hewlett was a Big Sandy timberman, reluctant religious convert, and fiddler: "music was in his body, and his body was big enough to hold all the music of the hills." (p. 45) His Grandma Clark was a herbalist

269

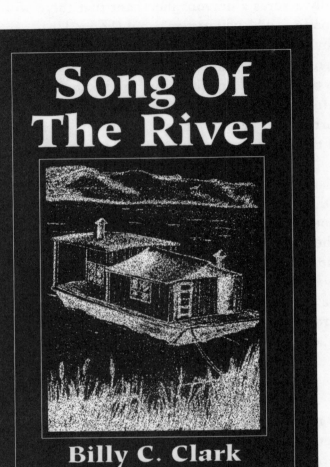

who knew the hills better than most men. There are also villains, notably the man who cheated his family out of their land and the "clique" that runs the town and scorns poor people like the Clarks, whom they call "river trash." Despite his poverty, Clark evokes a boyhood of adventure spiced with practical jokes and memories of his dog Drum and pet rooster Jeptha. It is a living museum of Eastern Kentucky folklore and a world of spirits and omens and good horse sense. And always there are the rivers of life and death.

Song of the River is another way of telling Clark's boyhood story. It is a novel about an old man named John who lives on a shantyboat on the Big Sandy. He is the nurturing, loving, benevolent spirit of the river; and he is on a quest to catch the legendary catfish called Scrapiron Jack, who inhabits the same woods and waters as Faulkner's bear, Melville's whale, and Hemingway's marlin. More imporantly, John is an independent, self-reliant, moral man who deserves to stand with such quintessential American characters as Cooper's Natty Bumppo, Steinbeck's Tom Joad, or Twain's Huck Finn—or such real-life naturalists as Henry David Thoreau and Kentucky's own Harlan Hubbard.

Because the book is so mature in its conception, because it is so consciously crafted in so many literary traditions, and because it is so carefully created in a lean and lyrical plain style out of honest nouns and verbs, it is hard to believe that such a book could have been written when Clark was only 14, as Gurney Norman states in his useful introduction. Whether written at 14 or 29, Clark's age when it was first published, this simple story is nonetheless a Kentucky classic and an American masterpiece. It deserves to be more widely known and read. If *A Long Row to Hoe* is a competent and engrossing autobiography, *Song of the River* is a national treasure. The Jesse Stuart Foundation is to be applauded for bringing both books back into print in handsome new editions. Billy C. Clark's boyhood may have been a long row to hoe, but it was a row that lead to a rich harvest— a productive life of teaching and writing, as these two books attest.

Wade Hall,
Professor of English
Bellarmine College

THE JESSE STUART
FOUNDATION

Incorporated in 1979 for public, charitable, and educational purposes, the Jesse Stuart Foundation is devoted to preserving both Jesse Stuart's literary legacy and W-Hollow, the eastern Kentucky valley which became a part of America's literary landscape as a result of Stuart's writings. The Foundation, which controls rights to Stuart's published and unpublished literary works, is currently reprinting many of his best out-of-print books, along with other books which focus on Kentucky and Southern Appalachia.

Our primary purpose is to publish books which supplement the educational system, at all levels. We have now produced more than thirty editions and have hundreds of other regional books in stock, because we want to make these materials accessible to students, teachers, librarians, and general readers. We also promote Stuart's legacy through video tapes, dramas, and presentations for school and civic groups.

Stuart taught and lectured extensively. His teaching experience ranged from the one-room schoolhouses of his youth in eastern Kentucky to the American University in Cairo, Egypt, and embraced years of service as school superintendent, high-school teacher, and high-school principal. "First, last, always," said Jesse Stuart, "I am a teacher . . . . Good teaching is forever and the teacher is immortal."

In keeping with Stuart's devotion to teaching, the Jesse Stuart Foundation is working hard to publish materials that will be appropriate for school use. For example, the Foundation has reprinted seven of Stuart's junior books (for grades 3-6), and a Teacher's Guide to assist with their classroom use. The Foundation has also published several books that would be appropriate for grades 6-12: Stuart's *Hie to the Hunters*, Thomas D. Clark's *Simon Kenton, Kentucky Scout*, and Billy C. Clark's *A Long Row To Hoe*. Other recent JSF publications range from college history texts to books for adult literacy students.

James M. Gifford
Executive Director